Judy Astley was frequently told off for day-dreaming at her drearily traditional school but has found it to be the ideal training for becoming a writer. There were several false-starts to her career: secretary at an all-male Oxford college (sacked for undisclosable reasons), at an airline (decided, after a crash and a hijacking, that she was safer elsewhere) and as a dress designer (quit before anyone noticed she was adapting *Vogue* patterns). She spent some years as a parent and as a painter before sensing that the day was approaching when she'd have to go out and get a Proper Job. With a nagging certainty that she was temperamentally unemployable, and desperate to avoid office coffee, having to wear tights every day and missing out on sunny days on Cornish beaches with her daughters, she wrote her first novel, *Just for the Summer*. She has now had eleven novels published by Black Swan.

www.booksattransworld.co.uk

SIZE MATTERS

Judy Astley

BLACK SWAN

SIZE MATTERS
A BLACK SWAN BOOK : 0 552 77185 6

First publication in Great Britain

PRINTING HISTORY
Black Swan edition published 2004

1 3 5 7 9 10 8 6 4 2

Set in 11/13pt Melior by
Kestrel Data, Exeter, Devon.

Black Swan Books are published by Transworld Publishers,
61–63 Uxbridge Road, London W5 5SA,
a division of The Random House Group Ltd,
in Australia by Random House Australia (Pty) Ltd,
20 Alfred Street, Milsons Point, Sydney, NSW 2061, Australia,
in New Zealand by Random House New Zealand Ltd,
18 Poland Road, Glenfield, Auckland 10, New Zealand
and in South Africa by Random House (Pty) Ltd,
Endulini, 5a Jubilee Road, Parktown 2193, South Africa.

Printed and bound in Great Britain by
Cox & Wyman Ltd, Reading, Berkshire.

Papers used by Transworld Publishers are natural, recyclable
products made from wood grown in sustainable forests.
The manufacturing processes conform to the environmental
regulations of the country of origin.

Thanks to Hedy for essential secrets
from the cleaning business.

And to fellow inmates of the Borchester Asylum
for welcome shots of daily lunacy. May Matron's
gin cupboard never run dry.

Contents

ONE

Cake

'Was it something I said?'

Well of course it was. When men have to ask that, it always is. It was the something Greg had said just seconds before as he'd rolled across back to his side of the bed. It was the something he'd added to his habitual post-coital 'Ooof!' (accompanied by tightly closed eyes and grin like a silly spaniel). Out he'd come with it, not a single bit of tactful pre-thought getting in the way.

'Hey,' he'd said, nudging Jay hard in the side. 'This is a first! *I've just shagged a granny!* Yee ha!'

Oh how he'd laughed; such a pleased-with-himself, aren't-I-witty tee-hee-hee of a cackle. It was all too clear in his jokey delight that he was thinking clichéd Red Riding Hood Grannydom as in cauliflower perm, frilly pinny and the late Dame Thora on a stairlift. Whereas Jay, since daughter Imogen had let them in on why she'd been groaning a lot and looking pale, had been lining herself up, grandmother-wise, alongside Bianca Jagger, Marianne Faithfull and Victoria Beckham's glamorous mum.

'I'm not a granny yet.' Jay was huffy and unamused. She turned over on her side, the one that didn't face

9

him. 'There's months to go. The poor girl isn't even showing yet.'

Poor girl? Where did that come from? Twenty-year-old Imogen had, with the simple words 'I'm pregnant' shoved her own still-young and unready mother along life's bench towards a generation beyond her own – and, you couldn't help thinking it, closer to where you fell off the end. You need time for being comfortable with that sort of thing. Time to start wondering about whether you're still allowed in Topshop without feeling you should give the excuse that the pink, lace-front cheesecloth top is for a Seventies theme party. Time to reflect on whether your Desert Island Disc choices should include a token classical number to balance out The Clash and Duran Duran.

'Isn't she?' Greg pummelled his pillows back into shape, propped himself up against the blue suede headboard and picked up the TV remote control from his bedside table. He started flipping through a few channels, searching for the last remnants of some sunny distant test match.

'I'd have said she was, a bit,' he said as he settled to suffer England being thrashed by the West Indies (again). 'But then I suppose, well, she's quite a big girl our Moggy.' He knocked a knuckle against Jay's thigh. 'Takes after her mum.' Greg laughed again, cheerily unmindful that this didn't exactly make her feel better.

'Don't forget though Greg, this is going to make you a granddad,' Jay pointed out. 'It works both ways.' Even as she said it she knew it *didn't* work both ways. This was another of the many things that were unfairly Different for Men.

'Yeah. That's right.' He smiled, picturing some distant happy scene. 'It'll be brilliant. I can just see it, me out in the park in the summer sun, pushing the buggy – we must get the baby one of those fab three-wheel efforts. And there I'll be, sitting on that bench at the playground with all the gorgeous nannies and slinky Slavic au pairs and bored young mums and they'll all be looking at me and thinking . . .'

'Thinking what?' As if she couldn't guess.

'That I'm its dad! They'll think I'm one of those cool old dude-dads who's still got a fully revved up turbocharger under his bonnet. *And* it's not running on unleaded.' The gleeful chuckle surfaced once more.

Jay sighed and muttered, 'Give me strength,' before burrowing down deep into the duvet, trying, unsuccessfully, to shut out flashes of light from the TV.

She surfaced briefly to ask, 'Are you actually watching that?'

'Mmmm.' Greg turned the volume up, bringing into the room the sound of an exuberant steel band.

Jay yawned. She felt exhausted suddenly, wishing she hadn't been so greedy with Imogen and Tris's baby-celebration champagne which had lowered the already feeble diet defences enough for her to pig out on that third slice of chocolate cake. It was lying heavily now inside her, accusing her of gluttony, slack discipline and a reckless disregard for seemly feminine behaviour. The strawberries didn't count – they were Only Fruit. But not even a token hesitation had she expressed about wolfing down all that sweet crumbly cake, the overrich, creamy filling, so very much thick chocolate and walnut icing. Failing all the rules of proper womanhood, Jay hadn't so much as murmured a reluctant 'Ooh I really shouldn't.' Now all those calories, enough to keep a polar trekker marching for several days, were getting their revenge, making their presence felt within her as they advanced unstoppably to cosy up alongside the fat deposits on her thighs. And there it would all stay for evermore, bulking up the flab and the inches. On top of all this,

Greg's thoughtless granny-comment was what a social commentator would call 'not helpful'.

There must be women, Jay mused as she closed her eyes and thought of sleep, in fact she was sure that there actually *were* women out there in that parallel fantasy realm of long-term coupledom, women who were blessed with a far higher level of after-sex appreciation than this. A hearty slap on the thigh, a jolly confirmation that 'slim as a wand' had bypassed 'gorgeously rounded' and morphed irrevocably into 'downright flabby', and a casual reminder about lost youthfulness couldn't be any woman's idea of the best post-coital moments. She'd have hated Greg to be one of those men who nuzzled in a creepily humble way and muttered 'thank you' as if they had just been granted a rare and filthy trample through the sacred female temple. And thank all the gods he didn't do that cringe-making 'how was it for you?' begging question that Barbara, her business partner, got from her husband every Friday night without fail. Good grief, if he couldn't tell by now . . . But just occasionally it would be pleasing if the sexual after-blast could include some close gratifying snuggling, some loving touchy-feely stuff as if there was at least the pretence of reluctance to let the moment go.

On the plus side of course, at least they still *did it* now and then. Half-joky hints from friends (and far too much nostalgic detail on how it used to be from Cathy next door) told her that several had partners who were not so much running on unleaded, as Greg would so charmingly put it, but whose metaphorical starter motors had rusted to a permanent standstill. Another plus with Greg was that he wouldn't give her pained glances suggestive of hypersensitivity when, as she did now, she gave up on sleep and reached down to the floor to pick up the book she was eager to finish.

As she was settling herself into a good reading position Jay caught the glint of reflected light through the bit where the huge glass expanse of the bedroom window met the huge glass expanse of the roof. So he was at it again. The Planet Man in the top-floor flat across the road was watching the stars from his home-built observatory and 'accidentally' doing his best to take in the views afforded by any neighbours careless enough to have far more window than curtain. Blinds. We should do something about getting blinds, she thought, making a mental note. It was time to do something more serious about privacy up in this roof-top fishtank of a bedroom than these flimsy organdie hangings.

What was it William Morris had said about home furnishings? Something along the lines of every domestic item being either beautiful or functional, preferably both? Close-to-transparent window hangings weren't anyone's idea of functional, even in this glorious shade of sandy gold scattered with tiny random pearly stones, so that the effect was a bit like a vertical stretch of beach with the sun glinting onto shimmering shell. They'd looked sensational in *Elle Decoration*, but you needed a full-time live-in stylist of your own to keep them as artlessly breeze-blown as in the seductive photos. Top of the list of what you definitely *didn't* need was a Burmese cat with a low boredom threshold and a crazed conviction that there must be a secret mouse hidden right at the top of any length of claw-sensitive fabric. Sad threads hung like half-fallen hairs, wafting this way and that in the breeze, reminding her of the folly of indulging a costly design whim in a house that was actually used for living in rather than looking at.

As ever, faced with domestic purchasing dilemmas, Jay thought of her cousin Delphine. The name made her visualize a brand of lavatory paper, in quilted lilac perhaps, with little gold fleur-de-lys printed on it. Jay imagined saying exactly that to Delphine herself and to Auntie Win, Delphine's devoted mama. Neither would find the analogy the slightest bit of a put-down. On the contrary they'd be thrilled at the very idea. If such a thing existed, Auntie Win would seek it out at once to match the purple and gilt Versace tiles in her bungalow boudoir's en suite. Still, loo-roll or not, there was still that tiny childhood remnant of envy when Jay recalled Aunt Win stroking her infant daughter's fine blonde hair and cooing 'Pretty name, a pretty girl.' When you're named plain old Jane on the practical basis that, as Jay's own mother briskly claimed, 'You can't shorten that' only to find even that reduced by all and sundry to the sound of a mere initial, it had been hard not to wish she'd been christened something madly fairylike, such as Philomena-Willow.

Delphine, far away as she was in Western Australia, used to know all that could possibly be known about sourcing domestic solutions. In her first marriage, twenty years before, she'd been the acknowledged Martha Stewart of East Sheen. You'd expect nothing less from a woman who by her early teenage years was saving her pocket money to buy drawn-thread Egyptian cotton sheets to stash away in her bottom drawer like a Victorian bride, and who had won a Blue Peter badge for knitting up a set of doilies, using the string bags that oranges were sold in. Delphine, were she not half a world away, would relish telling Jay exactly where she'd gone wrong with the window furnishings (and also gone wrong in marrying an architect who delighted in conducting his more outré design experiments on his own home. 'Using home as a showcase – it'll stun potential clients,' Greg had explained, jubilant with the early designs for this nearly-all-glass roof conversion.) Delphine would instruct Jay to source a long list of appropriate blind manufacturers for price comparison and she'd tell her exactly which fabric would look best. Unfortunately she wouldn't just leave it at that. In Delphine's case, advice always came firmly stapled to opinions, as in: 'What you should do *is*, you should . . .'

Also, Jay thought as she stretched first one leg down the bed and then the other, hoping it counted as calorie-burning exercise, Delphine's taste, interior-decoration-wise, had freeze-dried back in 1991. Or it had according to the photos she sent back for Auntie Win to show around the family. One appalled look-see at this sparkly new, huge, loft-style design-award roof job and she'd be lining up a brickie to replace most of Greg's much-loved glass and importing swags of floral chintz complete with tasselled tie-backs and gilded rose motifs on a limed curtain pole the diameter of a sturdy sapling.

Jay stared up through the sloped glass roof at the succession of planes making their way across the night sky towards Heathrow. She gave up on the book and switched off her light. It didn't make much difference, what with the light from the suspended plasma-screen TV and the orange glow from the street lights outside. Greg was still glued to his test match, headphones now considerately clamped to his ears, his hands still making barely conscious movements that indicated he was in there with the batsman, showing him how it should be done.

'Going to sleep?' he shouted at her, reaching across and squeezing her hand. 'Love you!' he yelled.

'Me too,' she told him, certain he couldn't hear and wondering if he'd have accurately lip-read if she'd said 'Sod you' instead. 'Granny' indeed, she'd give him bloody Granny.

TWO

Detox

Detox. The word had shimmied into Jay's head as she and her internal chocolate cake had slid away into sleep the night before. It was still there, waiting, like Daffodil the cat, to pounce on her the moment she woke. Detox, she'd read many a carefree time as the hairdresser snipped or the dentist was drilling the victim ahead of her, was where you started. It was an essential pre-diet body-cleansing in preparation for the ultimate weight-loss experience. If she was going to be a 'granny' as Greg so delightedly put it (and was it *that* hilarious? She didn't think so), she was bloody well going to be a gorgeous, slender, desirable one. No more would Greg slap her thigh as if she was a lardy pony and call her a Big Girl. Flush away the internal toxins, that was what she had to do, clear out the crap (literally, presumably, though she'd draw the line at colonic interference) and start again.

It was Monday, the ideal day for a fresh start. Now, in the early morning and an empty kitchen-stroke-family-room – if you didn't count the breakfast debris left by Rory and Ellie as they whirled through and attacked the cereal cupboard on the way out to school – she flicked through a colour supplement that had escaped the recycling box and found what she was looking for. A mug of camomile tea now sat on the big glass table in front of her, cooling fast. It tasted and looked and smelled like wee. Not appetizing, for sure, but virtuous certainly. She'd read somewhere that people actually *did* drink their own pee as part of a detoxification process. The thought did not appeal in the slightest and surely urine was already a whole lot of rejected toxins? Otherwise, wouldn't the body have found a use for it? Not to be thought of too deeply, she decided, contemplating the fist-sized heap of chilled white grapes which sat on the wonky pink plate that had almost failed Rory his mock Art GCSE. This was it. The inadequate sum total of detox breakfast. Here was where inner purification started.

'Mum? Got any Marmite?' Jay could hear Imogen shouting from halfway up the steps from the basement flat. Jay unlocked the long architecturally arty concertina of folding glass doors and her daughter rushed into the room clutching a pair of fat slices of toast. Melted butter dripped onto Mog's fingers and she licked at it, missing a bit that trickled down her chin. Jay inhaled slowly, eyes closed. Oh the smell of that toast. The blissful, sensual, warming gorgeousness of it. She shook her head briskly. Even if she gave into temptation, there surely wasn't time. She was due at the station in half an hour to pick up Anya and Katinka and drop them at Mrs Ryan's to do her Regular Clean. A wheel from the Henry vacuum cleaner had rolled to the back of the understairs cupboard and vanished among a pile of Christmas-decoration boxes. The van was only half loaded and it needed petrol. Jay, mindful of her job's requirements, reached into the cupboard under the sink, feeling for a new pack of J-cloths. At least down here there was only the non-alluring odour of damp and dishwasher tablets, nothing to seduce her tastebuds.

'Marmite?' Imogen said again. Jay backed out of the cupboard, hot and muddled. And hungry.

'For my toast? Me and Tris haven't got any. We thought you might.' Imogen was standing in the middle of the room, barefoot and in her droopy black jersey pyjama bottoms teamed with a blue T-shirt emblazoned on the front with 'Plumber's Mate' in rhinestones.

'You should have put shoes on.' Jay looked at her daughter's grubby toes with the chipped lilac varnish. 'You'll catch a chill.'

'God, Mum, it's only up the steps. So have you got any?'

'What? Oh the Marmite. I don't know. Have a look in the fridge, in the cupboards, wherever. I'm in a rush, haven't got time . . .'

'Great. Cheers. Thanks a lot,' Imogen growled, opening the fridge and taking out a can of Coke. 'Just cos I've got a *craving*, you'd think my own *mother* would want to spoil me a bit.'

'A craving? Good grief girl, you're only a few weeks gone. You wait till you're . . .' Jay ran out of steam, suddenly feeling her taste buds being overcome by the scent of Imogen's breakfast. She would kill to be sitting down for a long slow trawl through the newspaper, a cup of hot strong coffee in front of her along with a heap of lush toast, saturated with marmalade . . . Thick, lustrous peel-strewn marmalade. Sugar-sodden, a hint of bitterness, the tang of utter, utter pleasure.

But no. According to this article you definitely couldn't detox on toast and marmalade and the kind of coffee that made you think of Mediterranean mornings. She returned to her chair and sipped miserably at the tepid herbal tea. She thought of the chocolate and

18

strawberry cake from the day before, hoping to shame herself back into firm resolution. The thought only made her want to shove Imogen aside from the fridge and see if there was a sliver of the cake, a scraping of cream, left on a plate.

'Found it!' Imogen hauled a Marmite jar out from the back far reaches of the fridge, opened it quickly and plunged a knife into it.

'Maybe you should look at the "best before" date,' Jay warned.

Imogen paused in her toast-spreading and sniffed into the jar. 'Smells all right. Smells delish,' she shrugged, carrying on.

Jay munched dejectedly on the grapes, reading through the list of foods that were, for the next few days, utterly banned from her life. These included wheat, dairy products, eggs, fish, meat, coffee, tea, alcohol, sugar, cakes, biscuits. It didn't leave much. It left, as far as she could work out, grapes and apples and lemons and brown rice. Oh joy. Food to commit suicide by. Still, it wasn't for long. A limited amount of proper food (as she'd define it) could be introduced soon, gradually and with care. (Why? What digestive disaster would occur if she ate, say, a bacon sandwich, very fast and in quite reckless spirits?) Only six days in and for supper she could look forward to a small salad of citrus fruits with pumpkin seeds.

'Got any more bread?' Imogen clattered the top off the big old earthenware breadbin without waiting for an answer. 'I just fancy one more slice . . .' She turned to her mother, eyeing with pity the few remaining grapes and the sad tangle of scrappy stalks. 'Shall I do one for you? And wouldn't you rather have some proper coffee?'

Jay prodded her left thigh. The flesh gave beneath her finger, pleasingly soft and squishy beneath the denim of her favourite old jeans. Her resolve, as well as her plumpness, was dented.

'OK then, just one. And marmalade.'

Well she needed it, Jay thought as she took a long, languorous bite and savoured the fleshy chunks of fragrant peel and the gorgeous gluey orange ooze. There was a hard day's work ahead. Running a cleaning company wasn't exactly a sit-down doddle. Every single client seemed to think Monday was the ideal day for getting the housework done and then complaining about whoever had done it. After delivering the girls to do Mrs Ryan's Regular there was the Dachshund Man who wanted an Upstairs Blitz and two new clients who needed a go-see and a quote. Plenty to do. And anyway, Jay reassured herself, surely it was hardly worthwhile starting on a serious detox if you were already running on empty.

Rory was in trouble. He'd copied Hal Clegg's French essay on *'L'après-midi d'un chat'* pretty much full-on word for word. At the time he'd have said it was definitely Hal's fault, the loser; he shouldn't have left his bag on the bus. Rory had done him a favour really, picking it up off the seat, lugging it home, taking care of it overnight, phoning Hal to say he'd got it safe for him and then dragging the thing back into school (in his mum's Dishing the Dirt van, embarrassing or what?) the next day. Hal couldn't have expected there not to be some kind of reward in it. He couldn't really be surprised that Rory had had a good scrabble through its contents and selected various items that could be of personal use. These had included a packet of Marlboro (only two gone), Samantha Newton's new mobile number (result!) scrawled on a bit of paper and decorated with little hearts (you as well, Hal?) and the French essay.

Rory had had a quick look in his own homework diary. The essay title he'd written down was *'L'après-midi de Jacques'*. He must have got it wrong. Rory wasn't too keen on French (in fact what was French for understatement?) and would be the first to admit he probably hadn't been paying attention. Hal was ploddy and studious and the kind of boff that got roped into those evenings for Prospective Parents, so they could admire this prime example of the best a state school could turn out. French Jacques, on the other hand, or perhaps not now Rory came to think of it, was the dreary spoon whose sad life they'd been reading about in *Nos Amis Francais!*. Jacques lived in *une petite village* up *la montagne* with his *maman* and *papa* and *petite soeur* Marie. He was keen on his pet *chien*, on *le football* and *le skiing* and on playing *la trompette*. Coming up with even fifty words' worth of stuff of the remotest interest that Jacques could get up to in one afternoon was surely beyond anyone's creative range.

So Rory had copied the cat essay, because Hal was a swotty div and must have listened right. Hal had written some quite funny stuff about a cat called Celine who chased a mouse into a bar and drove the customers nuts by leaping at the TV screen when they were trying to watch a World Cup final. Hal's French vocab was quite impressive. Rory had to look up lots of the words and because of the differences in their basic language skills had changed the story a little bit, obviously, simplifying it down to somewhere closer to his own level. He wasn't completely stupid. He'd sent his personal cat (Fleur – neat touch that, even Hal hadn't come up with a pukka French name) chasing its mouse into a shop where David Beckham was trying on shoes (and did his dad – Rory's, not D. Beckham's – have to find it so hilarious when he'd asked what was the French for Prada? Like were you supposed to know *everything* at sixteen?). He'd thought he'd done OK and forgotten about it till the work had been handed back oh-so-publicly that morning. What a sodding way to start a week. Hal Clegg had got away with it, no question. Course he had, the blue-eyed boy who could do no wrong. 'Sorry, I must have misheard,' he'd said, all big smarmy grin, not that it mattered. 'Not a problem, Hallam; a highly inventive and entertaining effort,' Ms Lofthouse had cooed at her number one A-star dead cert. 'But as for you, Rory Callendar, what was your excuse?'

Detention. Two lunch hours. He'd looked at Samantha Newton, hoping for a glimmer of sympathy to raise more than his spirits, but she was doing nail comparison with Shelley Caine. Worse, during the detention he'd still got to come up with three hundred words on what Jacques did with his *après-midi*. So unfair. What, he wondered, was French for wank?

Katinka hadn't turned up again. When Jay picked Anya up at the station she had tapped her nose and sniffed hard, by which Jay gathered Katinka had caught a cold. It was her third in a month and somehow each time she'd managed not to let Jay know by the more usual means of phoning rather than by just not being there. OK, granted there was a language problem here (rustic Polish v English), but surely she had just one friend who spoke a tiny bit of English? This meant Jay now had to join in with the cleaning rather than getting on with some admin. Otherwise Anya would be at Mrs Ryan's for twice as long as she should be and they wouldn't get to the Dachshund Man before twelve.

It wasn't supposed to be like this, Jay thought as she lugged the vacuum cleaner up Mrs Ryan's plush-carpeted stairs. She was supposed to be the boss. She was supposed to sit in her little home office next to

Ellie's bedroom, to feel important and businesslike and Do the Accounts. She was supposed to take the bookings, hire and fire the staff, advertise, promote and generally motivate and organize. She was not supposed to be feeling hot, fat and sweaty, clad in itchy rubber gloves and shoving Harpic down the clients' skiddy lavatories. When Jay and Barbara-with-the-cats had set up Dishing the Dirt, investing serious money in their four little vans, the logos, the advertising, insurance and materials, the idea had been that their personal involvement should entail as little that was hands-on as possible.

Obviously they trained their staff on site, demonstrating the domestic arts and adapting them to any picky personal preferences of the clients. They made a point of settling in all their cleaners – working alongside even the most reliable, experienced ones – at any new bookings, partly to reassure clients that they took their requirements seriously but mostly so they were familiar with the premises and could fend off any unjustified complaints (such as the very many who assumed that by booking a Regular they'd be somehow getting a Blitz, including all books off shelves and all overcrammed kitchen cupboards emptied, scrubbed out and restocked tidily). But essentially Jay and Barbara would *administrate*.

Barbara didn't really have time for much more than that. She had her breeding queens (Burmese, the source of Jay's crazed cat Daffodil) to deal with, her cat-show schedule and her kitten list to organize. Jay had her chaotic home life, Moggie and Tristan making babies in the basement flat and two moody teenagers whose activities required a constant stand-by taxi service. Yet here she was at Mrs Ryan's, hauling a dangerously overfull bag of fish-stink garbage out of the swingbin. And Barbara was almost certainly, right now, up on

Putney Hill, showing the two newly recruited Brazilian language students how to differentiate between Lemon Flash and Beeswax Pledge (quite important that, when faced with a cherrywood dining table), and making sure they understood that Fairy Liquid wasn't what you used to clean the inside of Mrs Latimer-Jones's fat-splattered oven.

Up in Mrs Ryan's chilly spare bedroom Jay sank her behind down on the silky sky blue bedspread and attached a soft brush to the end of the vacuum-cleaner hose. The room was kept polished, dusted and as sprucely ready as a Hilton suite for visitors who had never, as far as Jay could tell, turned up. The room reminded her of cousin Delphine's teenage bedroom years ago, all co-ordinated fabrics – swagged Austrian blinds, fringed scatter cushions and quilted button bedhead – in blue and pink rose prints. Delphine had kept her room as immaculately tidy as this one now was, all her clothes were hung in colour order in a massive mirrored wardrobe that spanned an entire wall and had a light that came on when you opened the door. Her shoes had been perched inside on sloping racks, as if they were pertly tripping down a slope towards the thick cream carpet. Belts and scarves hung on a battery-powered gadget that turned like a tiny carousel.

'Lovely isn't it?' Auntie Win had sighed to her sister Audrey, Jay's mother, the day after the decorators had left and Delphine had at last arranged her silver-backed hairbrushes and combs on the glass dressing-table top.

Audrey had had a quick glance round and said, 'Yes dear, but where does she keep her books?'

'Books?' Win had looked at her, puzzled, then pointed to a white wicker contraption by the bed. 'Oh, over there!' she said triumphantly. 'The magazine rack. There's room for at least a years' worth of *Vogue*.'

Jay, now whooshing the brush round the unchipped white skirting, thought of her own teen bedroom. She'd shared it with her older sister April. Their mother had made a point of being uninvolved with nagging about cleanliness, on grounds of respecting their privacy, and their inadequate wardrobe space and overflowing drawers made the room resemble a serious burglary aftermath. Little scraps of fabric – fluorescent nets and vivid satins and sequinned taffeta – found their way all over the house, escaping from Audrey's sewing room where she put together elaborate costumes for the area's ballet schools, assorted competitive ice skaters and ballroom dancers. Jay and April's bedroom walls were carelessly Blu-tacked with posters of angel-faced rock musicians. Homework and paperbacks and socks and abandoned crumb-strewn plates obscured the floor. Surfaces were obscured by make-up, magazines, records, jewellery. Jay, faced with a tangle of wire hangers on which her clothes were hung three items at a time, longed and longed for Delphine's immaculate expanse of pristine cream carpet, the line-up of satin padded coat hangers, each one with a little lacy dangling bag of lavender, and the drawer dividers separating row after row of immaculate white pants.

She sat on the bed again to swap the vacuum-cleaner heads back and took her phone out of her pocket. Perhaps there'd been messages. Perhaps the office phone had almost rung itself off the desk with people clamouring for a few months' casual cleaning work. It was coming up to spring – you often got students getting in quick for a way of making summer cash, or affluent sporty boys back from the ski season ready to save up for the next big trip.

'Mog? Anything I should know? Any calls?' It was no surprise that Imogen was up in her mother's kitchen instead of downstairs in the basement flat. The heating there was free for one thing, so was use of the washing machine and the contents of the food cupboards. Jay could picture her daughter, sitting on the kitchen worktop reading her horoscope in a month-old *Marie Claire* and sipping at her fourth cup of coffee, very, very slowly getting herself in the mood for writing an onerous line or two of her final year university dissertation on drugs education for the under elevens.

'Hmm,' Imogen murmured. 'Yeah there were one or two work ones. I've written them down. They're on your desk.'

'Thanks. And Imogen?' A thought crossed her mind suddenly. The news of the pregnancy was coming up for twenty-four hours old for the immediate family, but there were others who should know. That was Imogen's job.

'Have you phoned Gran?'

'No? Why?'

'Well don't you think you'd better tell her? About the baby?'

'Oh. Right. Well I thought you could . . .'

'Oh no, Moggy, that's your job. She was bad enough when I got pregnant with you. It's your turn now for the "throwing away your education" lecture!'

'But you didn't throw it away. You got your degree. I'm going to as well. Uni is cool about it, I told you.'

'I know, I know. But Gran doesn't. Just give her a call, there's a love, get it over with. And tell Tristan to tell his parents. They won't want to be the last to know.' Why was she having to say this, she thought, why was it all so uphill all the time?

'Reminds me,' Imogen said, 'Auntie Win phoned and said you'd want to be *first* to know about this. She said Delphine is coming home. From Australia. To live.' It crossed Jay's mind that this must be a prime example of 'think of the devil'.

Jay looked down at her hand, flabby and oversoft from being encased in its stifling rubber glove. Delphine would look and tut and advise cotton liners inside the Marigolds. She'd be right, as ever.

'Mum? Did you hear me? Delphine's getting married again. God, at her age! She's leaving Australia and she's going to live near here. Win said you'd be really, really pleased.'

THREE

Chocolate Hobnobs

'This cousin. You two must be really close or . . .'

Jay watched as Barbara paused to adjust the wriggling cat she was grooming so that its fang teeth didn't succeed in chewing holes in the brush handle. The lithe little pinky-grey animal squirmed on its back under Barbara's big broad-fingered hand and gave a long disgruntled miaow of protest. Barbara cooed kindly and brushed away expertly at its short silky fur, smoothing out the cat's lean body across her lap.

'. . . you must be really close or it wouldn't be important, would it? She'd just be a distant family member back from foreign parts. You'd get together for a reunion tea with the rellies, she'd get stuck into living back here again and then everything would carry on as per normal.'

Jay sighed into her spritzer – it was a bit early for a drink, barely past four thirty, but Barbara considered Monday to be the longest, hardest day that needed to have its working end rewarded with alcohol as soon as was decently negotiable. While Jay had been standing in for the cold-stricken Katinka, sweeping spider nests from the back of the Dachshund Man's wardrobe, Barbara had been giving her overstressed employees a much-needed extra hand clearing the debris from a client's weekend-long eighteenth birthday party that no-one had thought to warn them about. 'It's quite staggering,' she'd told Jay, 'that anyone can imagine that cleaning up after eighty teenagers – and it looked like a bloody good time had been had – could just pass as "regular cleaning" and can be whizzed through by two students in their usual couple of hours.'

'The thing about Delphine isn't really about closeness. She was always a lot more than *just a cousin*,' Jay said, wondering how to explain. 'She was always *there* for a start, like a sort of shadow. Auntie Win had this idea that as Delphine was an only child, and I was the closest of my lot in age to her, that I'd have to play the sister part for her. "Your best friends are your family" she used to say to Mum, who didn't actually agree but there was no telling Win – whatever you said she didn't listen.'

'All families are like that,' Barbara said gloomily. 'My kids don't listen to anyone either. They're convinced they know it all.'

'Mine too.' What was it she'd said to Imogen about being on the pill? Something about it being a good idea so long as you were the sort of person who remembered to take it, every single day? And there was lovely Moggie, the sort of dreamy, scatty person who barely remembered that breathing out came after breathing in . . .

'Anyway, Delphine, well she defined my childhood. She was . . . how can I put it . . . she was what I *failed to be*, with the emphasis on the "failed".'

Barbara let the cat jump down to the floor and went to wash her hands at the kitchen sink.

'Oh come on now, who said you failed? Not your mum, surely. I can't imagine that. She's too laid-back. When she looks at you it's in an approving sort of way, like she's standing back and thinking she's pretty pleased with how you turned out. Don't tell me I'm wrong?'

Jay leant across the table to the plate of chocolate Hobnobs that earlier she'd pushed out of her own weak-willed reach. The outstretched hand looked pallid and bloated and rough-skinned and still smelled faintly of Mr Muscle (bathroom), in spite of a thorough washing and a rub-over with *La Remedie* hand lotion.

'Heavens no, Mum was fine, very hands-off but generally OK. She thought her sister Win and the pampered infant Delphine were a hugely amusing source of entertainment. She, well all of us, we used to giggle like anything over Win indulging her little princess. There were lots of things that used to have her in stitches, like Win telling us she hung Delph's school skirt inside a stocking every night to keep the pleats in place, and that she anointed Delphine's eyelashes with Vaseline every night to strengthen them.'

Barbara shuddered, laughing. 'Everything I achieved,' Jay told her, 'Delphine sort of managed to outdo, everything I had, she had a better version. If you were looking at it from a ten-year-old's point of view, Delphine was someone's life-work; she simply had it all, in spades. Everything from high-heeled silver ballroom-dancing shoes to a fluffy white fun-fur coat and her own pony down at the riding school. Sorry Barbara,' she laughed, 'I know this all sounds pathetically juvenile. It was really left behind years ago, finally taken away when Delphine went to Oz about twelve years back and she wasn't there any more to tell me I should have got proper carpets instead of wood floors and rugs that slip.'

'So do you think she'll bring it all back again? Like luggage?'

'*Just* like luggage – I hope not but it's possible. You

assume you change with the years but I know I'll have to work at not falling into the old patterns. We should be past all that. The grown-up thing would be to be delighted to see her. I will be.'

Barbara didn't look convinced. 'This is like sneaking into someone else's therapy session. What else bugged you?'

Jay eyed the Hobnobs then continued, 'Well, she was what Auntie Win called "perfectly formed". I, believe it or not, was an undersized, puny little thing, all bones and flatness. You can't believe how toe-curlingly embarrassing it was, having your aunt look you up and down and say something like, "Not developing yet then?" when you're pancake flat and nearly a year older than your curvy cousin in her first rosebud-patterned bra. I suppose I would've appreciated it if Mum had been a bit more in my corner, so to speak, but she wasn't at all bothered about my fragile little ego.'

'Yes but you're all grown-up now aren't you?' Barbara pointed out crisply, topping up Jay's wine glass. Jay mentally added another hundred calories to the day's intake. So much for detox. That must have been the shortest attempted pre-diet in history. How long had it lasted? Five minutes that morning? Seven at a push?

'Sure, I'm all grown-up. But these things linger, or their effects do.'

'And *don't* tell me you ever went in for competitive swanking about your own children's attributes!'

Jay laughed. 'Not at championship level, no, not like Win, but I'd have stuck up for them if anyone else had pitched their daughter against mine so they were in no doubt they were gorgeous – or at least I would have when they were that small. They deserve the odd boost to their confidence. Though just lately Ellie is so

31

grumpy and foul-tempered that if anyone compared her unfavourably with their own thirteen-year-old I'd probably agree wholeheartedly and offer to swap.'

'So you'll be pleased to see her then, this Delphine. Personally I can't wait.' Barbara laughed. 'I want to meet this woman who can still get you so rattled.'

'Gee thanks! Yes, I'll be pleased to see her, of course I will. Though only when I've had my roots done, lost a stone and we've got some more reliable staff so it won't be a complete lie about you and me running the business rather than it running *us*.' Jay looked down at her middle and poked it hard. 'You know there must have been a time, maybe only a day or a week or two sometime, when this body was just perfect, size-wise, not shamingly skinny any more and not wodgy like this either. I wish I'd appreciated it at the time and taken more trouble with it.'

'What you need is grapefruit,' Barbara said, tumbling another heap of Hobnobs onto the plate. Jay, with great difficulty, managed to resist helping herself to yet another one. Barbara, who was blessed with the shape and height of Joanna Lumley, took two, one in each hand.

'Grapefruit? Why?' Somehow, Jay was still thinking of her first 30 AAA trainer bra and imagined shoving fruit down her front, padding out her teen flatness just as she had with tissues, in the days when she'd raced into the changing rooms after school games to get safely back into her uniform shirt before anyone could catch her in her underwear.

'You eat half a grapefruit before every meal. I was reading about it,' Barbara told her. 'It's full of fat-burning enzymes.'

'Hmm. Are you sure? I mean they said that about cabbage soup. It's not true. And pineapple too, and they're full of sugar.'

'Well anyway, it's got to be worth a shot. You just have the grapefruit three times a day, oh and cut back on the carbs and the alcohol and drink lots of water. At least it's not antisocial like the cabbage soup.'

'Right – I'll get some on the way home. Before I go though, can I just have a peek at the kittens?'

Barbara laughed. 'Weakening now?' she teased. 'I did say when you got Daffodil that you should have got two of them. Burmese need company. Come on, they're in here. It's time for them to come through to the house anyway, for a bit of socializing playtime when the boys get home from school.' She opened the kitchen door and Jay followed her through to the old garage which Barbara had converted into palatial safe accommodation for her champion cats and their broods.

'Their colours are really showing now. Two lilacs, three blues and one chocolate.' Barbara picked up a kitten that was scrambling up the ragged back of a discarded velvet armchair. The nut-brown mother cat looked up from dozing on her cushion, blinked at Barbara and settled back down again, sure of her babies' safety.

'This one's almost pink!' Jay said, stroking the tiny creature's leathery nose.

'Potential champion, I'd say. A lilac. I'm thinking of keeping her, letting Bluebell retire from breeding. I've taken to calling her Lupin.'

Jay picked up another kitten, rolled it onto its back and tickled its broad plump tummy. The rattling purr sounded far too big and raucous for such a small animal.

'They're gorgeous. I don't know how you can bear to part with them.'

'I try to think of the money, what little there is of it after registration, stud fees, food and vaccinations. Really, you have to put it down to being a labour of love,' Barbara told her with a smile as she rounded up the rest of the kittens, gathering them up into her arms like a bundle of wriggly laundry and heading back to the kitchen. The mother cat trotted after her, mewing reassurance at her babies.

'Come on you fluffies, time for you to run round the house and learn about joining in. Just think, Jay, this time next year it'll be just like this for you but with Imogen's baby.'

'Hmm. Another long stint of house-training and mopping. Lovely,' Jay said.

Ellie followed Tasha round the shop. It wasn't easy to keep up – Tasha moved through the display racks fast and carelessly like a woodland creature through brambles. Tash looked this way and that, her streaky blonde ponytail swishing as she took in the stock and sorted it in her head into Wanted and Not Wanted. Ellie, following, picked her way more carefully, mostly looking at the floor and trying very very hard not to look up into the far left corner where she knew there was a security camera. She was, she knew, the idiot sort who'd go and smile up at it politely and probably end up on Crimewatch or in the 'Familiar Face' column that the local paper had been running to try and shame local shoplifting kids.

Tasha didn't care where she looked. 'Brazen Personified', that was what Mrs Billington, head of their year, called her. It had been meant as a huge telling-off but had somehow only added to Tasha's glory. Nothing fazed Tasha. She'd blag her way daily through lost-homework excuses, through being caught most mornings with a fag at the bus stop, for wearing four-inch pink platform slingbacks, and never ever having the kit for netball. You wanted to be like Tasha, for the sheer nerve of her, for the fat-lipped, sexy, big-toothed smile that everyone fell for (even Mr Redmond, who blushed raspberry pink every time he told her off for not handing in the maths homework and she just grinned and flicked her bum at him like one of Barbara's cats on heat). But then you so *didn't* want to be like her because of the things she did. She lied. She picked on people. She changed favoured friends like other people change their tights and she stole. She'd get A grade A-level thieving, no question. That's what they were out doing now, after school, still in uniform. Shoplifting. Tasha was after a new top, a restock on the Glamma Nails and some purple bangles to go with a dress she'd had (or said she'd 'had', who could tell? Her mum might have bought it for her) out of Topshop the week before. She was on a mission and Ellie happened to be the person picked to tag along, just because she'd lent Tasha some lipgloss in the cloakroom at going-home time.

There wasn't anything in this bright brash shop that Ellie actually wanted, not really. Everything, the jewellery, the make-up, the nail stuff, the thongy underwear that looked harsh and scratchy, it was all cheap and glitzy and just not worth the terrifying hassle. It looked like the kind of kit that nine-year-olds wanted, as if it would turn them into a fantasy play-Barbie overnight. Even if she'd got the money she wouldn't be spending it on this. If she had a wish list, say if it was coming up to Christmas or a birthday, she'd have written down something shamingly secret like soft cuddly pyjamas that made you want to get into bed with a good book (like *The Woodlanders*) and completely shut out school and the Tash-girls and all the fighting hard-boys and the being careful not to be the nerd-in-the-corner stuff. Every school day she felt as if she was pretending to be someone else. You had to, if you were a bit different. The bit that was different wasn't always easy to know till someone picked on you and made it clear.

After more than two years at the school she'd worked out that there were things she had to act about, to make up for. These were: One – being small, which included looking way too young to be a credible thirteen, going on fourteen. Ellie, taking after her mother, was one of the littlest in her year and still child-shaped, though (thank goodness) acceptably pretty and with long glossy brown hair and a curvy mouth that went up at the corners, so people always thought she was smiling even when she was in a fury. To be a credible thirteen you actually had to look old enough to get served in a pub, to look as if you'd already had so much sex you were bored with it (even though hardly anyone had) and to have had periods since you were in primary school. Ellie's hadn't even started yet, which was why she kept Tampax loose in her bag and let them fall out on the classroom floor now and then.

Two, you had to have home problems that you could moan about. Top of that, best, you needed a struggling lone mum who scraped by on the social, with men who were a pain and maybe even smacked her about a bit. Ace would be a stepdad on remand for something dangerous. Ellie had two nice friendly parents who liked each other. On the plus side, her mum was often seen around driving her Dishing the Dirt van, so she'd told everyone she was a cleaner, not that she owned the company. But they were borderline posh, a bit suspect for living in a house that was practically mansion-size by her classmates' standards. It didn't have many rooms downstairs. There was just the sitting room (square-shaped and comfy) and the kitchen (huge, with space for a sofa and massive glass doors and roof) but that was because her dad had had most of the walls taken out. It was also arty and mad-looking, with weird

36

glass bits designed by her dad tacked on all over the place. Imogen was going to be useful, now she was pregnant and only twenty and shacked up with a plumber. Ellie wouldn't bother to mention that she lived with no real difficulties at all (apart from cool student poverty) in their basement flat, and that her bloke Tristan might be a plumber but he'd been to school at Eton and had got five A levels.

'Whaddya think?' Tasha stood in front of the mirror, holding up a scarlet bra that had silver lace and a vicious-looking underwire. Ellie smiled, loathing her own deep need to please. 'It's OK. Looks a bit . . .'

Tash narrowed her eyes, daring Ellie to come up with something that would prove first opinions right: that she was snobby, spoony, different.

'It looks like it would show a lot through a top,' Ellie said, rushing her words. 'The lace, I mean, it's very knobbly.'

'Hmm. Yeah, I suppose.' Tasha put the bra back on the rack and calmly flicked through a few more. 'What about this one for you?' She held up a pale lilac one, a rigid balcony effort that Ellie wouldn't even half-fill. Ellie laughed, hoping she wasn't going red. 'Yeah right. And if anyone prodded me there'd be a dent!' It was the only defence, putting yourself down before someone else did. You learned that fast enough.

'OK, bored now, let's go.' Tasha crashed off again, out through the rails, diverting a bit to the right so they went out through the shop's side door. Ellie raced after her, puzzled.

'But what about . . . ? I thought you wanted . . .' she hissed at Tasha as soon as they were a safe hundred yards round the corner away from the store. Tasha grinned at her, glancing back slyly to where they'd just come from, then hauled Ellie into Starbucks doorway and grabbed her school bag from her shoulder. Ellie watched open-mouthed as Tasha pulled the zip back. Inside her own bag was a messy jumble of jewellery, bangles and earrings all still attached to their display cards and price tags. The silver and scarlet bra glinted from behind her maths textbook and a nail varnish selection clinked together like her parents' bottle bank donations after a typical boozy weekend. In spite of feeling a terrified nausea – God, if she'd been caught – Ellie was hugely impressed. Her eyes shone as she looked up at Tasha's cunning face, the big luscious smile and the slanted cool grey eyes.

'How did you do that? I didn't see . . .' Ellie managed to say at last as Tasha pulled out her haul and shoved it deep into her own bag.

'I know you didn't! That's the point. You're such an innocent, babes.' Tasha patted the side of Ellie's face, the way you would a cute toddler. 'No-one would ever point the finger at you. If there was anyone looking down those cameras, their eyes would have been only on me.' She grinned and handed Ellie a bottle of Hot Blush nail polish. 'Here y'are, keep this. It's more your colour than mine. See ya tomorrow!'

Ellie stared after Tasha as she strode down the road towards the station. What she was feeling now wasn't good. She wanted to feel used, to feel appalled, to feel hurt. Instead what she felt was exhilaration. Worse than that, she felt something even fiercer. Trying to work out what it was, she could only come up with 'love'. All the same, as she walked to the bus stop she pushed her hand into her bag, pulled out the small shiny bottle and, looking round sharply, though not really seeing who was around, hurled it into the bin outside McDonald's.

FOUR

Grapefruit

'You should be doing this yourself. I shouldn't have to drag you over to Gran's,' Jay told Imogen as the two of them drove to Thames Ditton to inform Audrey that she was to be a great-grandmother.

'I've been busy. Stuff to do, college work. I'd have got round to it – you don't have to take me there, I'm not a kid.' Jay wasn't so sure about that – Imogen had her feet up on the dashboard, making dusty scuff marks. Her trainers had no laces in them and she'd stuck Bob the Builder stickers – that had come free with pots of yogurt – all round the toe sections. Jay could just picture her, sitting there at the kitchen table, concentrating hard on tweaking the stickers into place. Still, at least today she wasn't wearing her Plumber's Mate T-shirt. Audrey would be sure to point out that Moggie might as well unpick the apostrophe, then she could go round as walking evidence that plumbers do exactly what it said on her front.

What kind of mother was Imogen going to make? Would she cope? She still slept like an adolescent herself, long into the mornings given the chance; how was she going to get up several times in the night to deal with feeds and nappies and the crying?

'Moggie, at the rate you're moving these days your gran would have found out about the baby by reading it in the *Times* births column. Tristan's told his family, it's only fair that you tell yours.'

'You could've. She's your mum,' Imogen complained sulkily.

'She'd be hurt if she didn't hear it from you.'

'But she'll *fuss*.'

Imogen was right, Jay conceded privately. Audrey *would* fuss. She would ply her beloved granddaughter with weak tea and leaden scones and, during the coming months, would collect every magazine on pregnancy and parentcraft she could find and hand them to Imogen in a couple of tatty Sainsbury's bags, presenting them with as much flourish as if she'd given her something priceless and gift-wrapped. In spite of having been a breathtakingly hands-off parent herself, Audrey had taken on grandmotherhood with a rather haphazard fervour. Only the Christmas before, she'd made Ellie a white velvet hooded cloak, trimmed with Barbie-pink marabou and lined with scarlet sequinned lamé fabric. Luckily Ellie had had the good manners to pretend to be delighted. In fact she would have been if the cloak had been given to her six years sooner, when she'd have stood on the table and given them a chorus of 'Winter Wonderland'.

'She means well,' Jay murmured, feebly. 'She'll be really thrilled.' She crossed her fingers and hoped this would be true. Like most of her generation, Audrey did prefer the major events of life to occur in a comfortably settled, traditional order. When Jay had become pregnant with Imogen, while she too was at university, her mother had been hugely supportive but mostly as a reaction to Win's gloating sympathy about her having a daughter 'in trouble'. Behind closed doors she'd given her a good telling-off for carelessness before getting down to the fun stuff like searching out fabric for Jay's wedding dress and doing her proud with eight subtle shades of blue chiffon in a design Stella McCartney would have cried with joy to have created.

Jay's mother lived in a bungalow that adjoined her sister Win's. This pair of widows had long ago accepted that their differing approaches to housekeeping made it impossible for them to share living accommodation, but they relished existing within such close grumbling distance. Living alone, Audrey saw no need to confine her sewing to its own specific room and so she lived happily among a shifting drift of fabric offcuts, shreds of flimsy paper patterns and trailing threads. Clumps of chiffon, satin, Lycra and net were heaped around the place, every fragment kept in case a tiny rose trim was needed to complete a costume, or to augment a hair decoration. Half-finished catsuits, leotards, fur-fabric animal outfits and voluminous classical tulle ballet dresses hung from every door frame. Stray threads of cotton wafted throughout the bungalow after her, ingraining themselves too deeply into carpets for the vacuum cleaner to reach.

Win, visiting from next door, picked sequins out of the sugar bowl and tut-tutted about A Place for Everything. On returning to her own home, she'd spend a good long time in her hallway tweaking minute threads and bits of fancy feathers off her shoes and clothes and making sure they didn't escape into her own im-maculate furnishings. Audrey saved her best domestic efforts for the garden. Whereas Win had covered her half of the semis' gardens with no-fuss obliterating gravel (so you could hear the approaching crunch of midnight burglars, not a joyful prospect that, as Audrey had pointed out), enlivened only with small plaster statues of miniature poodles and the occasional ugly variegated shrub, Audrey had cultivated gloriously thriving beds of flourishing perennials and arrays of spring and autumn bulbs that would bring a joyful tear to Alan Titchmarsh's eye.

'Watch out for pins on the carpet,' Audrey said as she opened the front door to Imogen and Jay, 'I've been on the go with four tutus since early this morning. It's a bugger, net. Nasty springy stuff. Tea? We'll have to go in the kitchen, I'm cutting out a lion in the sitting room.' Audrey led them through the hall to her kitchen.

Behind Jay, Imogen groaned quietly. 'No tea for me, Gran, thanks. I've gone right off it.'

'Oh really?' Audrey said, half-turning to look at her granddaughter and colliding with a pair of turquoise Lycra leggings that hung from the banisters. 'That's new. What's brought that on? Some kind of diet fad?'

'Er no. Nothing like that.' Imogen cleared a heap of paper patterns and a bag of knitting from the chairs and sat beside Audrey's old round pine table.

'You young girls, you're always on some new health kick or other. When we were young we ate what we were given and were thankful. But then of course,' Audrey said, scooping several packets of cakes and biscuits out of the cupboard, 'food was in a lot shorter supply in those days. You wouldn't think of picking and choosing and snacking on crisps.'

Audrey plonked her squat brown teapot down on the table and arranged three mugs in a triangle beside it. The nearest one to Jay showed a profile of the Queen's head and 'Silver Jubilee 1977' written in gold beneath it. Imogen's refusal of tea had been ignored, as they had both known it would be, and she was toying with the handle of a mug that instructed her to 'Protect and Survive' beneath a CND symbol.

How had this ancient mismatched crockery lasted? Last summer Jay, forever in pursuit of the kind of order so alien to her mother, had bought a dozen beautiful large handcrafted cups, each painted with bold brash bluebells, from a potter in Devon, only to see most of them vanish in less than a year, victims of clumsy handling, of unskilled dishwasher loading or of Rory carelessly chipping them against the sink. She feared for the sink too, at those moments. Corian was supposed to be a hyper-tough kitchen surface but if anyone could make a dint in it, surely the heavy-handed Rory would be able to manage it.

Audrey had barely poured an inch of tea into the CND mug when the back door was flung open. Win, plump and jowly, came bustling in and in one slick long-practised movement had whipped another mug from the cupboard, cleared magazines from a chair and sat down.

'I saw your car,' she said to Jay. 'Just thought I'd pop in and say hello.'

'You mean you smelled a pot of tea on the go through a brick wall,' Audrey muttered. Win was eager and clearly pent up with things to tell, and took no notice.

'You'll have come to talk about the news,' she said to Jay, smiling gleefully. 'Wonderful isn't it? I bet you're pleased. I said you would be.'

Imogen gasped. 'How did you know? Who told you?'

'Delphine of course. She phoned.' Win pushed her hand deep into the massive black patent bag she carried everywhere. 'And now she's written. She always does prefer to write – she's got such lovely handwriting and there's always lovely descriptions. The scenery . . .'

'But she . . . ah. Cross purposes I think.' Jay gave Imogen a warning look.

Win's hand was now scurrying again among the many zipped bag sections for her reading glasses. She gave up the search and handed an envelope (sugared-almond pink, lined with pale green tissue, purely and perfectly Delphine) to Jay. 'Go on, you can read it for yourself.'

But before Jay got the chance, Win announced the contents. 'She says she's going to live near Kingston, just by the river, in one of those lovely new apartments. Your Greg had something to do with those didn't he? *Penthouse.*' Win savoured the word as if it was part of a prayer. 'She'll be up the road practically, here for her poor mother in her old age.'

Audrey pulled a face at Jay, who stifled a giggle. 'And this new fiancé.' Win took a second or two to sip her tea, grimaced and reached back to the worktop (without needing to look) for the sugar bowl. 'This new fiancé, he's an *airline pilot*.' There was another small silence for her audience to absorb the 'hasn't-she-done-well' aspect of this occupation. It was obviously part of the same prayer as 'penthouse'.

'Anyway, Jay my dear,' she said, patting Jay's hand, 'he's away ever such a lot so she says it would be a good idea for your cleaning people to go in and do a complete scrub-through before she gets here. You do do that sort of thing don't you? Cleaning?'

Jay, feeling close to speechless, managed to mutter, 'Yes. Well the staff do, the girls I employ, you know . . .'

'Jay stop it, you're rambling,' her mother cut in. 'It's a perfectly good job, nothing wrong with cleaning.'

Imogen, looking round the terminally cluttered kitchen, spluttered over her chocolate mini-roll, sending crumbs scattering.

'Oh nobody said it wasn't.' Win nodded, briskly, her several chins wobbling and setting up a sort of ripple effect. 'Funny you should end up doing it for a job though, you being the clever one and all.' Jay held her breath and counted. 'What with your degree, and Delphine not even passing her eleven-plus. Not that it's held her back, oh no . . .'

'What about me?' Imogen stood up, went to the sink and poured her tea down the drain, then refilled the mug with water from the tap. 'What about my news? Doesn't anyone want to know?'

'Go on then dear, what have you done? Have you got yourself engaged as well? To that boy who talks nicely?'

'Win, do shut up and let someone else get a word in,' Audrey said.

Imogen laughed. 'Engaged? That's like sooo naff? Apart from the big fancy ring I suppose. That'd be OK. No. I'm pregnant. You two are going to be a great-gran and a great-great-aunt.'

There was a five second silence while the two sisters exchanged glances that seemed to include a mutual counting of too many 'greats' for comfort. They then duetted, 'So when are you getting married?'

Imogen looked puzzled, as if they'd mentioned a long-discontinued ritual that she'd only vaguely heard of.

'I don't think they've thought of getting married yet,' Jay said quietly, then making the mistake of adding, 'they're a bit young.'

'Not too young to have a baby though,' Win pointed out, lips pursed.

'They'll be all right. They've got the downstairs flat to live in and all of us around to help.' If Jay had her own doubts, she wasn't going to let on to Win. And did she have doubts? How could she not? What about baby-care when Moggie left college and started teaching? What about . . . oh what was the point? There was a long way to go yet, time to think it through, or rather time for *Imogen and Tris* to think it through.

'Well I think it's wonderful. A baby is always a welcome addition.' Audrey said, putting her arms round Imogen and hugging her tight.

'You've said that before,' Win reminded her sister. 'When Jay got herself into trouble and fell for young Imogen here. Still, at least *she* managed to get Greg to do the decent thing.'

Win poured herself some more tea and gave Imogen a somewhat pitying look. 'I'll get some wool, dear. The baby'll need a proper layette and I don't suppose you girls today have got the first clue with a pair of needles. Lemon. I'll get lemon. Boy or girl, you can't go wrong with lemon.'

Grapefruit. The kitchen was full of them. They were down among the oranges in the splintery old wooden fruit bowl, as if trying to hide for fear of being crammed on top of the juicer and having their soft innards cruelly gouged out. They lurked in the chiller box at the bottom of the fridge, too cold to hang onto their flavour, waiting their turn to be promoted to join the oranges and lemons. They also sat, these plump yellow globes, lined up like fat smug suns on the breadboard, occasionally lolling slowly to one side or another and down to the floor from where Rory kicked them at the fridge, with as much drama and posturing as if he had just been brought on in place of Wayne Rooney. Jay was sick of the sight of grapefruit. She was, however, three pounds lighter after barely a week. It was tempting to show off this fact, to strut about saying things like, 'Does my bum look small in this?' but she knew better than to tempt ridicule, more of which she frankly did not need.

'You're definitely going yellow, Mum,' Rory had commented as Jay tackled her pre-supper half-grapefuit the night before. 'You're going to end up the colour of custard.'

Jay had smiled weakly at him, feeling the cold sour juice stinging her teeth as she bit into the flesh. It was

surprisingly sticky stuff, grapefruit, and it got everywhere. Despite its searing sharpness it managed to
leave her fingers as cloyed as if she'd dipped them in
syrup.

After the second day, Jay had taken to eating the
grapefruit in an almost secretive way. It was all right in
the mornings; grapefruit with breakfast (or even *as*
breakfast) was a perfectly acceptable food item. But at
other meals grapefruit was a gatecrasher, to the extent
that there was something antisocial about sitting down
by herself and working her way through this diet food.
It rated somewhere between medicine and ostentation.
Ellie disapproved, scowling in the near-vocal way only
a near-fourteen-year-old could achieve.

'It's very bad for me to have a dieting mother,' she
told Jay. 'I'm impressionable. I'm at an age where I
might get a food disorder.'

'You make it sound like something you shop for,'
Greg teased her, 'In which case I'd have thought you
wouldn't be seen dead with something your mother's
got, seeing as you're at that age too.'

Ellie's scowl deepened – not that Greg noticed, being
deeply involved in trying to get the hang of something
deathly on Rory's PlayStation – to the point where Jay
wondered if she should warn her that she would be
queueing up for Botox by the time she was seventeen if
she furrowed her brow so dramatically and so constantly. Ellie had such a little face, her eyes and mouth
looked far too big for it, as if she'd been allocated
somebody else's in the pre-birth handout of features.
Every frown and grimace seemed to crumple too large a
proportion of her skin, as if her expressions were
already fully adult-size but the rest of her hadn't
yet caught up. On the plus side, when she looked
really happy she was glorious, completely alight with
pleasure. In repose, her expression might well tend

47

towards moodiness apart from those giveaway corners of her turned-up mouth.

Sometimes, in one of those horror moments that sneak up and pounce on all mothers' imaginings, Jay frightened herself by thinking that Ellie looked like the classic teenage schoolgirl murder victim. She was little for her age, sexy without knowing it, too pretty with only nature's help: overall a paedophile's wet dream. She was noticeably smaller than most of her contemporaries, inches shorter and skinny-bodied just as Jay herself had been. There were times, when Ellie came home with a friend (especially the hulking Serena who'd been last year's best friend) or Jay gave some of them a lift in the van, when it was hard to remember not to talk to these girls as if they were so much older than Ellie, as if they were the near-women they resembled.

At the same time, she had to be careful not to treat Ellie too much like a young child. She might look barely more than primary-school age, but inside her head there must be teen stuff going on, close to four-teen years' worth of growing and learning and thinking things out just the same as her blowsy, fleshy friends. Jay remembered well enough how hard it was to be the undersized one, to know she hadn't a hope of getting into an over-fifteen film or to be eyeing up the boys on the way to school but knowing they'd never look twice while she was still wearing pony-print knickers with 'age 11–12' on the label.

It was hard to know just what *did* go on in Ellie's head. She didn't give a lot away. Just recently though, she'd been looking as if there was something pleasing her in a secret way.

'She's up to something,' Jay commented to Greg as they lay in bed that night under the planes, the stars and the possible observance of Planet Man.

'Probably,' Greg agreed. 'She's getting to the Age of Secrets. A boy, do you think?'

'Doubt it. Even if she was more grown-up-looking she'd still be a bit young.'

'Maybe. Though there's thirteen, and there's thirteen-going-on-twenty-three.'

'She's got the rest of her life to be grown-up, give her a break. She's not even that interested in make-up and clothes. She's like me. I was no more than a wannabe pony girl at thirteen. Boys and make-up didn't figure at all,' Jay said, thinking back to the after-school hours she'd spent leaning on the paddock fence at Mrs Allen's scruffy junkyard riding school, longing and longing for Delphine to let her have her promised go on the plump little pony. This chubby toffee creature, with a cascading blond, flicky mane like the Timotei shampoo girl, was Delphine's pet and weapon of supreme manipulation. Jay owned a sweet and loving black cat that made Delphine sneeze in an exaggeratedly suffering manner, but from Santa, the year she was eleven, Delphine received every girl's dream of a pony complete with monogrammed blanket, grooming kit and fabulous, biscuit-coloured, squeaky leather tack. Only a child destined for sainthood could fail to be envious.

Even many years later, when she'd bought a My Little Pony Grooming Parlour for Imogen's fifth birthday with its miniature pink brushes, curry-combs, rosettes and ribbons, Jay had had a pang of nostalgic covetousness, recalling Delphine's real-life equivalent. Jay's mother Audrey had been sniffy about the pony's expense and declared it would be a five-minute wonder, that the creature would be abandoned in a matter of weeks to languish in a field, getting fat and grumpy. But in the months of meantime, the power shift between Jay and Delphine was even more horribly unbalanced.

The deal had been that Win would let Delphine stay for whole afternoons at the stables as long as Jay (being that bit older) was there to keep an eye on her. In exchange Jay was supposed to be allowed to share the riding time on Cobweb. Delphine wasn't cut out for sharing. She was an only child and the pony was only hers. She was the one who could say yes or no about who got to sit on its glossy saddle. She loved power much more than she loved poor Cobweb. At Mrs Allen's Delphine would canter round and round the sandy practice ring, flicking the pony over foot-high jumps, yelling instructions at Cobweb the whole time. 'Bad, stupid pony!' she'd roar, when she lost a stirrup or mistimed her approach. All the time she'd be eyeing Jay sideways, slyly smiling as she watched her hanging over the fence with an uncontrollable expression of yearning. Jay would always get her ride – it would be a brief twenty minutes or so till Delphine got bored and fidgety and demanded to go home in case Mrs Allen noticed she had nothing to do and allocated the less pleasant tack-room duties to her.

'I wasn't a bad rider, actually.' Jay was almost surprised to hear herself saying it aloud.

'Eh? What? Horses?' Greg looked puzzled. 'Or,' and his tone became more animated, 'motorbikes?' Horses to Greg were merely optional decorative items for a rustic scene and best viewed from a safe distance. Motorbikes on the other hand were objects of desire and he knew quite well that when the time came for an edgy male menopause to strike, a shiny, bestudded Harley-Davidson Electraglide would be top of his splash-out list and he would joyously embrace his inner biker before it was too late.

'Horses.' Jay laughed. 'What made you think I'd got a motorbike history that you didn't know about?'

'Dunno, but even after twenty-one years you can't

know everything about a person, can you? It was quite an exciting thought, picturing you zapping to school on a little Vespa or something, all straw boater held on with elastic and your skirt wafting up in the wind.'

'Sorry to disappoint you, Greg. I wasn't even a bicycle girl, let alone a motorbike one. I could never understand why on cold wet winter days some of the girls from school were pedalling down the high street having cars swoosh puddles all over them when they could be all steamy and warm on a crowded bus.'

Greg rolled towards her and snaked his hand under the duvet and across her stomach. 'That's you,' he said, snuggling into her neck. 'A keen eye for the comfort option.'

Jay wasn't sure what to make of that – it was disconcertingly close to telling her she was fat and idle. Fat (ish) maybe, she conceded (though working on it . . .) but idle, hardly. Another day out with Henry tomorrow, she thought as she pit-patted her Cif-whitened fingers down Greg's back. Such a pity Henry was a vacuum cleaner.

FIVE

Skinny Latte (Two Sugars)

Ellie waited at the bus stop in the drizzle, a suitable distance from her brother. They got on fine, quite well really considering, even if Rory believed deep down and unchangeably 50 Cent was the greatest star, music-wise, ever, ever ever. And he played the Darkness louder than anyone who wanted to keep their ears from shrivelling could possibly stand. All the same, you didn't travel on the bus to school sitting next to your brother. There was no written-down reason, you just didn't, End Of.

Rory was huddled into one of the bus stop's pull-down seats under the shelter, rudely ignoring an elderly woman struggling with two walking sticks and a handbag big enough to contain, Ellie shocked herself by thinking grotesquely, a severed human head. Rory looked about as miserable as it was possible to look, even at eight fifteen in the morning. Ellie watched from the back of the queue as he wrapped his arms across his chest, reaching them round as far as he could and shivering dramatically. He was really pale too, but then who wasn't in chill March. And he was fidgety, in that way she remembered he used to be when he was little and was about to throw up but didn't quite know it yet.

She started to feel hot and panicky – she needed to make sure he *was* completely OK about the state of his insides before they were trapped on the bus and it was too horribly late.

'Rory?' Ellie went to the front of the queue and tugged at his arm. 'Rory, are you . . .'

'Hi Ellie! You OK babes?' Tasha, all glittery gold eyeshadow and the chemical whiff of knocked-off market perfume, appeared beside her.

'This your brother, innit?' Ellie watched Tasha push her shoulder bag a bit further back so her breasts jutted forward inside her shiny black hooded jacket. She wondered if she was wearing the red and silver bra. Tasha had wolfy teeth, big, grinning and predatory, gnashing up and down hard on Barbie-pink gum. Rory was now staring at the floor, his head in his hands, elbows resting awkwardly on his knees.

Please don't, Ellie thought suddenly, please don't chuck up on Tasha's perfect kitten-heeled square-toed boots that must have cost a mint, if she'd actually paid for them. With them she was wearing diamond-pattern black tights. Cool-as and also not to be sicked on. Rory glanced up, looking bleary, and grunted something at the two girls, then raced off down the road, back towards home.

'What's he say? What's wrong with him? Have I got eggy breath or something?' Tash was staring after the running figure of Rory, which ducked down an alleyway out of sight. I was right, Ellie thought, he was feeling pukey. He was probably right now leaning on the fence round the back of Oddbins barfing his toast and raspberry jam all over the alleyway's dog shit and wind-blown Macca wrappers. Better not to mention it to Tasha, it would be all round school in a something-to-laugh-at sort of way.

'He said he'd forgotten something. His brain possibly.'

Ellie laughed. 'If he ever had one. And anyway, how come you're here? I thought you lived over the other side of the bridge. This isn't your usual stop.'

Tasha linked her arm through Ellie's. 'My dad was going to drop me off and then I saw you. Thought I'd come and say hi. Don't mind do you?' Tasha squeezed Ellie's arm. There was pressure from Tasha's hard, bony fingers even through her school sweatshirt and padded jacket. It was a pressure that was emphatic; it underlined that Tasha had made a thought-out choice to be with her, not just turned up by accident or coincidence.

Across the road another uniformed girl was hurrying towards them, racing to get to the stop before the approaching bus. Amanda Harrison, Ellie's friend, the girl she usually sat with – not just on the bus but in most classes and at lunch – was waving as she ran. There was a choice to be made here and as they all clustered to board the bus she knew with a sort of elated helplessness that it was no contest. Tasha slid into a double seat, patted the one next to her (sugar-mouse-pink nails with added heart motif in silver) and Ellie sat beside her. Amanda was great, she really, really liked her but sometimes you just needed a bit of danger in your life.

Delphine's handwriting was neat, upright and spiky. The envelope was pale lilac and suggested that it contained a pretty greetings card rather than the business-like list that Jay found herself reading.

'Bloody cheek,' she muttered to Tristan, who had come up from the basement flat to have a look at the leaky tap in the attic shower room. In twenty minutes he'd made his way only as far up the house as the kitchen and was making himself a cup of tea, claiming that no plumber could be expected to work without a sharpening shot of caffeine. Good thing, Jay thought, that I don't have to pay him by the hour.

'Listen to this, Tris,' she said as she scanned Delphine's instructions. 'She wants me to have this Charles person round for drinks before I go and give his flat the professional once-over. "Make a bit of a party of it," she orders me. "Welcome him into the family." Hmm.'

No wonder Delphine preferred to write instead of phone (or e-mail, how come she hadn't caught up with e-mailing?). She knew perfectly well no-one could argue with safely distant written instructions. You can't simply slam down a letter like you can a phone.

Tris swooshed hot water three times round the tea-pot then poured it down the sink before carefully measuring four flat spoonfuls of Twinings Darjeeling into the pot. Jay wondered what he did when he was out on his regular plumbing jobs. Did he wince at householders' cheap tea-bagged offerings (Staff Tea – she'd seen it stashed away along with a jar of super-market instant coffee and plenty of white sugar in many of the houses she'd cleaned) provided in thick heavy mugs? He and Delphine would get on wonder-fully. They'd bond over fine bone china and an abhorrence of twice-boiled water.

'But you have great parties. It'll be well cool,' Tris said, placing Jay's late grandmother's silver strainer on top of a rose-patterned Coalport cup and saucer that were so delicate you could see through the glaze. It had been a perfect joky find at the school car-boot sale, bought specially to indulge Tristan and his taste for dainty traditions. (Win had seen it on the worktop, turned over the cup and said, 'Ooh lovely, Cole Porter') What on earth he was doing living with slapdash, untidy Imogen – apart from the sex and procreation thing – she could hardly begin to imagine.

'We do, we do,' she agreed, though recalling that on the last Christmas Eve, the big garden flares had set fire to next-door's fence. All the oldest ladies from the retirement home up the road had turned out in their dressing gowns to warm themselves at the blaze and shout naughty comments to the firefighters about the size of their hoses.

'But all I really need to do is check over his flat, arrange this cleaning blitz that Delphine wants, give him a price and allocate a couple of the girls to do the work. I didn't think it was going to involve . . . well *involvement*. I assumed we'd do the socializing bit when she actually gets here. After all, surely the introductions are her job.'

'Well you could just, like, tell her that?' Tris suggested, with the simple logic of youth. 'Tell her no? E-mail? Phone?'

Jay stared at the letter again. 'Oh I suppose I could phone – she doesn't "do" e-mail, but . . . you don't know Delphine – she's always got an unarguable reason for having things her own way. She says here it would really help her out if it's me who introduces him to Win. Listen to this; she says, "He'll be the third husband I've brought home for Mum to give the once-over. I know she'll say something completely barmy if it's just me and her and then he'll think that in marrying me he gets part share in a family of nutters." I hope she's not including me in that. And she goes on, "Get it out of the way for me, Jay, would you. She'll be on her best behaviour if she's got a smart frock on and a g. and t. in her hand. Just make sure it's her first, not her fourth." Oh and get this, Tris.' Tris took a long sip of his perfect tea, closing his eyes blissfully like Daffodil the cat after she'd had a go at a dollop of tuna.

'She says – can you believe it – "You might need to know that Charles is allergic to smoked salmon."' Jay laughed, 'Instructions, instructions – that's Delphine. She was born in the wrong era. She should have been a Roman with teams of slaves. I'm surprised she didn't give me a list of acceptable canapés and a map showing a correct buffet-table layout.'

'She sounds a . . . a . . .' Tristan was groping for words as he carefully washed his cup under the hot tap.

'A control freak?' Jay finished for him. 'Oh she's that all right. No question. But I'm supposed to be all grown-up now. I can say no.'

Tristan raised an eyebrow (the one pierced with a small gold bar).

'I'll think about it,' Jay insisted. 'Anyway, gotta go. Got a mutiny among the staff to sort out. See you later Tris, good luck with the tap.'

Rory felt better now. He'd made an executive decision not to go to school – well he was doing the teachers a favour really, they wouldn't want someone in their classrooms who might puke on the floor and scupper the lesson. He spent a peaceful hour in the park having a cigarette or two, a can of Coke and a mooch about by the pond to see what the ducks were up to. He'd watched two of them mating and it looked like a sadistic sort of process. Date rape at best; the male had grabbed the female by the back of the neck and shoved her head under the water while he did the deed. Then he'd let go, left her on her own to fluff up her feathers again and done a lap of honour, racing round and round, squawking. The triumphant drake reminded him of blokes at school on a Monday morning, the sporty ones like Ben Pickard and Alan Simmonson when they'd got some action at the weekend. They came in all cocky with a swaggery walk and a smirk, looking for someone to guess what they'd done. Some of them even said it, not even a lead-in, just in-yer-face with things like, 'You know that Kelly in 5R, the fit one with the tits?' and straight in with the details to whoever was in the way.

He himself had nothing to report as yet, well apart from party snogging and the odd feel, nothing at the Ben-and-Alan level anyway. Not that he *would* report. He'd decided to be a bloke girls could trust, so that they could all agree when they talked about him and coo to each other, 'Oh Rory, he's just so *lovely*', not a bastard who practically ran his conquests' pants up the school flagpole for everyone to snigger at. His way, they'd like him as a friend, they'd trust him and know he wasn't just out for what he could get. Also, being A Nice Person, he might pull more of them. Not cynical at all then, he chuckled to himself as he sat down on a damp bench next to where a couple of rooks were efficiently emptying a garbage bin with their beaks.

Rory was starting to feel a bit sick again. It must have been that toast – he should have given the bread a proper look when he got it out of the pack, made sure there weren't any mouldy bits on it. Jay had said she couldn't be responsible for ensuring the bread was inside its sell-by – especially as she wasn't eating it at the moment. Bloody diets. Or it might have been the jam. Sometimes you found stuff at the back of the fridge and it looked like someone was trying to grow their own antibiotics. Lots of the food was still Imogen's, special sorts of honey that she liked, blueberry jam, lime pickle. She had her own fridge down in the basement, why didn't she move all her poxy food? He hoped she'd be a bit more germ-free when the baby arrived, otherwise the poor kid wouldn't have a chance.

Holding onto his aching stomach, Rory put his feet up on the bench and stretched out, lying full length along the seat to see if his insides would feel better when they weren't scrunched up. Two of the old park biddies that were always in there gave him a look and a dose of tutting as they went past. They were in full olds-out-walking kit of all-weather woolly crochet hat and tartan scarf, dragging their Scottie dogs that were supposed to be white but looked yellowy round the edges, like snow that's been pissed on. He felt worse, if anything, lying down. The biddies would feel sorry for him if they knew; they'd pat his head and say grand-motherly comfort stuff. He wished he was at home now, groaning miserably in his own bed. The pain in his gut was getting sharper and was there all the time, not just twingeing sometimes like before. Whatever he'd had for breakfast would have to be evicted from the fridge the minute he got home, before everyone in the house got ill and the whole place was declared a deadly disease zone and headlined on the local TV news.

The women had done their circuit of the pond and were coming back for a second round. You'd think he'd meant to do it, by the look on their faces, the pulling back the dogs and the shudder of disgust like he was some junkie on a downer. After all, you couldn't control the moment when you barfed on the pathway. No-one could, he was willing to bet, not even this outraged pair of old wifeys.

How wonderfully useful it was to have a functioning artisan as part of the family, Jay thought as she drove out to negotiate with Mrs Caldwell, Dishing the Dirt's serial complainer. How much more handy that Imogen had fallen in love with Tristan the plumber rather than someone such as, for example, a City money trader whose expertise was only in the coffee futures market and how to get a good deal on an Audi TT. When the time came for career choices to be made by Rory and Ellie she would encourage them firmly away from sit-down office occupations, and try to point them in the direction of carpentry and electrical work. In an area such as this, affluent, educated and devoutly non-practical, there would never be a shortage of work. There was a course at the local college grandly entitled The Built Environment, whose students, over the past few years, had constructed a whole new art block and some very fancy walling round the car park.

Ask most bright kids about their futures and they said they wanted to be 'lawyers'. Did they really know what that entailed? Did they have a clue how many hours they'd waste trying to find someone to degunge the washing machine just because they'd got no simple hands-on skills of their own? How many lawyers could a country need anyway, she wondered as she made her way over the bridge and down to the Common to sort out why every one of her staff had now refused to do so much as another hour's work for Mrs Caldwell.

Jay pulled into the pale gravelled driveway of the double-fronted quasi-Georgian house and parked beside Barbara's Volvo estate that still had the Cats on Board sticker in the back window from the West London Area Burmese Championship qualifiers, held the weekend before. There was a window-cleaner's truck as well. His ladders were propped up against the house front and Jay could hear the faint squeaking of chammy on glass. Another essential worker, she thought. After all, how many householders these days were prepared to risk going up ladders with the Windolene Wet Wipes? Greg got dizzy at the top of his own glass staircase and had to drink half a bottle of Rescue Remedy when he was out on an architectural recce and had to shin up some scaffolding.

This meeting had to be a two-hander, for Mrs

Caldwell had a wide circle of book-group friends and she could, if she accumulated enough grumbles to report them, be extremely bad for business. The area had several van-and-mop businesses like Dishing the Dirt, and clients went from one to another as recommendations came and went. The casual cleaners did exactly the same of course, which meant that a client, changing companies simply because a girl had missed a dusty skirting board once too often, might well get the same girl back again but wearing a different logo on her apron.

'Do come in.' Mrs Caldwell had the door open before Jay was out of the car. Disconcertingly, Jay noticed she was wearing almost identical clothes to her own – black trousers and top with a honey-coloured fine wool cardigan. She'd guess Mrs Caldwell's was cashmere as opposed to lambswool and that her trousers were Joseph, not M & S. Oh and two sizes smaller than her own. Bloody grapefruit, she thought, giving Mrs Caldwell what she hoped was a smile that combined both a business-like attitude and reassurance. Neither offering was returned with any warmth.

'Come through to the kitchen. Your business colleague is already here.' Jay could see Barbara sitting at a long oak table and looking uncomfortable behind a row of folded garments. She caught her eye as she followed the cashmere cardi into a kitchen full of cerise lacquered units polished to a standard of blinding reflectiveness. If Dishing the Dirt's Monique had done this, it would be impossible to agree she was incompetent. Barbara gave her a weak smile that wasn't easy to interpret. Jay hoped fervently it didn't mean 'total nutter'. She still shuddered at the memory of the woman who'd made a Battenberg-effect birthday cake for her dog out of chopped liver and tripe and then offered her cleaner a slice.

'We have a problem.' Mrs Caldwell almost pushed Jay into a chair beside Barbara and stood looking down on them like a headmistress facing a pair of persistent truants. She was straight in, no faffing about being social. Coffee would have been nice, Jay thought, and a biscuit selection that she could virtuously resist.

'Ironing.'

'Ironing,' Barbara repeated, leaning forward and looking attentive.

'Ironing,' Mrs Caldwell said again.

We're going to be here all day, Jay thought, fighting the urge to look at her watch. Her phone was vibrating in her pocket too; it might be a new client. Perhaps she could sneak off to the loo (left of front door, under the stairs, walls decorated with cases of gloomy stuffed trout caught by Mr C. To be taken down fortnightly and all glass polished) and see if Mrs Caldwell could be dealt with by a pleasing deletion from the rota.

'Ironing.' Mrs Caldwell pointed a square-nailed sapphire-ringed finger at the assortment of items in front of her on the table. 'Your girls don't seem to get the hang. I've left notes, I've had words – not that they understand, most of them – I've even shown by example, as here. But do they take notice?'

Both Barbara and Jay opened their mouths to reply but Mrs Caldwell was in first. 'No they do not. Shirts.'

'We've taught them the right order: collar, cuffs, sleeves and body.' Barbara defended her trade, her voice as crisp as starched fine linen.

'Oh I'm sure. But then *they hang them up!*'

'Well yes, of course. As instructed.'

'No, no, no! I want them *folded*, I want them presented as if they've just come from the shop, freshly bought. You must tell them. And blouses and pyjama tops.' Mrs Caldwell patted the top of one of the folded heaps.

'It sounds rather time-consuming,' Jay commented slyly. Time wasted on one job was time taken from another.

'But it's how I want them!'

'Of course. We'll have a little chat with the girls. Now is that . . . ?' Barbara made a move to get up but Mrs Caldwell hadn't finished. Outside the window cleaner clattered down his ladder and Jay heard water swooshing into the outside drain. For his sake, she hoped the man hadn't carelessly slopped any over the doormat or he'd be joining them in the kitchen line-up for a telling-off.

'Not it's not all, not quite.' Mrs Caldwell reached for another garment. 'Underwear,' she declared, holding up a pair of fine mesh pants, pink-flowered on a blue background and edged with cornflower lace. 'They should be folded *thrice* like so . . .'

The window cleaner knocked on the kitchen door and pushed it open, putting his head round and grinning at Jay and Barbara. Mrs Caldwell whirled round, knickers still held aloft.

'All done, love. That'll be thirty quid.' He gave Mrs Caldwell a lascivious wink. 'Nice knickies darlin', but I think I'll give our usual little extras a miss today, ta, if it's all the same to you.'

'Well that went well, I thought. Not,' Barbara said to Jay as they sat in Starbucks celebrating their telling-off with some much-needed coffee.

Jay stirred her skinny latte (plus two sugars) and laughed. 'It is *her*, isn't it? I mean, it is Mrs Caldwell who's overdemanding, not us who're sloppy and hopeless?'

'Are you serious? The woman's obsessive. Barking. She told Monique off once for winding the flex on the iron the wrong way. I mean, for heaven's sake, get

63

a life, woman. Some of them . . .' Barbara shook her head.

'Some of them you just want to shake.'

'And vac,' Barbara spluttered. 'I had a dream once that the Dachshund Man had been freeze-dried, scattered on the floor and hoovered up. Gruesome.' She grabbed Jay's hand suddenly. 'Don't tell anyone that, please, you promise?'

'You got it. It's just between us, that little fantasy. What shall we do now? I don't much feel like going home and adding up how many bottles of Mr Muscle we're going to need next month – it'll probably start me on some mad train of thought about why it isn't called Mrs Muscle, or Ms at the very least. How about you? Have you got cats to de-flea or de-worm or shall we comfort ourselves some more with a bit of retail therapy?'

'I can manage an hour or two – let's not do clothes though, let's go and do cosmetics. We could get mad-witch eyeshadow colours to scare Mrs C. next time she hauls us over the coals.'

The two of them wandered through the town centre and into the luscious scent-soaked cosmetics department of the biggest store. 'Mmm,' Jay said, closing her eyes and inhaling. 'The smell of lots of purchase possibilities. I need, and that's *need*, not merely want, some new lipgloss.'

She tried several, covering the back of her hand with smears of colour till she resembled the paint chart she'd used when decorating Ellie's bedroom the year before. It seemed, she thought as she paid for her choice, a ludicrous amount of money to hand over for such a titchy pot of bronzy-pink goo. No wonder women bought so much – at that price you just had to hurl all your faith into it.

Barbara declared herself well pleased with a new

perfume and some smudgy purple-grey eyeliner. 'Makes a change from browns for me,' she said, 'I keep buying all these taupe shades. I get them home and realize I've been influenced by the colours of my cats. Ridiculous.'

'What's so wonderful,' Jay mused as they walked towards the car park, 'is that make-up can't make you fat, drunk, pregnant or ill. It's a near sin with no punishment and no side effects. Perfect.'

'If you go . . . and I'm not meaning you, this is rhetorical, you're nowhere near a candidate,' Barbara said, 'If you, *one*, went to a sort of Overeaters Anonymous, do you think you have to rely on a Higher Power, like they do at the Alcoholics one? What do you think?'

'I hadn't thought,' Jay told her. 'Hadn't given it a moment's consideration. I suppose you'd have to. I just know I haven't got the right sort. My Higher Power, the one in my head that I listen to, is a jolly live-and-let-live soul who likes a drink and a good social nosh-up. It likes chocolate and doesn't even try to tell me not to have it. It says, go on, eat that doughnut, a bit of what you fancy can't hurt. He or she isn't on my side about the diet at all.'

Barbara stopped by the window of a new shop. There were all sorts of vitamin potions piled up in the window display along with diet remedies, powders and pills and drinks all claiming to be essential for toxic cleansing and inner purity. Photos of slender, bikini-clad women playing beach volleyball tempted body-envy. She and Jay wandered into the shop where soft persuasive music was playing and looked at a huge toy-like selection of primary-coloured tummy toners, exercise wheels, hand weights and elastic straps, every gadget promising to change your body shape, to tone, stretch and lengthen muscles till, presumably, they had to be folded double to fit inside your skin.

'You could waste your whole life playing with this lot,' Barbara said, picking up a broad elastic band, putting one end under her foot and hauling hard on the other end. It escaped from beneath her shoe and snapped back at her viciously, sending her flying into an artistically arranged stack of cartons that clattered to the floor.

Jay, overcome with laughter, started picking them up. 'Hell's teeth, look at this! Cellulite patches!'

'You can buy it in *patches*?' Barbara said, misunderstanding and grabbing one of the boxes. 'Oh I see, you stick them on and it gets *rid* of it.'

'I shall get some. I must try it.'

'You're mad, Jay, you know it can't work! It couldn't possibly!'

'Hey, it's just like the make-up, isn't it? You've got to believe in the magic. Of course I'm going to try it. What can it hurt?'

'About twenty-five quid, it says here. Lucky you're not trying to give up smoking as well, you could be all patch and no skin.'

'Lucky it's not summer as well,' Jay agreed, pulling her debit card out of her wallet. 'I'd get a spotty tan and end up looking like an albino leopard.'

Jay's phone rang just as they were leaving the shop. 'Not more disgruntled clients, please,' she said, not recognizing the caller's number. It was the hospital, telling her not to worry.

'Why do they say that?' she wailed to Barbara as soon as she'd finished the call. 'Why do they tell you not to worry when there's obviously something to worry about? I've got to go, Rory's ill. They said they don't think it's anything "too serious", as if you're supposed to be able to interpret that and come up with any sense. Oh God, I must dash . . . where did I leave the car?'

'It's round the corner on the green, just next to the Cricketers pub. I'll see you soon,' Barbara said, hugging her. 'Let me know how he is and send him my love. And I'll summon up my own higher power, put in a word for him.'

SIX

Patches

From just inside the stuffy waiting area, beside the League of Friends shop (selling an amazing array of intricately knitted pastel bedjackets) Jay could see Greg sauntering towards the Accident and Emergency department, bouncing slightly with his loose-legged old-hippy walk straight across the busy car park, without looking to see if any vehicle was backing out of a space and likely to turn him into a patient. She wished he'd do a bit of stop, look and listen; people who were driving to and from hospital premises usually had more on their minds than avoiding marauding pedestrians. Some drivers in these cars would be caught up in deep new grief, others would be here to join in with a birth, some could be jubilant with relief that an invasive and much-dreaded procedure was now over and then there'd be those, like her, who'd been hurled into a sudden, unexpected worry about their sick child.

'So. Appendicitis. You don't hear much about that these days, do you? Poor old Rory!' Greg greeted Jay quite cheerfully as the automatic doors opened and a blast of cool air whirled into the building with him. He sounded, Jay thought, as if Rory had had nothing more than an unlucky run-in with a stinging nettle. This, from a man who had taken to his bed with 'gangrene' the previous summer when he'd contracted a touch of athlete's foot. The air outside smelled fresh and robust and she wished the doors could stay open, reconnecting the inmates with the world of health and wholeness beyond.

The waiting room was hot to the point of inducing torpor, and Jay could feel the skin on her cheeks shrinking as any natural moisture and all that morning's Clinique evaporated. She had the impression that if she picked up a magazine from the pile on the low table it would flake away to shreds. If she squeezed the back of one of the cracked, blood-scarlet chairs its stuffing would tumble out beneath it in heaps of desiccated foam. The room was dotted around with minor-injuries customers; some were clutching bloodied cloths to their wounds and others were pale, silent and sickly with maybe an arm in a makeshift sling or a bare, swollen foot propped up out of damage range.

'Waiting time, 2 hours' flashed past over and over on a startlingly bright electronic sign. No-one commented or grumbled; two hours didn't rate any kind of fuss. This was not the Saturday night post-sport and pub-fight slot where you squeezed into a space on the floor and settled in for the duration. The place was scented with something sharply antiseptic and lemony, masking the full range of years of bodily spills that was, Jay decided, best not thought about.

'Rory's through there,' she told Greg, pointing to a row of curtained cubicles, half-hidden round a far corner. 'Someone's just having another look at him before he goes up to the theatre. I don't think he'll even get a pre-med.'

Greg chuckled. 'That's a good thing. Keep him away

from all pleasurable drugs at his age. Don't want him getting a taste for them.'

'Greg! Be serious, the poor boy's in a lot of pain. This could have been really bad – think of peritonitis.'

'Ah Perry, met him at a party once . . . Sorry.' Greg summoned up a scrap of sensitivity. He gently squeezed the back of Jay's neck. 'Just staving off the worry with a bit of misplaced flippancy. Have you seen him? Is he . . .' Greg stopped for a moment, watching with a grimace as a nurse bustled from one of the cubicles carrying a covered kidney bowl.

'Ugh. Hospitals, doncha just love them?' Greg turned away and shuddered.

Jay pulled him to a row of seats close to the reception desk, a little apart from the waiting patients, where he wouldn't feel the temptation to engage them in chat about what they were in for and some mutual fault-finding about health service policy.

'We've to wait here, then someone'll come and tell us what the plan is. And then we can see him before he goes up to have the thing out.'

'Do you think he'll want to keep it?'

'Keep it?' Jay said. 'Are you mad? It's not going to get any better, it's got to be taken out.'

'No, no I mean in a jar,' Greg said. 'You remember, when you were a kid, if you had your appendix out they'd give it to you to take home.'

'I hope he *doesn't* want it.' Jay thought about the state of Rory's room. The carpet, the surface of which was rarely visible, was like a many-layered cake with magazines and CDs sandwiching clothes, trainers and schoolbooks. A mouse, slaughtered by Daffodil, had rotted to a skeleton among his rugby kit under the bed last summer holidays. 'It would just end up spilling all over the floor like all those abandoned coffee cups. The cat would get it . . .'

70

There was a loud groan from a teenage boy sitting within hearing range. He was a year or two older than Rory, covered in mud and wearing school sports kit, and with his arm supported in a sling made from two football socks tied together.

'Sorry!' Jay called brightly to him and the woman accompanying him – a teacher from the school, she assumed, looking as if volunteering for hospital duty wasn't, after all, an improvement on force-feeding quadratic equations into Year 8. The woman glared back, issuing a clear non-verbal warning that if the pain-struck lad had to overhear one more gory word she knew who she'd hold responsible for the resulting mess on the lino.

'Mr and Mrs Callendar?' A tiny blonde doctor who, in Jay's opinion, looked far too much like one of the pert teenage-girl finalists from *Pop Idol* to be taken seriously as any kind of professional, approached with a clipboard and an encouraging smile.

'Rory is ready to go up to theatre now? You can come up and wait if you like? Or maybe you could come back later? He'll be a bit out of it for a while? Say two or three hours till he's properly back with us again?'

'Um . . . we could just stay with him? Hang around till we know he's OK?' Jay suggested, catching the quasi-Australian question tone. She didn't like the sound of 'back with us'. It made the general anaesthesia sound too much like a long hike in the direction of permanent oblivion. Suppose something went wrong, suppose Rory knew as he faded, fighting, from life that his family weren't anywhere close to him but had gone carelessly swanning off to pick up a trolley-load at Sainsbury's, while surgeons frantically scoured the district's blood banks for the right gallon of cross-matched plasma?

'Come and see him for a few minutes before you

leave.' There was no question this time, this was an order; the authorities didn't want the place cluttered with hangers-on. 'He's a bit woozy.' Miss Pop Idol (the badge said 'Melissa') led the way to Rory, who lay on a trolley with a needle taped to his hand and a tube snaking up to a drip. He waved vaguely, smiling slightly and looking beatific.

'Yo, parents. Missing History. Result.'

'What've they given you, man? You look miles away.' Greg perched on the edge of the trolley. Rory winced.

'Greg, don't sit on the poor boy!' Jay shifted sideways, looking for a place in the small cubicle to get close to Rory, and knocked into the drip support.

'Mind your big bum, Mum,' Rory murmured.

'Sorry, sorry.' Jay felt flustered and squeezed past a stack of cardboard kidney bowls to sit on the one creaky chair. She caught sight of young Dr Melissa smirking and pursing up her pretty mouth to suppress a giggle. Oh great, she thought. I'm here at the bedside of my possibly-could-have-died son and all people can do is notice my lardy arse. Did her darling son have to use the word 'big'? Just bum on its own would have been adequate, thank you. More than.

'We'll be back just after you wake up, Rory,' Jay told him, stroking his damp hair back from his eyes. 'Is there anything you want us to bring? Pyjamas and things, obviously and . . .'

Had he actually *got* pyjamas, she wondered? His sleeping attire seemed to be what looked like surfers' baggies and faded, ripped T-shirts. There must be something at the back of a cupboard that was hospital-suitable, surely, something one of Greg's aunts had sent many Christmases ago. Every household but hers was probably equipped with a decent emergency supply. They had to be, otherwise the hospital wards would be full of women in black transparent teddies trimmed with marabou and old men in holey grey vests. That League of Friends stall would be wise to have a constant stock of sensible patient-garb in all sizes.

'*Pyjamas?*' Rory looked as if he'd never heard the word before. 'I just want . . . like music and stuff. And Mum?'

'Yes?'

'If, I like don't make it . . .' Even as he said it, he was eyeing the delectable Melissa in search of comfort-reaction.

'Rory, removing an appendix is a routine thing, they do it every day.' Jay had her fingers crossed all the same. Fate shouldn't be tempted. Rory took no notice, 'Samantha Newton, she can have my *Pink* CD, OK?'

'Right, time to go up now?' Dr Melissa threw back the curtain with the kind of flourish that game-show hosts usually keep for Tonight's Star Prize and ushered in a porter. 'Say farewell, folks?'

Jay and Greg watched as the trolley was trundled away and disappeared into a lift.

Outside in the real-life sunshine, Jay felt tears stabbing at the back of her eyes. She took a deep breath and tried to steady her thumping heart.

'He'll be fine, truly,' Greg said, hugging her close to him. 'He'll be back at school in a couple of weeks, bragging about fancying the nurses. Or at least . . .'

'What? Tell me!'

So Greg wasn't so hundred per cent sure either. It was going to be like *Casualty* or *Holby City*; a slip of the scalpel, a quavery surgeon covering up early-onset Parkinson's. They'd be ushered into the Relatives' Room to be told a sorrowful tale of unforeseen complications and given tepid tea, all sticky with too much sugar.

'I was just wondering . . .' Greg looked puzzled, 'This *Pink* CD . . . it's a band is it? Not a sexual orientation?'

'Rory will be unbearable when he gets home. He'll expect room service,' Imogen complained to Jay from where she was slumped over the kitchen table surrounded by open books, a disembowelled pencil case, an empty biscuit packet and several mugs, each one half full of cold tea. This was Imogen in full-steam college-work mode, spread across all surfaces, marking out maximum territory. She'd got a perfectly good desk and computer down in the basement. It too had probably disappeared under strewn-about books and college-work notes.

Tris, on the other hand, had unstacked the dishwasher and was now cleaning the sink. He'd get into all the corners too, not miss out the scuzzy bit round the overflow or ignore the undersides of the taps. Jay would have been thrilled to employ him on the Dishing the Dirt workforce: he'd be a godsend, an inspiration. But then every single client would sidle up and try to get him alone in their hallway, offering him serious cash incentives to become their personal domestic treasure. And possibly not just for cleaning – he was a good-looking young thing with the kind of tight neat bum that still distracted her from driving when she saw one like it on a boy in the street. 'Just window shopping', as Barbara called it. She also knew that upstairs, having fixed the tap that morning, Tris would have swept away any gritty debris and have made sure the shower door had had a spritz of cleaning stuff to sparkle it up a bit after the dust had gone down. And there in the kitchen sprawled slobby Imogen with her bare feet up on the seat cushion next to her, without a clue how lucky she was.

'Oh, Dad, while you were at the hospital that mad

woman from next door came round. Cathy Thing,' Imogen said vaguely, waving her pen in the general direction of the garden. 'She said to tell you the sun's reflecting from your office roof again and getting in her eyes when she's doing her yoga.'

Greg shrugged and grinned. 'What does she want me to do? I can't move the sun, can I? Heaven and earth maybe, but . . .'

'She could just salute it,' Tris suggested. 'That's what you do in yoga, right?'

'We'll invite her round. I'll do a Sunday lunch for this Charles bloke of Delphine's and Cathy can come too. I'm not up to a silly cocktail-type bash, not with Rory the way he is. Lunch, though God knows when . . .' Jay said as she went off to find suitable hospital outfits for Rory.

'What Charles bloke? What lunch?' Greg called up the stairs. Jay closed the bathroom door after her, leaving it to Tris to tell Greg about Delphine's letter. For now, it was more than enough to contemplate the jumble that tumbled from the airing cupboard the moment its door was unleashed.

First though, she opened the small packet of anti-cellulite patches that she'd brought upstairs with her and sat on the edge of the bath to read the instructions. They were very small, the patches, and, thank goodness, they didn't smell. She'd imagined going around wafting a potent, mildly medicinal scent of eucalyptus and cloves as if she was treating a bad cold. She was to stick four on each squishy plump thigh every morning and leave them to do their magical thing, choosing a different bit of skin each day. This would be fun – should she circle the bits she'd already done in biro so that she didn't inadvertently keep applying the patches to the same bit? And if she did would she have a lovely smooth slender circle of thigh that contrasted with the rest of the general blobbiness? And how long would it last? Would she have to wear these things for ever and, if she went to the pool, have people speculating that she was covering up a host of domestically inflicted bruises?

Quickly, she peeled off the first few stickers and applied them to her bottom and upper thighs, stretching the skin slightly as she stuck them on. They felt OK. Better still, they were actually pretty much invisible, so that she had visions of herself hunting for them via the mirror when removal time came. That would be one for Planet Man – perhaps she could get him to make a note of exactly where she'd fixed them in case she needed something to refer to later.

Jay stashed the remaining patches back into her pocket and started the search for appropriate hospital wear for Rory. Somewhere at the back, behind the mismatched towels, long-lost swimming kits and tower of defunct blankets , sleeping bags and worn-out pillowcases kept for their potentially useful lace edgings, there must be something that would get him through a few days in hospital without either mortifying him (classic striped old-man PJs, 'God, Mum, suppose someone *sees*?') or appalling the other inmates (his favourite 'Yo Muddah-fuckah' T-shirt).

She would also, while she was up here filling in time before returning to Rory, make an eviction heap of stuff to be thrown away. For once, just once, it would be so satisfying to have the cupboard full of tidy piles of bedlinen all stashed together in colour-coded size order, with little sachets of scented beads scattered among them. So very *Delphine*, she thought and such a small but fulfilling task that she and her team quite often undertook for the Dishing the Dirt clients but somehow never got round to at home. On your own premises, where you chose the keeping and the chucking, how long could it possibly take? And more to the point, once perfected, how long could it possibly stay like that?

Tasha was waiting outside the school gate. Even from halfway down the tarmac drive Ellie could see she'd got the full face on – her eyelashes must weigh a ton under all that mascara and the eyeliner was loaded so thick she looked like a panda. She'd got her hair clipped way up on top of her head and spiked into place with a scarlet and white beaded scrunchie. It was all pulled back so hard Ellie could swear the skin over her cheekbones was higher and thinner than usual. She must be waiting for a boy. You didn't make that much effort just to go home on the bus with no-one to impress.

Ellie wasn't in much of a hurry. There'd be no-one home anyway today, nothing to rush for. She wasn't going to race back just to do homework and watch the early soaps and listen to Imogen going on about the baby having grown, this week, to somewhere between the size of a bean and a Brazil nut. She sauntered along by herself, wondering if Amanda had gone out by the school's side door to make a point or if she really had, like she'd said, got to meet her mum and help her do Tesco's. If it was all about not sitting next to her on the bus that morning, well get over it, Mands.

'Ellie! Over here, babes! Where you been? I been waiting.' Tasha pounced on her and took hold of her arm. Ellie felt claimed: claimed and confused. Confused and flattered and a little bit nervy. What did starry Tasha see in her? Ellie could only guess she was to be a stooge for more shoplifting. She didn't want that. One day they'd be caught, and in the milli-microsecond before the store tec's hand landed on her shoulder Tasha would have offloaded all her swag from her own bag into Ellie's. In the brief time before she spoke to her, Ellie had imagined the whole sequence, from the first questioning in the shop's back room to being taken down the courtroom stairs to start a long and horrible sentence at some dismal young offenders' institute.

'You were waiting for *me*?' she asked Tasha, deleting the mental image of massive, hard prison-girls beating her up for her chocolate ration.

'Course. I'm going your way.' Tasha looked round. 'What happened to your brother? I didn't see him around today. Not in lunch, not in the corridors. I usually see him.'

'What, Rory?' Why did Tash want to know? Rory was *so* not interesting. 'He didn't come in,' she told her. 'I got a text from Dad, Rory's gone in the hospital to have his appendix out.' She shrugged. 'I don't suppose he'll be in school for a couple of weeks.'

Tasha stopped in the middle of the pavement and turned to Ellie, her face huge-eyed with drama-queen shock. 'His *appendix*? What, like having an *operation*? So why are you here? Shouldn't you be outside the operating thingy, waiting for when he's awake, see if he's OK?'

'I dunno. I don't think so.' Tasha was being a bit over the top. Still, probably better this than robbing River Island. 'I rang Mum, she just said he got really ill in the park and some women got him an ambulance. She said he'll be all right, your appendix, well it's just like a tooth or something.'

'An ambulance! Wow, poor Rory!' Tasha's eyes were glittery. 'Why didn't you say something earlier? You could've told me in Maths.'

Ellie laughed. 'But you don't even know him!'

'No, but . . .' Tasha dashed forward suddenly, pulling Ellie with her so she almost fell. 'We'll go and see him!

Now! Which bus is it? The 36 I think, right? Come *on* Elle!'

Ellie had never seen Tasha move so fast. She trailed behind trying to get her to stop. She didn't want to go to the hospital. She'd hated it when old Auntie Win had been in for what she called 'Down There' problems and kept making big eyes at Mum whenever she said things Ellie wasn't supposed to understand. Medical stuff made her feel queasy – all those dangling bags of liquid everywhere and people lying around looking like they'd already died and with needles sticking out of them and the thought that someone might be sick.

'Tash! Stop, I've got to go home. Mum wants me to start supper.'

'*Supper? Ooooh* aren't you posh?'

Ellie blushed, mumbling, 'Tea, dinner, supper. Whatever you call it, I've got to start cooking it.' Well it was almost true, she'd have a look in the freezer, see what was mike-able.

This was a big mistake. She'd now have to go with Tash to the hospital or next thing, Tash would come to the house and tell everyone about her dad's mega Mercedes and the glass staircase. In fact the glass nearly-everything: shelves in the sitting room, kitchen table, the thing the television sat on, the pale blue basin in the downstairs loo, the mad roof extension, Dad's office down the garden. Where had he got this thing about glass? Did you have to have it if you were an architect? Why couldn't he have had a thing about bricks or wood, then at least no-one could look up your skirt when you walked up the stairs.

'I'm really surprised you don't want to be with him. Don't you care about your brother?' Tasha sounded slightly menacing now. She was standing very close with her hands hanging straight by her sides. Ellie could smell her cherry-mint bubblegum and felt conscious that she was between Tash and the road where school-run traffic was swooshing past, thick and fast. Big cars, huge, heavy four-wheel drives full of kids off to piano lessons, t'ai chi, extra maths, ballet . . . One push . . . But Tasha wouldn't do that, not while there was something she wanted; but there'd be other times when you couldn't be so sure.

'OK, OK, we'll go down there and see how he is. Don't know why you want to come though.'

That so wasn't true any more, Ellie knew as she stamped off towards the bus stop. Tasha fancied Rory. Vile thought. Brothers weren't for fancying. Still, that shouldn't last long. One look at Rory slobbed out in a hospital bed wearing one of those gowns that looked like a giant bib and Tasha would soon go off him. And she'd leave her alone again. Right now that really felt like something to look forward to, even though that weird adoration feeling from the thieving day was still there deep down.

'Good thing I phoned Imogen, otherwise I don't sup-pose I'd have heard about it till he was home again. I am his grandmother, you know.' Audrey was waiting in the corridor outside Ward D3 and accosted Jay the moment she and Greg stepped out of the lift.

'Oh Mum, there's no need for you to be here. I don't suppose Rory will feel much like seeing visitors, not today.'

'Well *you're* here. He'll have to see *you*. And it's not as if I'm not family.' Audrey sniffed. 'Win drove me, I was too upset. She's in the loo, powdering.'

'Oh God, both of them,' Greg muttered, making Jay want to giggle. She hoped they'd behave. Win and Audrey shared a deep fondness for hospital premises and considered it only generous-spirited good manners to strike up intimate conversations with every ward resident. They were never happier than when a friend of theirs went in for some op or other and they got the chance to catch up on current medical procedures. They'd been particularly delighted a few months previously with Win's dog-walking companion Molly, who'd explained in a loud whisper that the endoscopy she was having was so named because the camera was to be inserted into the *end* of her. Which end, Jay had managed not to ask.

As they went into the ward Jay could see that she and Greg were not the first of Rory's visitors. Ellie, to Jay's surprise, was already there, leaning on the end of the bed, picking at the skin round her thumbnail and looking bored. In what Jay couldn't help thinking of as the Chief Visitor spot, up at the head end and on the only chair, was a blonde girl, made up as if for serious party-going and gazing without blinking at Rory's face. Surely not a girlfriend of his, Jay thought. And if so, possibly not for long. The sight of Rory waking up would certainly put anyone off.

Rory's eyes were closed but he looked reassuringly pink and healthy – or at least Jay thought he did, until it crossed her mind that being a bit flushed might, according to something she'd once read, be due to inhaling too much of a particularly dangerous gas. She wished she could recall which one.

'I don't think he's allowed so many visitors at once,' she warned Audrey, who, with Win, had followed her and Greg so closely into the ward she could almost feel their breathing on the back of her neck. It was like being trailed by a pair of eager wolfhounds.

'Oh they won't mind. Not after a nasty operation,' Win said, parking her vast handbag on Rory's feet.

'Oy whoozat?' Rory opened his eyes and glared at his great-aunt.

'Poor kid probably thinks he's died and gone to hell,' Greg whispered to Jay.

'Are you all right? How do you feel?' Jay asked him, taking his hand. Rory slid his hand out of hers – a good sign, she thought. Only a Rory who was close to giving up the ghost would allow his mother to touch him fondly in public.

''M'all right. Tired.'

'No change there, son,' Greg commented.

'Why're you all here? Have I got Complications?' he asked, suddenly interested and opening his eyes properly. He looked at the blonde girl beside him with a small recoil of surprise as if he didn't know who she was, causing Jay to worry about what the anaesthetic had done to his memory. What else had it obliterated, his (already fragile) grasp of basic maths? Every French verb he'd half-learned?

'No, no, you're fine. We thought we'd just come and say hello, make sure it all went well,' Jay told him. 'We won't stay long. Is there anyone about? Anyone medical we could ask?' She looked around. It was all very quiet in the eight-bed room. Two beds were vacant, neatly made up for the next incumbents. Someone lurked behind a *Daily Telegraph* and a couple of ancient men lay back on their pillows, headphones on. There was no-one of Rory's age to enjoy his recovery with. She was surprised they hadn't put him in a children's ward, where he'd grumble about being with little kids but at least (presumably) not risk the possible trauma of the patient alongside him dying in the night.

'We've brought you some things.' Win leaned over the bed and patted Rory's forehead. 'Some raspberry jelly. I know it's hard to eat when you've had an op.'

'No it's not, not for an appendix,' Audrey argued. 'You're thinking of tonsils. I've brought you a pack of cards. You can't beat Patience for passing the time when you're stuck in bed.'

'And it'll take your mind off what the others . . .' Win cut in looking around the room. 'What *they've* got wrong.' She made a face at Jay then murmured, 'Some of them might have *prostrate* . . . He doesn't need to get involved with any of *that* at his age.'

The blonde girl giggled and Win glared then turned her attention back to Rory. 'And don't listen to your gran; a jelly is always nice. Young people like jelly. My Delphine always did, especially with her appendix. I used to make it whenever hers grumbled. You remember, don't you Jay?'

Jay did. Delphine had been, as her mother had boasted, a martyr to her grumbling appendix. Audrey had been dismissive, asking why Delphine couldn't just have indigestion like everyone else, why did she have to dress it up with a fancy name. That complaining appendix had been cosseted and coaxed all through Delphine's childhood. Every morning – and it now came back to Jay as clearly as if it was last week – Win had got up at dawn (or 'before God' as Audrey had scathingly put it) to make Delphine's muesli for her (nothing so simple as opening a packet) so it was ready on the table before school and with plenty of time for proper digesting after. She remembered the daily refrain from Win: 'Have you *been*, Del*pheen*?' Jay and her sister April used to sing it at her as a tease.

Whenever Jay had stayed overnight and witnessed the palaver of the process, it had amazed her that anyone could go to so much trouble for a bowl of cereal. Every morning Win would mix up a selection of nuts and and whole oats, carefully measured from glass storage jars (kept out of harmful direct sunlight) with a copper scoop. She'd peel and chop a scarlet apple (never a Granny Smith: too sour) and add dried fruits and ripe banana and, in summer, strawberries picked from a planter which was kept close to the back door and covered with green net and flapping silver streamers to keep the birds off. Then she'd stir the whole lot together with gluey buttermilk that had been out of the fridge for at least an hour to make sure the chill was off and the state of Delphine's delicate appendix wouldn't be compromised.

'I've done plenty for you as well, dear,' she'd said to Jay. Now, remembering, Jay felt ashamed at her lack of graciousness at the time. 'Yuck no!' she'd yelled, backing away, queasy at the sight of the fatty butter-milk. 'Haven't you got any Weetabix?'

Delphine had looked at her with something too close to scorn. 'Weetabix? *Bought* cereal?'

'Yes. It's what I like. *And* with proper milk,' Jay had retaliated, brave for once and defensive that her own family's breakfast habits were being criticized.

'You should try this, dear, while you're here,' she remembered Win insisting, firmly sitting her at the table in front of a dreaded bowlful of Delphine's con-coction. *'Especially* with this lovely buttermilk. You could do with a bit of fattening up.'

My, thought Jay, that was a long time ago. How she'd love to hear someone say that about her now.

SEVEN

Shape-Shakes

He hadn't made a very good start, this Charles bloke of
Delphine's, Jay decided as she read the brief, typed
note that accompanied the keys to his apartment. He
could have rung the bell, introduced himself and come
in for a chat. That way they could have fixed a date for
the as-demanded-by-Delphine lunch. Just pushing the
envelope through the letterbox and buggering off without so much as a hello didn't exactly make for the best
impression of friendliness. Imperious, that's the word
that comes to mind, she thought, im-per-i-ous. Not
unlike Delphine herself, come to that, so at least the
two of them had something in common. Where her
letter had been bossily instructive about party-giving,
this one contained a businesslike list of cleaning requirements and a request for a thorough all-areas
blitzing to be done on any one of half a dozen possible
dates between now and the end of the month, when
Delphine would arrive to set up home with him and his
immaculately turned-out cupboards. It was probably
better done later rather than sooner, Jay decided, giving
Delphine less opportunity to run her fingers along
radiator edges and scoop up a triumphant smear of
dust.

'Perhaps he doesn't want us to see him till the wedding,' Greg suggested from the far side of the *Sunday Times* Home section, where he was reading a piece on one of his own designs, a semi-subterranean grass- and glass-covered dome for an old rock star, headlined 'Going Underground'. 'Perhaps he thinks it's bad luck.'

'I'm pretty certain that's only the bride's frock,' Jay told him, making notes in her diary for a price quote for Charles's flat.

'Frock? Surely Delphine will be the one wearing the trousers,' Greg said, laughing.

'He says he's on his way to Hong Kong,' she read, picturing him stepping out of a cab in full-on pilot kit and tiptoeing up the path to push the note through the door. Perhaps it had been the very early hours, she thought, trying hard to feel inclined to forgive, in which case he'd hardly have liked to bang on the door and bluff his way in for a cup of coffee in the interests of making himself known to his future wife's extended family.

'Ah well.' Greg murmured, turning to a page of Italianate villas for sale on a man-made Dubai island. 'There you go. We can't expect to compete with a 747 full of passengers revving up on the Heathrow runway.'

Jay wasn't in a good mood. Those stupid anti-cellulite patches kept falling off every time she stretched. Barbara had said she was probably not applying them to her skin at the right tension, which made her think of knitting and how her mother had taught her to knit up little sample squares to try to get the stitches even. And then the night before, Greg had run his hand across her thigh, laughed and said it wasn't the hottest form of turn-on, being in bed with someone who brought to mind Rory's old World Cup sticker book. Besides, the patches were a constant stick-on reminder of her own disgraceful shallowness. What kind of mother, she asked herself in the guilty pre-dawn wakefulness, what kind of self-centred, terrible, worthless mother gives even those few moments of attention to fighting flab at the moment her beloved child is in the middle of a serious operation?

All the same, now Rory was well into recovery, Jay felt she could once more allow herself to feel grumpily certain that acquiring a more streamlined body should be easier than this. She wasn't going to become obsessive about it (no, really, she wasn't, she insisted to herself), but surely it wasn't too much to ask to be back to a flab-free size 12 by the time Delphine and her pert curves, unfurrowed by childbearing, arrived.

She could just imagine her cousin looking her up and down and coming out with the single doomy word 'matronly'. It brought to mind Win and Audrey, years before over cups of tea and pink wafer biscuits, gossiping that one friend or another had 'let herself go', somehow a worse crime against feminine propriety than going on the game or running off with the insurance man. Of course, it shouldn't matter – and wasn't it Mick Jagger (or his dad) who said it was all right to let yourself go, as long as you could get yourself back again? – Delphine was going to snigger anyway and call her Granny.

In intellectually rational moments it didn't matter at all. But no-one's existence is made up entirely of such moments, and somewhere on the reel of Jay's Life-So-Far movie there was a scene from when she was fourteen and secretly passionate about her best friend Sandy's older brother Neil. Neil was having a party, a full-scale, parents-out, free-house (if you didn't count the au pair taking care of their seven-year-old sister Emmy), all-teen debauch session. He was a boys' school pupil and the consequent shortfall of girls in his life meant that Sandy and Jay were invited, in a desultory, if-you-feel-like-it way, to join in and help balance the numbers. Neil had warned them to keep in the background and not get embarrassingly drunk or silly, or they'd be banished upstairs to Emmy's room to watch TV with Birgitte.

Sandy and Jay got the silly bit over with during the afternoon in the cramped and cluttered half of the bedroom Jay shared with her sister April, who generously lent her a new lime green ra-ra skirt and blow-dried their hair for them. Delirious with anticipation of the night's possibilities, they got themselves ready in a riot of shrieks and giggles with an all-stops-out orgy of face packs, manicuring, hair primping, clothes choosing and accessory selection. Neil and his friends were to be gob smacked by their glamour, their sophistication, their hitherto unsuspected sheer *fanciability*. The glorious teen world of snogging and boyfriends was about to begin. Only as they were leaving the house did it start to go wrong: Win turned up in need of a comfort chat with her sister and Delphine was handed over to Jay to keep her out of earshot of sensation-filled adult conversation.

'But me and Sandy are going out!' Jay had wailed to Audrey.

'Sandy and *I*,' her mother admonished automatically, then hustled the three girls out of the the door, insisting, 'Just take her with you. She'll be no trouble.' In the background Jay could catch the sound of Win starting to be tearful. The words 'other woman' and 'that bastard' had been murmured more than once between the two sisters, and Delphine's father was away a lot these days. 'On Business', as Delphine tended to explain, grandly, leaving whoever was listening to assume he was saving a major industrial conglomerate from certain ruin as he travelled the world on a private Concorde.

'So at last you're wearing a bra, Flatso,' Delphine observed as they clattered down the road, Jay and Sandy tottering on their uncomfortable and new platform heels and Delphine in her favourite gold dance sandals that weren't supposed to grace any surface other than polished parquet, 'What is it, a 30 triple-A?' Jay blushed and folded her arms across her body. Her new, first, bra and its embarrassing lack of contents were that night's terrifying chinks in her confidence.

'Take no notice. Just ignore. We'll send her up to Emmy's room and they can watch *The Generation Game*,' Sandy muttered, furious at the imposed tag-along.

'And who's this?' Neil leered at the interloper as soon as they arrived. Delphine, taller and precociously curvier than the two older girls, simpered at him and asked for a cigarette.

'Definitely *not*, Delph,' Jay said, then turned to Neil. 'It's OK, this is my very much *younger* cousin, only *just* thirteen. I'm babysitting her so she's to go upstairs and hang out in Emmy's playroom.'

'I'll get you for this.' Delphine glowered as she was bundled up the stairs by Austrian Birgitte with a bottle of Coke and a monster bag of crisps. Jay took no notice – she was already caught up in the music and the possibilities. She soon forgot about Delphine and about the bra.

Much later, Jay was in the midsummer-warm candle-lit garden sitting on a bench by the fish pond, satisfyingly spoilt for choice, boy-wise, being thigh to thigh between Neil and someone called Aaron who was stroking her bare arm from wrist to elbow. Around her were the heady mixed scents of cannabis and carnations and the sounds of couples groping their way into each other's clothes beneath the rhododendrons. Jay grinned across at Sandy who sat on the grass entwined with her own quarry for the night, and wondered if the summer could get any better than this.

'*Jay*. I'm *bored*, can we go now?' Delphine appeared at her side, hands on hips and an expression of petulance on her face.

'A bit later Delph, just half an hour, OK?' Jay was feeling mellow and almost inclined to be generous. 'Would you like a proper drink? Just the one? I promise I won't tell Auntie Win.' But it was too late for generosity – the earlier damage still told and Delphine glowered, distrusting. Then she sneezed 'I've got hay fever,' she whined. 'I want to go *now*.'

'*Look*, Delphine, I know it's past your bedtime . . .' Not a kind thing to say, Jay would be the first to admit, but she hadn't asked to be lumbered with her cousin.

'Any tissues out here? I keep sneezing!' Delphine interrupted her. She was almost shouting, making a big play of searching around, picking up glasses from the table, putting them down again, sneezing with loud, exaggerated drama and generally making sure everyone was looking at her.

'Be quiet, Delph, you're being . . .' Jay hissed.

'Oh I know where there's some!' shrieked Delphine, 'Look everyone!' Too late, Jay clutched her hands to her skinny-strapped low-cut top. Delphine, like a conjuror executing his grand finale trick, delved her hand down her cousin's front and pulled out a wad of tissues. She then blew her nose loudly and pocketed Jay's shaming bra stuffing, squealing in triumph, 'So *now* can we go home?' through the waves of surrounding laughter.

Well at least that was one thing that had changed, Jay thought now as she adjusted a cutting-in strap; these days it was genuine D-cup flesh that spilled over the top of her gorgeous lacy underwear, not Kleenex.

The grapefruit diet had been abandoned on grounds of paltry results and a growing certainty that it contained no magic calorie-zapping ingredient waiting to be discovered by the obese Western world. Instead, the Shape-Shake Jay had had in place of breakfast was lying heavily on her stomach. She felt as if she'd drunk a vat of wallpaper paste, vanilla-flavoured. It had been horribly sickly too, cloyed up with artificial sweetener as if all slimmers had such a deep-seated cake and chocolate habit that they could only be weaned away from it by a replacement that brought to mind the stickiest childhood sweets. This must be, she was sure, the dieter's equivalent of methadone. She was supposed to have another one for lunch as well, and then something 'proper' in the evening, by which time the food would be fallen upon and scoffed down greedily as a well-deserved reward. Tonight's 'proper' was going to be lamb roasted over shallots and rosemary-scattered potato slices, julienne carrots glazed in tarragon butter and courgettes pan-fried in olive oil with garlic, tomatoes and a generous squeeze of lemon juice. There would be a sauce made from the lamb juices, deglazed with port and with a smidgen of redcurrant jelly added. She knew this because she had bought all the ingredients the day before, just as the grapefruit was wavering out of favour and an hour before she'd stocked up on a bargain special offer of twenty-four assorted-flavour cans of Shape-Shake. It would be all right; she wouldn't eat the pudding, even though it was a lush and sticky lemon tart, bought from Maison Blanc by Richmond station, and would take Olympic levels of will power to resist.

Rory was being discharged from hospital early that afternoon. It would be a relief to get him safely home and on his own again, away from that strange blonde girl who seemed to have grown roots by his bedside. He'd started to look a bit desperate. He'd only been in for a few days but there she was, this Tasha person, eternally sitting on the orange plastic chair by his bed, her legs crossed so high that he could hardly miss seeing right up to her knickers. The girl chewed gum with a ferocity that had made Greg say (fortunately only in the privacy of the glass bedroom) that he feared for any future boyfriends she might happen to fellate. She didn't appear to need to make any conversation with her prey either, but sat bouncing and bobbing in rhythmic silence beneath a set of headphones. Rory looked as if he had barely a clue who she was. Perhaps he hadn't. It was no good asking Ellie either. When asked, she'd just grunted, 'That's Tasha,' and frowned (oh those embryonic wrinkles), discouraging any further questioning.

The state of the house wasn't improving Jay's mood. Even with Rory absent, the usual weekend tidal wave of free-roaming possessions found its way from rooms and cupboards and shelves. These items – books, coats, shoes, CDs, undealt-with mail, magazines and avoided homework – distributed themselves over every available surface and lay around like washed-up beach detritus, waiting for some reluctant inhabitant to be nagged into clearing up and putting it all somewhere else. The somewhere else too often turned out to be the bottom of the stairs, the bench in the hallway, the shelves in the sitting room (how did so many DVDs get themselves from shelf to floor? Did they jump down from their boxes in the night and take themselves for a spin on the rug?)

How did they do it, Jay wondered, these people whose homes appeared in magazines like *Elle Decoration* and *Living Etc.*? Did they have a skip outside the front door crammed with things they didn't want the camera to see? All those photo-articles she gazed at so longingly, amazed and bemused that the immaculately tasteful Jeremys-and-Susannahs with their assorted under-six children (Polly, Dolly, Molly, Olly) existed without a single extraneous item or colour-unco-ordinated Lego brick. There really were people out there, so she was led to believe, who successfully combined sticky infants and a moulting black Labrador with a shaggy cream rug and pale lavender suede curtains. She knew it was possible – some of the houses that Dishing the Dirt took care of looked as if no-one did any real living in them. Any children in such houses, she sometimes thought, must be kept in attic cages until they were old enough to heed the words 'Don't Touch'.

These were people who didn't have fourteen half-used shampoo bottles on display in the bathroom (as did Rory and Ellie in the one they shared), whose baths had aromatherapy candles lined up seductively along the edge rather than a rusting selection of disposable razors, a paperback that had fallen in the water and a dented pink plastic duck of some weird sentimental value to Ellie. Where were these people's newspapers? Their junk mail? Their ironing pile? The children's luminous Barbie palace and lime green plastic pedal car? Why did their window ledges behind the kitchen sink always look so gleamingly bare, with possibly one carefully placed slender glass vase containing a single perfect lily?

If the No Clutter look was a sleek twenty-first-century wanna-have, Jay remembered that a certain order had been possible even in the country-pine kitchens of the early Nineties. Delphine's domain had been crammed from floor to loft with dinkiness and faux-rustic knick-knacks. Baskets of dried flowers had topped every kitchen wall-cupboard. A row of floral-painted kettles had graced the kitchen window ledge. Eggs had nestled on the worktop in a frilled basket. An antique coffee grinder had stood to attention, shining and polished beside a stencilled mug tree. Jay didn't remember so much decorative paraphernalia ever looking a mess. There'd been a lot of stuff, but Delphine's house had never descended into the chaotic, lying-where-it-falls sort of state that her own house constantly veered towards. It was easy for her, Jay told herself. With only two adults trit-trotting neatly around the place, any fool could keep the domestic scenery in check. Throw in a few kids and all anarchy broke loose. Delphine hadn't taken that little factor into account the day when, watching Jay trying to get a casserole into her own (decidedly neglected) oven while spooning baby rice into six-month-old Imogen, she'd come out with a classic 'Surely it's only a matter of a proper routine' comment.

Jay looked across towards her own sink, trying to see it with a fresh eye, pretending for a moment she was the woman from *House Doctor* advising on clearing out before potential buyers came to give it the once-over. A scrunched-up J-cloth hung over the slim arched neck of the tap like a drunk over a gate. On the ledge behind was half a bottle of Fairy Liquid, a squirty Mr Muscle, two tubes of hand cream, a two-year-old Mother's Day card, a pile of mail-order catalogues (Toast, Boden and something from the garden centre) and a row of six cling-filmed flower pots in which morning glory were supposed to be germinating but didn't seem to want to emerge. There were several bottles of fancy vinegar which should really be kept out of the light and a small jar of truffle oil which had been there for several years and was unlikely ever to be used. A pack of holiday photos waited for someone to claim it. Imogen had left the bread out, yet again, along with the Flora and at least three knives. Not a decorative selection, all round. All these random items, she decided, except for the sulking morning glory, could be redistributed to various cupboards. The plants could be banished to Greg's office where they might be enticed to grow beneath the glass roof. Ellie could do all this (well you could ask, you could hope) while Jay was at the hospital collecting Rory.

'I'm starving. When's lunch?' Ellie strolled into the kitchen still wearing her years-old, shrunken and faded Hallo Kitty pyjamas. Her wet hair was wrapped in a vast blue bath towel, making her look like a weird, wrongly proportioned cartoon figure. If Ellie had only got to the hair-wash stage by 11.30 a.m., it would surely be mid-afternoon before so much as a CD found its way to its rightful container – Moggie and Greg would have to be roped in for clearing-up duties as well.

'I'm not doing lunch,' Jay told her, 'I'm collecting Rory at two after the doctor's had a last look at him, then cooking roast lamb for us all at about six. Have a look in the fridge if you're hungry now, see what you can find.'

'But . . . uh.' There was a sighed outburst of frustration as Ellie opened the fridge and gazed blankly at its contents. 'Ooh there's a lemon tart,' she said, livening.

'That's for tonight, Ells, don't touch that. Look, there's some sausages – you can have those if you want.'

'Mm. That sounds good,' Greg said, folding the newspapers and (oh, there is a God) piling them into a neat heap ready for either the next reader or the recycling bin out by the front door. 'Can you put a couple on for me as well, Ellie pet? And I'll do a few onions to go with them. I've a fancy for a hot-dog and I think there's some rolls in the breadbin. Lots of ketchup, and that lurid American mustard,' he was now saying to himself, inspecting the jars and bottles on the fridge door shelves. Jay could feel her taste buds pricking dangerously. This weight-loss business was torture. She muttered an old slimming-club mantra: 'A moment on the lips, a lifetime on the hips'. It didn't help: it just sounded arch and smug.

Ellie switched on the grill and loaded up the sausages (organic, leek and apple) while Greg chopped a big juicy onion, ready for slow-frying in a butter and olive oil mixture. The real will-power-killer was going to be the aroma – onions slowly caramelizing, the treacly ooze of the sausages . . .

'Um – I'm just going next door to see Cathy. See what I can suggest about the sun and her yoga,' Jay said, and fled. By the time she got back they'd have finished eating, the kitchen would be filled with unappetizing dirty dishes and it would be time for her next Shape-Shake. Oh the joylessness of it, the tragic avoidance of mouth-watering anticipation. How much, she wondered, could a nice fast blast of liposuction hurt? Quite a lot, she imagined as she plodded down the front steps, quite a lot in both body and bank account.

None of the nurses were even halfway fit. And if he had been the type who was into women in uniform, Rory would have been disappointed. These wore shiny shapeless, pale blue overall things and looked like supermarket checkout staff. Whenever they touched you they put on thin Durexy gloves as if you were dodgy meat that was going off. There was only one with a bit of a foxy look to her (a slinky walk and pouty pale lipstick) and even she looked like her back end was made of concrete under that outfit. And hardly anyone from school had been in. Of his mates, only

Alex and Mart had bothered to turn up but they hadn't stayed long, just long enough to lob him a tatty-looking sympathy card which Ellie had said you only sent when people died ('From the whole form' they told him, but it only had twelve names in it and two of those looked faked), before they sodded off to watch Arsenal coming to well-deserved grief on Mart's dad's massive widescreen Sky set-up.

There was no Sky TV in here and even if there was, he'd never get near it for all the elderlies glued to *Emmerdale*. There was no sign of Samantha Newton. He hadn't expected her to come in (but you could dream . . .) and her name wasn't on the card – it was the first thing he'd looked for. He pictured her now, doing Sunday things at home. She might be sitting on her bed, all newly showered and scented, painting her toenails sparkly pink. Her body would be naked under a not-quite-big-enough fluffy white towel with little beady drops of water still scattered across her shoulders. She'd probably got a couple of soft toys on her pillow – a squashy teddy and Garfield or a polar bear, maybe both. And she'd probably got a picture of that Timberlake tosser on her wall. Somebody older anyway, somebody with a gristle-hard body and too much attitude. He hated being sixteen – your head and your dick were going on twenty-two but to women you might as well still be seven.

Rory wished he was at home. He felt OK now, though he didn't want to go back to school yet, not while the stitches were still in. School was a hard place if you felt a bit vulnerable. Some wanker or other would think it so *amusing* to leap on your back in the corridor and hurl you to the floor just to see how much your wound could bleed. What he wanted was to be at home on one of the big pink sofas in the sitting room, with his feet up and the telly on and the smell of

97

Sunday-type cooking wafting in from the kitchen. He'd even like to see Ellie looking cross about something Not Being Fair.

Rory didn't really understand this Tasha girl who kept coming in and sitting with him. I mean, he thought, she was no minger but she was only a kid, in Ellie's year. Did she have a thing about hospitals? Did she want to be a doctor or something and was soaking up the atmosphere? Of all the things there were to soak up in here, atmosphere wasn't the one there was most of. He'd seen more stuff come out of people in the few days he'd been in than he'd thought any human body could possibly hold. That poor old bloke in the end bed – no wonder he'd died. Pulling the curtains round his bed hadn't really helped – he could still hear all the mopping and wiping and imagine all the tubes and stuff. Jesus. And when they'd trolleyed him away to the morgue the wheels had creaked and clanked like a ghost's chains. It was enough to give you nightmares, and he'd know where the blame would start if he spent his adult life in therapy dealing with an aversion to high white metal beds.

It wasn't long to go now. Dr Melissa would be round soon for a final check – she'd said some time after twelve thirty – and then his mum was coming and he could go home. A small childlike bit of him hoped she'd been in his room and given it a surprise make-over. Clean sheets and a start-again vacuumed floor had a hugely comforting appeal. Though any surprises were likely to be Jay's, he suddenly thought. I wonder, he mused, if she's ever read *Out for the Lads* before.

If Jay longed for a minimal look when it came to household furnishing, then it could be said that Cathy in the house next door opted for maximal, if such a word existed. Dishing the Dirt had clients like this –

premises which Jay and Barbara referred to as the heart-sink homes (that is, from a cleaner's point of view – their occupants tended to be jolly folks with happy lives as full and colourful as their houses), crammed from cellar to attic with ornaments and mementoes, every one of which had to be moved and dusted and washed and polished. Cathy's philosophy was that if you'd had a lovely time, whether it was a simple fun lunch with a friend or a full-scale holiday, then it was essential to bring back something to remind you of it. From the stuff stacked on each room's wall and surface – everything from an extensive plastic snow-dome collection to hundreds of pretty jugs, wooden carvings and postcards tucked onto every ledge – Jay would say she'd had a lifetime of daily outings filled with delight.

'Come in, come in! Fancy a drink? A Sunday morning livener?' Cathy was pulling faded hyacinths from a pot at the top of the front steps. She was a welcoming soul with her hair tied back in a long black plait, and a smoker's off-white smile occupied a good half of her small bony face.

'No thanks, I've got to drive later. Wouldn't mind some of that lovely tea you have though.' There was a spicy scent in the hallway, cinnamon, Jay guessed, something warming and Christmassy and probably grated into an apple pie.

'Camomile?' Cathy suggested.

Jay shook her head, 'Actually *not* camomile, thanks. Reminds me of my five-minute detox – don't ask!'

'OK, you sad dieter. I've got a wonderful blackcurrant and elderflower mixture – come on through to the kitchen, but you'll have to excuse the mess.'

Every surface in the kitchen was covered with unwashed plates, glasses and cutlery. Wind chimes clanked lightly outside the French doors and a pair of overfed stripey orange cats lay on the wooden rocking chair, entwined on a velvet leopard-print cushion.

'I had a few people in last night and got too pissed to do the dishes.' Cathy grinned at her, looking sheepish. 'It must look like your worst professional nightmare.'

Jay laughed. 'Just reminds me of what's in my kitchen. I'd love to say I never bring my work home, but with my job it's impossible. It's easier to keep up with other people's cleaning than it is with my own. When I get home and trip over the bags and shoes in the hall I sometimes long for an empty white space with nothing but a lilac leather chaise longue, hours of nothing to do and one single brand new copy of *Vogue*.'

'Impossible with a family, and anyway you'd hate it. You should come to my yoga class – take some time to chill.'

'Do you know, I just might. Talking of which, what's this about the sunlight and the office roof? Can I have a look?'

Jay followed her neighbour's taut-muscled bottom up the purple-carpeted stairs to the big back room that Cathy had converted into her yoga and meditation sanctuary. The stairwell walls were filled with well over two hundred framed art offerings by Cathy's now grown-up children, ranging from nursery powder-paint handprints to classy A-level life studies. With her persistent professional head on, Jay found herself working out that the best you could do for the highest ones would be to tie a feather duster to a broom handle and give them a whoosh-over to keep the cobwebs down.

Cathy's yoga room was an unexpected contrast to the rest of the house. It was an almost bare, empty space painted a soft sage green and containing nothing but a pair of pink yoga mats and a selection of candles on the window ledge. Crystal prisms hung on threads at the window, reflecting baby rainbows across the dark polished wood floor. The two women stood and looked down into Jay's garden, at the end of which was Greg's glassy two-domed office, reminiscent of a small version of the Eden Project.

'I always thought he should have made the two sections the same size,' Jay commented. 'To me they look like a pair of badly matched breasts.'

'Have you told Greg that?' Cathy laughed. 'What did he say?'

'He said it was better than what the last person had told him, which was that they reminded him of caterpillar eyes. He quite liked the idea of glass breasts. I caught him doodling possible ways of giving them nipples.' She shielded her eyes as the sun came out from behind a cloud and a spear of light bounced off the glass below. 'I can see your point about the light reflecting into here. Greg needs to smear some mud over the surface or something.'

'No, no, definitely not. You can't have muddy knockers in your garden,' Cathy said. 'I had a bit of a think about it last night and I've got some old silk prayer flags I've had for years. I'm going to hang a couple of them from a batten up here at the top of the window. That should do it. Look good too – they're orange, colour of peace.'

'Hmm, peace, serenity. Imagine that – you know, Cathy, I think I just might join your yoga class. When is it?'

'Thursday evenings, seven fifteen, down at the leisure centre.' She squeezed the top of Jay's arm gently. 'I think you'll enjoy it, it's time out just for yourself. Recharge those batteries and get a tone-up at the same time.'

Jay laughed, prodding her hips. 'A tone-up would be very welcome and as for the batteries, well they're the only things about me that's flat these days.'

Rory still looked pale and Jay could swear he was a good couple of inches taller than when he'd left home to go to school that day he'd got so ill. He seemed thin too, as if he hadn't quite enough nutritional resources to keep up with the extra growth and had simply stretched. It might not be an illusion – her mother and Win had always been Old-Wife certain that any time a child spent lying ill in bed would guarantee a growth spurt. I must have been a supremely well child, in that case, Jay concluded as she shoved Rory's washbag into his rucksack. And possibly that would account for why Delphine had grown so fast so young. That grumbling appendix of hers (along with Win's conviction that she was in danger of 'outgrowing her strength') had kept her languishing in bed on many a rainy school day. She'd been fed so much comforting Heinz tomato soup and Lucozade at these times that Audrey had once said she was surprised the girl hadn't turned orange.

Jay was glad to see Dr Melissa in the corridor as they said goodbye to the nurses and left the ward. The little blonde Kylie lookalike was click-clacking along in a pair of powder blue kitten-heeled mules that looked as if they were left over from a much more exciting time the night before.

'Going home, Rory? Sad to be outa here?' Melissa treated him to a stunning smile and he grinned back, though directing his blushing expression towards the floor.

'Um – could I just ask you something?' Jay ventured. 'Do appendix problems run in families?'

Jay tried not to interpret Dr Melissa's expression as that of someone pitying ignorance, but it wasn't easy.

'Not that I'm aware of?' she told Jay, the Antipodean upward lilt back in place. 'Is there someone else at home with symptoms?'

'Oh no, no, everyone's fine,' Jay said. 'It's just my cousin, when she was a child she suffered a lot from what was called a grumbling appendix. I just wondered . . .'

The echoes of Melissa's laughter bounced off the walls in a kind of quadrophonic cackle. 'Hey that old myth? Appendixes don't grumble? They're either quiet and well-behaved or they explode, like Rory's did? There's no middle ground. Your cousin probably had a bit of irritable bowel going on? Or constipation, that's all? Grumbling appendix – no way, ha ha ha!'

Well it surely wasn't that hilarious, Jay thought as they made their way down in the lift, the echo of shrill Queensland mirth following them. She thought of her mother suddenly and wished she'd been there – how completely unable she'd have been to stop herself wagging her finger at clever little Dr Melissa and putting her straight: 'It's appen*dices* dear, not appen*dixes*.'

EIGHT

Yoga

'When she gets here, do I still have to call her Auntie Delphine, like when I was a kid?' Rory asked Jay, as Barbara drove them in a Dishing the Dirt van to have a look over Charles Walton's apartment.

'No, just call her Delphine. I'm sure she won't mind. And if she does . . .'

'If she does,' Barbara cut in, 'just call her madame. She certainly sounds like one, from all you've told me.'

'A *madame*?' Rory's voice was so full of astonishment that it skittered over several octaves. 'What, like in a . . . ?'

'No, no, I meant demanding, difficult. A bit of a prima donna,' Barbara said, laughing.

Jay didn't have to wonder how he knew about the brothel sort of madam. She'd had a quick flick through the *Out for the Lads* magazine that had been poking out from under the scrunched-up single socks (why did they all blame the tumble-dryer fairy? Couldn't they just *look*?) the toast crusts, and the homeless CDs that had been under his bed when she'd given his room a tidy-up while he was in hospital. It had been quite fascinating and informative, that article on Bawds in the 'Burbs: Out of Town Pleasure Palaces. She'd wasted a comfortable twenty minutes sitting on Rory's bed, reading about unexpected down-your-avenue red-light venues, and, although they didn't exactly print the address, there'd been one mentioned that could only be a couple of streets away from home. She was pretty sure she recognized the big mimosa tree that was just visible in the picture. 'Pleasure Palace', it had struck her, seemed a grandiose description for a house that looked like a typical, if over-decorated, four-bed Victorian villa. No wonder its upstairs windows had those tarts'-knickers blinds. She should put a Dishing the Dirt card through the letterbox to see if the proprietor was in need of a cleaning service and in possession of a sense of the ironic.

'We should tell Planet Man about it,' she'd suggested to Greg. 'Maybe he'd like to point his telescope the other way for a change.'

'Oh no, don't let's. I'd quite miss the old perv.' Jay hoped he'd been joking, but you could never tell with Greg and he hadn't been laughing at the time. Peculiar things went on in his head – as she imagined did in the heads of most men – and it might well be that the thought of being watched was giving him a bit of an edge, sexually speaking. She'd let it pass, Jay decided, seeing as things were currently going well in that department, but she really must do something about those useless, flimsy curtains: the *fantasy* of being watched was one thing. The near-certainty of it was quite another. Planet Man might also be equipped with a high-tech camera and a streak of impish madness. She could end up starring as an unwitting Reader's Wife for Rory to find in one of his lad mags, or, possibly worse, flyposted mid-coitus to the side wall of Waitrose.

Rory was staying away from school for a couple of weeks and didn't appear to intend wasting his time catching up with any studies. He complained a lot, as if it was to be expected in his condition, although not about itching stitches or his aching wound. What annoyed him was that his viewing of *Diagnosis: Murder* and *Bargain Hunt* was too often interrupted by Imogen coming up from the basement with the Mothercare catalogue to ask his opinion on cots and changing mats. It may have been a pretty desperate avoidance of potty-selection that led him to choose to come out with Jay and Barbara, but as this was merely a costing exercise and there was no danger of him being asked to lift a duster and apply polish to a surface, she'd understood that even he, with a teen's capacity for junk-viewing, could become bored with daytime TV.

'Is he loaded, or what, then, this Charles geezer?' Rory asked as the van swung in through the security gates of the Swannery, the block where Charles Walton lived.

'I was wondering the same myself,' Barbara said, peering upwards through the windscreen towards the absurdly futuristic penthouse. It was perched at a dangerous-looking angle on top of five storeys of other-wise reasonably staid red-brick and deep-windowed flats, converted from a former riverside storage depot. Charles's penthouse was, most of it, two floors high, partly set back from the block's edge to provide a deep deck, and looked as if the building contractors had decided: hey, to hell with it, let's commission the top layer from a different architect, one who'd had nothing to do with the design of the rest of the building. It was a mad structure of glass slabs and lime green concrete with a silver sail-shaped roof, quite recognizably, to Jay, the work of Greg.

Greg had laughed at the agent's brochure description of it as the Ultimate Penthouse. He said that the best fun in redesigning a big block like that was that you got to play with the bit at the top. It was very much, he explained, like being a kid on the beach embellishing a whole hot day's worth of carefully built sandcastle. The bottom bits, the hard work of digging out and shoring up and scooping out a moat (or in this case a car park), were about providing stability and structure, but at the top you got to be as fancy as you dared with as many turrets and flags and shell patterns as you wanted. Buildings were much the same. The ground-level ones that would never have got through the outline stage without guffaws of hilarity from planning committees were passed without question when they were 100 feet up. You could stick a massive purple metal marquee up there for all they cared, as long as it topped off the building in an icing on the cake, flash-cash-attracting sort of way.

Jay remembered Greg's excitement as the building took shape – the flats being a fairly run-of-the mill former industrial conversion, but the roof apartment being a work of pure architectural indulgence for him. And now, she thought as Barbara drove the Dishing the Dirt van into the underground car park, now her nice, neat, matching-bag-and-shoes cousin Delphine was going to be living in it. The thought had very much pleased Greg. He was delighted at the chance to go and keep an eye on how his design was shaping up as real-life living space, rather than as hyper-smart glossy-magazine fodder.

'Do you think it's really *her*, though, Greg?' Jay had said to him when he'd pulled the original sketches out of his files to show her the layout. 'I mean we're talking about a woman who was keen on floral tapestry cushions and asked for a hostess trolley on her wedding list.'

'Hmm. Good point. If they put in chintz sofas and a marble fireplace I'll be going down for murder, I swear,' he'd said, leaving her wondering why he sounded as if he almost relished the thought. Jay was less keen: she was, after all, going to be the one who oversaw the loos being properly bleached and the inside windows (and there were so many square metres of them) properly Windolened. At least there were no pets. She'd lost count of the times she'd had to explain to picky householders that it really was a waste of her time and their money to expect her staff to deal with scummy fishtanks or long-neglected gerbils.

'When Delphine moves in I just want to be a background consultant-type person. I'm not doing any of the hands-on stuff. You do know that, don't you?' Jay reminded Barbara as she swung the van into a visitor's parking bay.

'It's OK, you've only said that about nine times. I do sympathize, I wouldn't want to be my cousin's skivvy either, not for a million quid.'

'*I'd* do it for a million. I'd do *anything* . . .' Rory muttered.

'I don't doubt it,' Jay teased him as they all climbed out of the van. 'Don't forget I've seen your bedtime reading material.'

It was mega. Unbelievable. Completely, mind-stonkingly stylin'. Rory could almost feel his jaw dropping in amazement. Why, he thought, would any-one live in an ordinary house if they could live in something like this? Why didn't his own family have this flat? His dad had designed it, after all. So he obviously knew there was this kind of option out there and yet they all existed in a house that was (mostly, he conceded, OK it was only mostly – no-one he knew had that much glass) like everyone else's in the road.

'It's amazing how much space in a house is wasted by an ordinary stairwell,' Jay commented as she stood in the kitchen (white lacquer, cloud-grey slate) and gazed through the double-height sitting room towards the deck outside. 'You get a lot of acreage in a flat. I mean it's only two bedrooms but it gives an illusion of being massive.' It wasn't an illusion, not entirely. The sitting room must have been fifty feet long, even if part of it was under a sort of mezzanine floor at the end: home-office space, she presumed.

'There's a lot of mirror in here,' Barbara called from the main bedroom, sounding distrustful. She flicked open a wardrobe, looking a bit nervous. Rory joined her and peered in, curious. What had she been expecting to see – a row of blow-up dolls hanging like dresses? A dead body all cut up in binbags stashed away for disposing of later? The geezer had plenty of shoes, that was for sure. They were mostly old-man shoes, brown or black polished and with laces, though there were some that looked a bit more beaten about, sports shoes and sailing ones and those horrible things with the little fringy flaps at the front that he'd seen on golfers. He couldn't see any pilot kit, but then he supposed he must have taken that with him.

'What do you think, Rory?' Barbara asked him.

'What? The shoes? A bit girly, all on racks like that . . .' Rory had an inner conviction that a real man would have them chucked around at uncaring random under his bed.

'No, I meant the flat!' She was laughing at him. 'First impression: do you like it?'

'Brilliant,' he shrugged, feeling gloomily conscious that if he was ever going to get a place like this for himself he'd have to get a billion exam passes at grade A, possibly as an ongoing, rest-of-his-life exercise, unless he turned to crime or gambling. Obviously it's sodding brilliant, he thought. How could it not be? It had pale blue-grey suede sofas, long, low squashy ones that looked more for lying on than for sitting, and see-through tables with bits of weird twisted silvery sculpture on them. The telly wasn't just a telly – it was a whole cinema set-up about ten feet across, up on the end wall between chrome speakers that looked like the radiator grilles off the front of an American truck. There were huge splodgy paintings and these mad lamps here and there, looking like the sort they had in old film studios. On the treacle-brown wood floor there was a socking great blue rug, all long curly strands of tuft. A perfect shagging-rug, he couldn't help thinking, for when you'd got bored with doing it on the sofas and the enormous bed. Well you couldn't help thinking that about the whole place. It was a wildest-dreams *lerve*-venue. It would be impossible to bring a woman back here and *not* get lucky, surely.

What the hell was this Charles bloke doing with old Auntie Delphine? Unless she'd morphed into a complete fox since he'd last seen her, which was not possible, being as how she was the same sort of age as his mum and he remembered her as the type who only wore on-the-knee straight skirts. She was going to look as out of place as a nun on a racehorse.

'It's a bit like *Through The Keyhole*,' Jay said as she came down the curved staircase from the mezzanine level. 'You can just imagine Loyd Grossman asking who lives in a place like *this*. I'd never in a million years guess it was anyone who'd be about to marry my cousin. This is more of a young City-type's place. Though of course . . .' She stopped and laughed.

'What?' Barbara prompted.

'Well OK he's a pilot – but none of us has actually seen him. He could be half her age for all we know. Should be interesting . . . I can't wait to meet him. And have you seen . . .' She grabbed Barbara's arm and led her back up the stairs. 'Up here, look at this painting over the desk – do you think it could possibly be original? Do you think they all are?'

Rory followed them up the staircase, his feet slipping slightly on the aluminium treads. Design fault, that, he noted with satisfaction, you could break your neck falling down these stairs. He'd mention to his dad that it could do with a carpet – and then he'd run and· hide behind the sofa before the missiles that Greg threw hit him. The two women were looking at a smallish oil painting, hung out of the way of the light from the huge main windows. He'd seen something like it before.

'Picasso?' he ventured. They'd been doing him in Art at school. Mrs Gillibrand had been sly enough to get them interested by detailing the artist's woman-count.

'Oh well done Rory,' his mother said, with that smile they do when you've made them proud. He scowled, feeling he should remind her not to be patronizing but deciding it was a trivial thing compared to being in the presence of a real Picasso painting. He was impressed, very very much so. Along from the Picasso was something else that looked familiar. David Hockney, that was the one. But with him, he recalled, Mrs Gillibrand had mentioned a man-count. He didn't say anything this time, in case his mum patted him on the head.

'And a Bridget Riley in the main bedroom, no less,' Barbara commented rather quietly. Rory said nothing, but assumed it was the big black and white thing that made his eyes hurt.

'Hmm. They're not prints. Top-rate copies, possibly? Surely not originals?' Jay said. Rory could see she was looking thoughtful. She was probably, he decided, thinking about how much this place didn't need cleaning. It looked perfect already. What was there left to do? Even the shower room (just a big space, no naff cubicle or anything) only had a couple of towels lying on the floor and a few marks on the taps. It also had a telly set into the wall. It actually hurt, how very, very much he envied that. He hoped she'd charge him a bomb though, this guy. He was, obviously, truly mega-loaded.

At last. Ellie had been waiting for this day for the whole of this school year so far. She'd even practised what to do about it so now that it had happened it was – almost – no hassle. At last, at long bloody (ha ha!) last the Tampax in her bag wouldn't be a bluff. When she sympathized with friends about period pains and feeling a bit too fragile for netball she wouldn't be faking it any more. She felt a bit silly about that now, a bit embarrassed, as if all that pretence was part of a child-Ellie who had now pushed her way through a one-way turnstile into Adult-World. She thought she'd tell Imogen that she'd started, but not her mum. Mothers fussed about things. She remembered when Mog had got her first period (twelve and three quarters, lucky her), Mum had cried and hugged her and told everyone over supper that Imogen had Become a Woman. Ellie hadn't had much of a clue what they were talking about at the time. She'd thought it meant that Mog would have to leave school and go out to work and start driving the car. She remembered asking, 'Is she going to have a baby?' and everyone had laughed except Rory who, at eight, had also thought it a perfectly reasonable question.

It made a difference. She could feel it. The new, fully-functioning-female Ellie strode around the school that morning as if she was hyper-charged with fresh energy.

'You're practically running everywhere,' Amanda complained, trying to keep up on the way to French. 'What's the matter with you?'

Ellie couldn't tell her because then she'd know the truth and Amanda might tell. At very nearly fourteen, she was possibly one of the last in her year to start, if you didn't count the anorexics. Her mum had told her that she'd been over fifteen, herself, but that was probably usual back then, before there were all the hormones injected into chicken and tons of junk food and everyone's tits started to bud at nine. She'd only been trying to make sure Ellie didn't worry but it just made things worse at the time – how mortifying must that have been? You really wouldn't want to admit that your womanly inside bits hadn't kicked in till way after you started to think about snogging boys.

Ellie and Amanda came out of the French class and went into the girls' cloakroom. Ellie lined up alongside the other dozen after-school preeners, studied her face in the mirror and thanked God for her lack of spots. Her skin was baby-smooth with no need for the kind of heavy-duty camouflage that Tasha went in for. When she saw her piling that stuff on she wanted to do a mother thing – tell her she shouldn't cover up and smother her pores like that (especially with that grubby little sponge) but let her skin breathe so the grot had a chance to escape.

'You coming or what?' Amanda cut into her thoughts as Ellie gazed at herself in the mirror. 'What are you looking at yourself like that for? You look just the same as yesterday. Come *on* Ells, stop admiring yourself, it's time to go home.'

Ellie smiled as she fluffed out her hair with a brush, then pulled a lip-gloss out of her bag and smoothed it across her mouth. It was true, she did look the same. But she wasn't the same. Not even close to it.

'April's coming down for the weekend. She's bringing Freddie to look at a university and she's buying one of

113

Barbara's kittens and she says she'll be staying with you.'

This succinct answerphone message from Audrey was the first Jay had heard of it, but she didn't mind. She hadn't seen her sister for a few months, not since April and Oliver's twenty-fifth wedding anniversary party up in Cheshire, where they lived among footballers' wives and a connoisseur's choice of cosmetic surgery clinics. April would probably remember to phone and let her know just as her car was pulling into the driveway, breathily apologetic and dizzily forgetful as ever. She was easy to forgive. Jay was always delighted to see April because being with her reminded her of the many comfortable bits of her childhood – the giggling in the dark in their untidy bedroom, the week-long games of Scrabble (along with Matt who did not at all temper his competitive streak for the sake of his younger sisters), the time they'd painted a wall to resemble a Rousseau jungle scene to accommodate the lifesize cardboard tiger April had pinched from her school's production of *The Jungle Book*. The five-year age gap and their mother's sewing commitments meant that it had been nine-year-old April who had read the Magic Faraway Tree books aloud at night to Jay, giving her a lifelong certainty that every deep dark wood contained at least one tree full of talking owls and fairy folk. Later April passed on to her her own collection of Monica Edwards's pony books, which had made her go to sleep dreaming of stealing Delphine's Cobweb and galloping him through the fields and woods in pursuit of robbers and villains.

Jay had left a note at Charles's apartment inviting him to a Sunday lunch. He could pick his own Sunday; not knowing exactly when he'd be back, she'd left that to him. His was the answerphone voice that followed Audrey's: 'Hi, Charles here. Thanks *so* much for the

114

kind invitation . . .' He had a smooth, creamy voice like an actor. Possibly an actor typecast back in black-and-white-movie days as a bit of a cad, so that Jay instantly pictured him in a maroon spotted cravat and having a tendency to stand just that bit too close when he talked to women. He'd opted for the following Sunday, hoping (slight hint of throaty chuckle in voice) that it was all right with her. Well it *was* all right, the sooner the better as far as Jay was concerned, and with so many people in the house there'd be plenty to fill in any conversational holes. It would feel less like an awkwardly contrived inspection event.

'Listen to his voice, Greg, he sounds too old for that apartment,' Jay told Greg, playing the message back again for him to hear. You couldn't call it a flat, that was too mundane a word for it, reminding her of tatty student accommodation and makeshift conversions in gloomy Edwardian houses.

'Perhaps . . .' Greg mused as he stirred a handful of coriander leaves into a saucepan full of blissfully aromatic chilli con carne ready for that evening. Jay tried not to let her taste buds get too excited – they'd only be disappointed later when she got back from yoga and they were allowed just a small and virtuous portion.

'Perhaps he was minding it for a much younger millionaire friend and the friend died in tragic and mysterious circumstances and left it to him and he hadn't the heart to leave, preferring to stay and cherish the memory of this brave young . . .'

'Stockbroker? Footballer? Drug dealer?' Jay laughed. 'Who else could afford something like that?'

'I'm surprised a pilot living on his own could,' Greg said. 'Those places went for quite a hefty price, even off-plan two years ago. Maybe he came into an inheritance from that same young, tragic, mysterious multi-millionaire. Male friend or female friend, do you think? Any traces of girliness there? Any photos? Any old bras knocking about?'

'No notable girliness that I could see, not that I poked about in any drawers. The place was pretty neutral, a bit anonymous like a hotel suite. Any inheritance would have to be a big one – you should see the art collection. Even Rory went quiet.' Jay backed away from the kitchen, and the tempting tang of food, to pull the bag containing her new yoga mat out from the under-stairs cloakroom in readiness for her first class with Cathy, 'God, just listen to us,' she called back to Greg. 'We sound just like Win and Audrey – speculating like mad about a complete stranger and making two and two add up to a dozen.'

Charles was probably, she decided, a massively good catch for anyone. As she stashed her yoga mat into the car she tried to put together some kind of picture of him and came up with a cross between Roger Moore (in *The Saint* days) and the Duke of Edinburgh. Mentally, she separated this incongruous pair of men and placed Delphine between them, flirting girlishly at each in turn so that Jay could work out which one she was better suited to. She dressed the men in stagey velvet smoking jackets and Delphine in . . . It was no good. Somehow Delphine refused to join in, sliding away from anything seductively, strappily silky and remaining stubbornly in a sensible piecrust white shirt and a straight, on-the-knee skirt. The most frivolous twist her imagination could manage was a dinky kick-pleat at the back. She'd just have to wait for the real thing.

Cathy's yoga class was held in a big aerobics studio at the back of the local leisure centre. The studio had glass doors covered by sheets of coloured paper. Jay assumed this was because people had complained about casual gawpers in the corridor staring at the activities inside. She sympathized with these imaginary complainants, identifying with the unco-ordinated and plump of thigh, furiously puffing through their paces and mortified by the background mirth. As it was, she considered there were far too many mirrors. You really couldn't miss seeing yourself from angles you'd rather not know about, and she resolved to focus on her Inner Being or whatever it was you were supposed to do to make you feel that essential yogic peace. Those who had arrived before her were already doing just that: lying around the room on their mats, under blankets and with their eyes closed. Music played softly in the background. It was the tuneless, wafty sort that Jay associated with beauty salons where she'd had facials. Greg called it 'ambulance' music, aware it was known as 'ambient' but judging it mournful to a suicide-inducing degree.

'Hi Jay, I'm so glad you could make it!' Cathy greeted her as she greeted all her pupils, with a gentle hug and a feather-light kiss on each cheek. Cathy smelled faintly of vanilla and was looking inspiringly slender and fine-muscled in a tiny strappy vest and black stretchy trousers that just about balanced on her bony hips. Jay was amazed – out and about at home Cathy tended to go for the layered look, clothes-wise. To be this thin underneath she must have been piling on her entire wardrobe on a daily basis.

'You know I haven't done yoga before, apart from a taster session on holiday once,' she told Cathy. She was beginning to feel nervous as the room filled with the sound of deep slow breathing from those on the floor.

'Don't worry, you'll be fine. This isn't the advanced class – we've got all sorts. You should take the moves to the level that makes you feel comfortable. Where do you want to be? At the front?'

'Er . . . somewhere in the middle, I think.' What Jay meant was, out of range of the mirrors.

'Fine – oh good, you remembered to bring a blanket. What we do at the start is, we lie down and just take a few minutes to settle our bodies and our minds into a calm, centred place, to leave the outside world and the events of the day behind us.'

Jay left her shoes by the wall, headed for a piece of floor a safe couple of rows from the front, unrolled her mat and lay down beneath her blanket, closing her eyes and trying to make her mind go blank. It wasn't easy. She could feel the floor's solidity through the mat, and the blanket had a shamefully dingy-looking brown furry patch. Daffodil must have been leaping into the airing cupboard to sleep on it. People were still coming in, fussing with coats and mats and huffing about as they settled into position. A body flumped down quite close to Jay and she forced herself not to open her eyes and turn to greet it, for surely that would be only polite; lying down next to someone under blankets like this was quite intimate in the same way that being in a hospital bed was, or a hostel dormitory. She also tried not to think about the chilli Greg was simmering on the cooker back at home – her stomach, starved since the gruesome lunchtime Shape-Shake (malted chocolate), was in grave danger of rumbling its way through the entire class.

She would give up those Shakes, she decided as she lay there trying to breathe evenly. She felt as if they were turning her insides to glue and her body to a beige, toneless sponge. 'Shape-Shake' was a disappointing name for such stuff too – it made her think of the lively kind of dances popular in the seventies, where teen magazines would show you the moves with a series of footprint drawings to follow. It could only disappoint, really, if dance-type liveliness was what you had in mind when you drank it.

'OK everybody, welcome to the class . . .' Cathy had turned off the music, turned down the lights and pitched her voice into a soft, low tone. 'We're going to start with some alternate nostril breathing.'

Oh I'm sure I can manage that, Jay thought. She felt confident she wouldn't fail at that bit. She might not know her chi from her chakras but it surely wasn't possible to be hopeless at breathing. She opened her eyes to see everyone else already sitting pertly on their mats, blankets neatly folded by their sides. Quickly she sat up, rearranged herself and returned to full attention, feeling rather flustered, just in time to hear Cathy completing her instructions with '. . . then the middle finger of the right hand to close off the left nostril as we breathe out . . .'

Oh Lordy, she thought, trying to co-ordinate her efforts and work out what she was supposed to be doing. The word 'why' also came traitorously to mind, for surely, whichever of these two small orifices it went in through, all the air got mixed together at the back of your nose? Apparently not. Well then. She'd put that down as a 'fail'. To think she'd assumed breathing was the one thing you couldn't get wrong.

NINE

Cabbage Soup

'Mum told me you were on a diet so I brought you this instead of chocs and cake. I wouldn't want to be the one to put temptation in your way.' April giggled as she handed Jay a fat Jiffy bag containing something bulky but lightweight and slightly crunchy to the touch, like a bag of autumn leaves. She'd just arrived, breezing cool spring air with her into the house, scented with almond flowers and loaded with an assortment of canvas bags and a bunch of rhubarb-and-custard tulips. Her dark red hair looked wild and windswept, as if she'd raced down from Cheshire on horseback rather than driving in her peculiarly sedate way in her Honda Civic. 'So *why* are you dieting?' she continued, standing back a little to have a proper up-and-down look at her sister. 'You look fine to me. We just happen to be a family that morphs with age into unexpectedly rounded stock, that's all. You'll get used to it in a year or two. I did.'

April was a good bit rounder (though compensatingly taller) than Jay, an effect exaggerated by her being dressed in many quasi-hippy blue-and-purple-shaded layers: floppy trousers, an ankle-length bias-cut strappy Ghost dress over a T-shirt, all topped off with a rather pretty little pale grey lace-edged cardigan. It crossed Jay's mind that she wouldn't want to be in a queue for a thorough medical examination behind too many people attired like that. You'd be there all day while they faffed about, scrambling in and out of a stack of clothing.

'Well it's things like that for a start: I'm challenging that morphing process,' she told April. 'Plus it's realizing I'm going to be a grandma and not wanting to look like one . . . oh and there was a silly little throwaway comment from Greg. So I thought I'd see if I could trim up the body a bit before it's too late and it runs out of control into permanent decline.'

Jay tore the tape off her package and rummaged inside, pulling out the first of several sealed bags. So it *did* contain leaves, small crispy green ones. 'Thanks for this, but . . . um what is it exactly?' She turned it over, searching for a label.

'It's cabbage soup!' April had dumped her baggage on and under the glass table and now raced around the kitchen, switching on the kettle and poking about in cupboards for tea and sustenance. 'It's brilliant – or so I'm told, I haven't actually tried it myself. I got it from Bio-Beautiful round the corner at home – you should see the stuff they sell. They make their own no-carb cakes and there's a juice range with combinations of things like ginger, pear and artichoke – or was it broccoli? – and if you want to do a detox they'll take a blood test and package up all the right nuts and berries to balance your yin and yang. This cabbage stuff's all pre-packed and freeze-dried and ready to go. Saves you chopping it up and messing about for hours. You just boil up a bagful with water, simmer for twenty minutes and there you are: instant breakfast, lunch and a nice soothing bedtime drink!'

Chocolates and cake would definitely have had more

yum factor, Jay was pretty sure, but April – as always – meant well and was looking thrilled with her choice of gift.

'Apparently it works – so long as you do it right,' she went on, not at all abashed by Jay's lack of immediate delight. Jay was still wondering how much of a taste blast the juiced artichoke (or broccoli), pear and ginger would be. It sounded quite appetizing – but then almost anything would to a woman whose breakfast had been a plain no-fat yogurt and uninspiring flaky bran.

'And I'm told it's all a myth about filling you up with noxious gas, so you won't become socially unwelcome.'

'Thanks April – you're a treasure. I'll give it a go; it can't be any less effective than grapefruit. What I'd like to know though is how Mum knew I was dieting? I didn't say anything to her; she'd only have a go about "at your age you should be past bothering" or something.'

April laughed. 'Obvious. Ellie told her. She complained to her that you've been stuffing down Shape-Shakes and looking miserable and that you refuse to keep biscuits or crisps in the house. She claims she's feeling deprived.'

'Ellie said all that to Mum? Heavens, that's more than she says in a month to me! Which reminds me, where's Freddie? I thought he was the point of the trip?'

April stopped riffling through a cupboard and looked at Jay. 'It's all true, isn't it? I can't find a single naughty thing to eat in here. I'd kill for a doughnut. I might have been impressed by the Bio-Beautiful store but I prefer to admire it from a bigger distance than I can throw a Hobnob.'

Jay opened the fridge and pulled out a box of sticky, dark Florentines, handing them over quickly to her sister. 'OK, you can eat these. I got them for Sunday but I accept it's an emergency. So tell me about Freddie.'

April ripped open the packet with her teeth. Jay handed her a plate and they carried their mugs of tea through to the sitting room, where April balanced the plate of gooey Florentines on the arm of the pink velvet sofa. She looked, Jay thought, set to munch her way through the lot – which was good. Really it was. She'd just watch. And she'd try not to dribble.

Daffodil sat on the floor at April's feet, sniffing the air and looking up at the overhanging plate, calculating whether it was worth leaping up and giving it a swipe. Another, deeper, sniff told her there was no tuna in the air and she padded away in disappointment, flicking her tail rudely at them. April watched her go, 'Wonderful cats, Burmese. They do a great line in scorn. I can't wait to get mine – we're picking it up from Barbara on Monday on the way home. Now Freddie, well I dropped him off in Egham for an open day at the Royal Holloway College,' April said as she munched and licked melting chocolate off her fingers. 'I offered to go in with him – most parents did – so we could compare notes and discuss it afterwards, but he just did that look that they get and I handed over his train fare and left him to it.'

'I know that look – Rory does it and Ellie's is coming along nicely with plenty of training. His fare back home or to here?'

'Oh to here. He likes seeing your three.'

'They like seeing him. Perhaps, oh imagine, just perhaps they'll be all smiles all weekend.'

'Imagine it?' April laughed. 'A house full of peaceful, jolly, cheery teenagers? Unless they're smarming around like cats at feeding time in pursuit of hard cash, then no I can't!'

*   *   *

Freddie and Rory lay side by side on the scratchy seagrass floor of Greg's office and stared up through the glass to where the young elm saplings at this far end of the garden were waving their whippy branches in the wind. Nirvana's *Smells Like Teen Spirit* raged around them from Greg's new surround-sound B. & W. speakers. Greg was out at a site meeting and Rory liked to let himself in and enjoy his father's clean, cool, arty workspace with its classy glass desk, espresso machine, brushed-steel plan chests, indigo leather sofa and icy Macintosh computers. He'd love – in an ideal world, of course – his own room to be as streamlined as this, free from scattered clothes, littered homework, stray shoes, Cheesy Wotsit packets and scuzzy old boxes of childhood leftovers under the bed. He promised himself that after his exams he would junk all his superfluous possessions, even his first-ever skateboard, Tracy Island and the Lego pirate ship, and turn his room into something like this – or better still, that Charles bloke's place, if he could pick up some fancy art. Kylie would have to go, sadly, but he'd get some posh-framed black and white photos, some excellent arty nudes, lots of shadow and attitude.

'Trance, man,' Freddie murmured softly, inhaling on his roll-up and gesturing upwards with his thumb. 'Who needs drugs when you can gaze at nature moving about and just lose your brain in it?'

'Dunno,' Rory said, watching a wood pigeon clinging to a rocking bough. 'Haven't tried any drugs. I think I might be the only one in my year.'

He could admit this to Freddie. When your cousin lived two hundred miles away you could trust your every sad confession wouldn't get all round year 11 between lunch-break and home-time.

'You won't be,' Freddie reassured him. 'At least half the ones who say they have will be lying. Same with all

124

those surveys they panic the Government with: "Ninety per cent of over-elevens are off their nuts on E." All bollocks. They should worry about booze, stop wasting their time on the rest. We got girls of fourteen up our way doing a bottle of voddy every Saturday night and giving bj's to any bloke who looks halfway fit and claims he plays for Man. U. juniors.'

Rory thought of Tasha. Did she do that? Or would she do that if she was living her teen years in South Manchester? She looked a bit rough, but . . . no, it probably wasn't true. Freddie was just bragging in a mad sort of way, most likely. Doing the same as the survey people, exaggerating for effect.

'Why did he do it, do you think?' Freddie had moved on. 'Kurt Cobain – why do you think he shot himself?'

Rory considered for a minute, listening to Kurt ranting some more before answering. He felt flattered to be asked for his opinion. There was a two-year difference between him and his cousin, one that seemed to be getting gratifyingly smaller as they got older. Another couple of years and it would be practically nothing. This year they'd both got exams coming up; OK, Freddie's were A levels compared with his own baby-level GCSEs, but they were both at life-changing stages.

'I think . . .' he started, 'I think he just wanted to know what it was like to be dead.'

'Well he knows now,' Freddie said, chortling quietly.

'Ah but *no* he *doesn't*.' Rory sat up, wincing as his stitches pulled. The curly chrome radiator on the wall in front of him seemed to shimmer like a heat haze and his head was spinning slightly, which he put down to getting up too quickly. Unless it wasn't just Golden Virginia Freddie had rolled into the Rizla. He'd like to have been told if there was anything else, so he could savour the moment and check out in a proper aware state the things that spliff was doing to his head.

'He doesn't know what it's like to be dead,' he said, 'because when you're dead your knowing time is *over*. Kurt knows nothing. He did it for nothing.'

'He'll be regretting it then,' Freddie said.

'No, he won't be regretting it.' Rory was emphatic, excited at feeling sure he was close to some profound insight; sometimes you did that, got just the tiniest whisker's width away from what was the true meaning of the whole of life, the universe, everything – as the book went. 'See, your regretting time is over too. Your everything time is. He's beyond aware.'

Freddie laughed and looked at him. He had eyes like Ellie's, blue and overknowing. 'Beyond aware. *So* not imaginable. Waste of good time and a bullet then, right?'

Rory punched him on the shoulder. The insight moment whizzed on by, escaping his grasp yet again as he said, 'Man, are you ripping the piss?'

'When polishing the top of the dresser, please DO NOT place the goldfish bowl on the shelf unit in front of the mirror.'

Pretty decisive capitals, those. Anya was sitting next to Jay in the van and looking worried, waiting for an explanation. Jay read the note again, a note that Mrs Cooper had insisted Anya show to Jay 'In Person' which meant that after a anxious phone call from Anya she had driven over to the Coopers' hacienda-style bungalow to meet her and see what the problem was, leaving April boiling up a test batch of the cabbage soup.

Obviously it was of enormous importance to Mrs Cooper, this thing with the fish, although when Jay had previously been to the house herself, the small, plastic tank had seemed no different from any other standard-issue petshop number containing a pair of very ordinary goldfish shimmying around looking bored among pondweed, gravel and a miniature shipwreck. Hard as she tried, she could recall no outstanding features about them, and unless the underside of the tank was covered in razor wire, there was surely nothing that could do damage to a perfectly sturdy-looking beech-veneer Habitat unit. Perhaps Mrs Cooper didn't want the fish getting overexcited. Possibly she was a keen student of fish psychology and knew it would upset them deeply to see themselves reflected, only to be disappointed when returned to their usual spot to find their new 'companions' had vanished.

'Mrs Cooper says the fish is "fish ooey" and I am not understand,' Anya told her. 'Is money, she says. A money fish? They's not gold, only fishgold.'

Light dawned and Jay laughed. 'Fish ooey? Oh, I get it! *Feng shui.*'

'Huh?' Anya was no closer to understanding and there seemed no point in going into deep, linguistically tricky explanations about the mystical science of placing household objects. This might, Jay realized, also explain the mysterious coins Mrs Cooper kept under her doormat which Anya carefully removed and piled up on the dresser each week, only to find they were back in place again next time she washed the floor. Jay had assumed it was a test of trust. She suspected several clients did that, sneakily leaving pound coins around or a crafty fiver to catch out a light-fingered employee.

'It's OK Anya, I'll talk to her. Just put the fish on the floor while you wipe down the dresser and then put them back again. I'll talk to Mrs Cooper.'

'OK, you talk.' Anya smiled, relieved though none the wiser, and twiddled her finger beside her temple. 'Mrs Cooper has loose head,' she said.

Jay laughed guiltily, feeling she should not really be conspiring with her staff in questioning the clients' sanity. Anya was right though, it was a fine line, the one between having high domestic standards and being obsessive. This wasn't Mrs Cooper's first complaint regarding Anya. Only a fortnight before there had been a stormy phone call demanding that Anya return *at once* because she'd left the dining chairs pulled out a little way from the table instead of pushed in underneath as far as they could go, in Mrs Cooper's preferred way. Of course she'd made the girl do no such ridiculous thing and got out of the situation slyly by offering to send someone else the next week instead. That had Mrs C. backtracking – Anya was a top-rate cleaner, fast and thorough, and Jay would have been thrilled if all her staff were like her. The placing here or there of the set of heavy ladder-back chairs suddenly became less important than hanging onto a highly valued and sought-after worker.

On her way back, Jay drove past the Swannery and glanced up at Charles Walton's apartment. He'd be home the next day so there wasn't really time to sneak April in for a quick look round, much as she'd like to. They'd have to wait till Delphine was in residence and hope she didn't swap the fabulous grey suede sofas for gentleman's-club earth-brown chesterfields with matching pouffes. April would love the Picasso (if it actually was one) and she'd giggle about the en suite wet-room with the TV built into the glass wall. A natty addition would be one of those Philippe Starck perspex Ghost chairs, then you could sit and watch *EastEnders* in comfort while you rinsed conditioner out of your hair.

Jay had still got the Swannery keys in her bag, which wasn't very efficient of her. They should really be tagged with a code number and hung on the rack in the cupboard in her office. None of the keys had their relevant addresses on them – if they did, and there was a burglary in her or Barbara's office, the theft of the keys could result in dozens of households having to get the locksmiths in.

At the traffic lights, Jay had a quick look in her bag for Charles's keys. She intended to put them on the dashboard to remind herself to take them straight up to the office when she got in. It didn't bother her that she couldn't immediately find them; the bag was dark and deep and full of the usual clutter that most women, except the obsessively tidy, accumulate. She pictured her shamefaced horror if snoopers such as airport security staff asked to peer into it. The lights changed to green and she had to stop the search as a Range Rover behind beeped peevishly at her. She would wait till she got home. The keys were either somewhere in the cavernous bag or already up on her desk.

Ellie was in a rush to get out of school. It didn't matter about upsetting Amanda, not today, not on a Friday because whatever it took, she just had to get out and away before Tasha caught up with her. Ellie didn't want to be with Tasha today. Well, she didn't and yet she *did*. Being out with her, even just walking down the street, had such a dangerous edge that she got all pent-up and nervy. Carly Andrews had told her she and Tash had just been walking along talking about school stuff and the next thing Tasha was running, racing off with some old woman's handbag that she'd snatched off her as they passed. She hadn't kept it or taken anything; a hundred metres further on she'd hurled it over a hedge and laughed. Just practising, she'd told Carly, as if it was an OK normal thing for anyone to do.

Tasha liked doing her weekend shoplifting on a

Friday so she'd have something new to wear on Saturday night when, she claimed (who really knew what was true?) she went out clubbing all night and got ratted. She'd given Ellie a sly look, telling her this at lunchtime, as if wondering whether to trust her with some extra information. If it was anything to do with sex, Ellie really didn't want to know. She felt quite squeamish about sex; it was all right to think about getting close to boys and snogging, but only with clothes on and with no big fumbly hands trying to get at her skin. So far she didn't at all fancy the thought of any boy putting any naked bits of himself into or even close to any naked and very private bits of *her*. Picturing this made her squirm with horrified shyness, and the idea that one day not too far ahead she would actually *want* it to happen was almost beyond her wildest imagining. If Tasha started to tell her she'd been doing stuff like that, she would want to put her hands over her ears and sing loudly.

Tasha was older than the rest of them, very nearly fifteen. She'd been kept back a year at primary school after she'd missed two terms when her mum took her to Lanzarote in a converted ambulance to live with a man she'd met in Lineker's Bar in Puerto del Carmen. Tasha made it all sound really glamorous and said that her mum and dad had fought it out in court and she'd been in the papers as a tug-of-love child ordered to be brought back home. It might be true, Ellie thought, but it might equally not be. She might have been kept back a year because she was thick, and been bigging herself up with this story as a cover. That was both the problem and the attraction with Tasha, she'd got a story full of drama for everything; true or not, you couldn't tell but you wanted to hear it.

Ellie almost didn't recognize Freddie; for one thing her cousin was about the last person she'd expect to see outside the school gate, and for another he'd abandoned his last year's blond surfer look and got his hair all sticking up and with a dark red stripey bit down the middle, like someone she'd seen on telly playing cricket. He was leaning against the wall with Rory, smoking a skinny roll-up and eyeing the girls. The last time she'd seen him had been at his parents' mad party up in Cheshire, when all the cousins had gone outside and made a snowman in the middle of a late night blizzard. Freddie and Juliet's dad Oliver had lit a wood fire in the rusty barbecue and they'd topped off their snowman with a leather cowboy hat (Greg's), then given him a champagne bottle and made him look as if he was swigging from it. In the morning his head had slumped down and he looked like a sleepy drunk with a horrible hangover. Greg had gone out and put his arm round the snowman and told him he knew just how he felt.

'Hi Freddie, great to see you!' Ellie dropped her school bag on his feet and Freddie grabbed her and gave her a big squeezy hug. She looked around sneakily to see if anyone she knew was watching. He was very good-looking, for a family member – girls in her year, and not *just* her year, would be highly impressed.

'We thought we'd come down and meet you,' Freddie told her as they set off towards the bus stop. 'And Rory's got a cunning plan.'

'Well, not exactly,' Rory said, pulling her with him across the road.

'Hey, this is the wrong way, aren't we going home?' Ellie was hungry. She wanted to get home and make some cinnamon toast, her current favourite snack and one guaranteed to drive her truly annoying diet mother loopy with comfort-food craving. Serve her right, she thought, for the cruel absence of crisps and biscuits.

'Not yet,' Rory said. 'First we're going visiting. I'm

going to show you this incredible place where old Aunt Delphine's going to be living. I've got the keys.' He threw them high in the air and caught them, one-handed.

'But . . . you can't just walk in! Suppose someone's there!' Ellie really didn't want to do this. It would almost have been better to be with Tasha. At least with Tasha whatever they did would be just teen crime at worst and somehow she'd have a chance to persuade the police that it wasn't her. If she and Rory got caught in Charles's flat, it would all come down on her *and* Mum and the great business empire that was Dishing the Dirt.

'Rory, no, please don't let's. Mum would kill us if she knew.'

'She won't find out and anyway the geezer's away till tomorrow, flying his big jets. He's expecting people to go in – well, Mum and Barbara.'

Freddie stopped walking and looked at her, smiling and kind. 'You go home if you like, Ellie, honestly it's fine. We'll go on our own.'

That was even worse. She'd have to go with them, make sure they didn't jump on the beds with their shoes on or leave a fridge door open or something stupid. Boys didn't seem to have the thinking gene. She knew this from school, where it was always the boys who 'accidentally' smashed test tubes and mucked up the textbooks. They didn't look ahead and imagine that their stupidity might have results beyond making a few sad fools laugh. Her mum had pointed this out too, though in her case she'd been talking about the making of accidental babies. Luckily she hadn't been directing her comments at Tristan at the time. It would only have upset him when he and Imogen were so happy.

'OK, I'll come with you. But we're just looking for a

minute or two. And it's no touching anything, no messing about, then straight home, all right?'

The two boys mumbled a promise and they took the next bus towards the riverside complex.

Ellie had great hopes of the security gates being locked and that they wouldn't be able to get in. Either that, or there'd be a sentry guarding the place who would send them away for looking suspicious, but there was no-one around. The drive-in gates needed a special card but the walk-in one was open.

'It's not like we're not just slightly entitled to be here,' Freddie tried to reassure Ellie. 'We're just visiting our soon-to-be step-uncle.'

'Who we know for sure happens to be on the other side of the world – unless he's changed his plans. Have you thought of that?' Ellie said, feeling that she was about to go into a deep sulk.

'Chill, Ellie,' Rory told her, swaggering into the lift and keeping his finger on the 'doors open' button for her.

Well it was worth a look, Ellie had to admit as she stepped cautiously across the hallway and into the sitting room. It was like something out of her dad's design magazines. Aunt Delphine would tut about all the shiny surfaces and start putting crochet mats down.

'Great place for a party,' Freddie said, peering into the giant fridge and taking out a can of Stella.

'Freddie! Don't take his stuff!' Ellie panicked, terrified he'd spill beer all over the sofa. Instead the two boys went into the bedroom and sat down on the silky blue throw that was folded over the end of the bed. She wished she hadn't come. They'd had a look, they should go now, not hang about.

'I was thinking that, about a party or something,' Rory agreed. 'Even Samantha Newton would turn up if she got asked here.'

Freddie opened the can and took a deep swig while Ellie held her breath, waiting for an explosion of froth on the silk.

'She a bit special then?'

Rory glanced at Ellie, who was keeping terrified eyes on the main door. 'S'pose so.' he shrugged. 'She's in my year though.'

'Ah. Well that's bad and good.' Freddie nodded like a man of deep wisdom. 'Bad because chicks generally prefer older men. It bigs them up with their mates. But it's also good because she's actually the right age for you. Unless you can get an old one who's seen some action, someone really old like mid-twenties. All you need to do, old son,' Freddie said, getting up and, to Ellie's relief, pulling the cover straight. 'All you've got to do is really, really impress her.'

The smell hit Jay as she walked through the door. It stank like the bin bag of leaves she'd kept from two autumns ago so that they could rot down for quick compost. Too much rain had got in – they'd gone slimy and stank of mould. What she'd been expecting was the shady scent of hot, late-August woodland – fresh, mysterious and musky. This hadn't even been close. Even when she'd spread the leaves under the camellias the smell had lingered over the summer, and each time it rained the air was filled with a stench like a rotting pond. And now it was in her kitchen.

'April? What's that smell? It's vile!' The concertina doors were wide open and Imogen and April were in the kitchen, shrieking with hilarity and making dramatic, grand wafty movements with their arms to help clear the air. The extractor over the cooker was going at full blast.

'It's your soup!' April laughed. 'I started simmering it and I was just having five minutes on the sofa with

Daffodil and this month's *World of Interiors* and I sort of forgot about it! Sorry, Jay, but I think it might be fermenting.'

'Have you chucked it out?' Cathy next door would think there was a drain emergency.

'It's in the garden, still in its saucepan!' April wiped away a laughter tear. 'You could go outside and try it if you really want!'

'Better do it quick, before it gets up and runs off, all by itself,' Imogen squawked through her giggles.

'It's probably really nice, if you can get past the smell,' April said. 'I'm sorry about mucking it up.'

'Hey it's OK. I appreciate your efforts, but you know, tonight is sorted and it's a diet-free time.' She opened the fridge. 'One I prepared earlier – proper, luscious, gorgeous lasagne. With a *salade tricolore*. Just got to find these keys . . . And where are the kids? They're very late back.'

Imogen went out to pour the soup down the outside drain. It certainly wasn't allowed back in the house, and Jay admired very much that a girl in the early months of pregnancy could both watch and smell the foul stuff being poured away without throwing up. Just as the last drop disappeared and Imogen turned on the hosepipe for a final rinse, Rory, Ellie and Freddie crashed in through the front door. Jay watched in her usual daily amazement as her children carelessly flung their school bags at the bottom of the stairs, and they all mooched into the kitchen leaving a trail of debris. Rory was carrying a bunch of keys.

'Found these outside on the ground by your car, Mum. Getting careless in your old age.' He patted her gently on the shoulder. 'We'll put it down to a granny moment, shall we?'

TEN

Nigella's Strawberry Ice Cream (featuring ten egg yolks and a pint of double cream)

'I hope you're getting a good view of this,' Jay muttered in the general direction of Planet Man and his telescope as she bent her body in half, put her hands flat on the floor and spread her legs apart. 'I hope you're copping my bottom in your sights from up there in your lair.'

This, she was certain, should put him off and have him turning his viewing attention to the other end of the road. Perhaps he'd discover the local house of ill repute and decide to focus on activities far more exotic than those to be seen in the glass bedroom. What was on offer for his viewing delight today surely couldn't be a pretty sight for anyone: a plump (but working on it, working on it . . .) middle-aged woman in her bra and knickers puffing away at sun salutes on her bedroom rug at eight on a sunny Sunday morning. They were gorgeous knickers though – Elle MacPherson silky boy-briefs in mint and black. Planet Man would have got an excellent view of them (possibly even been able to read the label if his equipment was of outer-galaxy quality) as she went into Down Dog pose with her back to the window and warmed up with some hamstring stretches, bending one leg in first, straightening it, then flexing the other before sliding her body forward into Cobra.

It was harder work than it looked, this yoga. After Cathy's class Jay had come home feeling exhilarated and a bit light-headed (which she'd put down to thirst and sorted out with a reviving glass of white wine) but not particularly overstretched or exhausted. For a while she'd felt quite proud of herself – all that hauling vacuum cleaners around and leaning down to clean scummy baths must have been more aerobically punishing than she'd imagined. A couple of days on and her muscles were now letting her know that they were rebelling in serious protest at the disciplined stretching and bending, and she'd completely changed her mind about yoga being a gentle, not particularly demanding, activity.

'Mmm! Lovely! Your bum's gone all sleek and solid.' Greg, dripping and naked from the shower, came up behind her and clutched her flesh to check her workout results. It was pleasing to have your efforts admired but Jay was close to squealing with pain on behalf of her newly taut *gluteus maximus*.

'I don't think Kylie should start worrying just yet,' she told him as she stood up straight, turned herself sideways and took up a Warrior stance. 'But give me a few more weeks and who knows . . .'

It would take a lot more than a few sessions of yoga. Jay had now lost five pounds (of an aimed-for fourteen) but at such a slow rate it felt as if every ounce of her spare flab was a tiny plump animal, each one clinging tight to her body as if its life depended on it. Even the smallest lapse in vigilance – such as that post-yoga wine – seemed to result in the return of the weight that must lurk somewhere close by, possibly under a convenient stone. You might as well, she thought, just keep it in your handbag and invite it back on board with every titchy biscuit.

Grapefruit was useless and Shape-Shakes unappetizing so she would have to take up a new regime; but which? The yoga class had been a fun and friendly experience and made her feel she might get better results if she was in the company of other like-minded people. She would have to join a slimming club. The discipline – and potential humiliation – of a weekly weigh-in would surely do more to focus her mind than had so far been achieved.

'When people lose really serious amounts of weight, you know like almost half their body or something,' Imogen had said the night before, 'does that make the person, like, half-*dead*? Cos I mean, fifty per cent of them's vanished, hasn't it? So where's it gone to, all that chunk of body? Heaven? The same special body-parts afterlife that amputated limbs go to?'

This was a modified version of the question all children get round to by about ten, the unanswerable, 'Where do we go when we die?'

'Fat's gone down the bog, I suppose,' Tristan said, condemning life's greatest mystery to the council drainage system.

'Yuck, mingin'.' This idea had not appealed to Imogen.

'Or into sweat or energy or whatever,' He conceded. 'It's not like really dead is it, because your brain and all your organs and all the bits that make you work are still there and you're still breathing. Same as if you have a bit cut off or out, like Rory's appendix. Right, Jay?'

Did he think she had the last word because she was nearer to God, at least in the lifespan way, than he was? Cheery thought.

'Hmm, that sounds about right. Nothing's *dead*, as such, just sort of . . . melted.'

It reminded Jay of Hamlet, pleading for his 'too solid' flesh to melt. She sympathized with the poor man, even as she now realized that if she ever saw another production of the play she'd be hugely disappointed if he wasn't played by a big lardy darts-champion type, rather than the usual skinny, angst-ridden sort. All the same it was a thoroughly horrible picture, this melting thing. She imagined oily, hot grease, a vast oozy lake bubbling with the offloaded blubber of an entire nation; or, still solid, heaped up in pound blocks, like Hamlet's, a colossal bank of fat deposits. Which was, she concluded, pretty accurate, considering the way so many people regained the weight they'd taken trouble to lose, as if it was never really something you could disown permanently but merely stored in a current account, ready to be withdrawn and reattached as soon as anyone carelessly imagined it was safe to start wolfing down normal but unmoderated food again.

'Remind me, what time's he coming, this Charles?' April rinsed her fingers under the tap and started hulling strawberries ready for Jay to turn them into ice cream.

'I told him one thirty. But I told Mum and Win two o'clock. Oh and Cathy next door's coming too. I thought we could give him a drink and get him settled before those two get hold of him and start in with their questions.'

April laughed. 'And we can force him to answer all our own nosy-parker stuff first. Poor Charles. You could almost feel sorry for the man. By the time we've all finished with him he'll wish he'd been born in the nice, gentle days of the Spanish Inquisition.'

Jay took the mixing bowl with the egg yolks in them out of the fridge. This was not going to be a mimsy-pimsy low-fat, healthy-option ice-cream mixture: Nigella's sumptuous recipe required ten egg yolks and close to a pint of double cream. The whites had gone into making meringues which were lined up, ready to be sandwiched with the ice cream, raspberries and blueberries. And there was a hearty, traditional apple pie that April had made the night before. Audrey would comment on the pastry, having never knowingly consumed a piece of pie without saying something about flakiness, lightness of touch or crumbliness of texture. There seemed to be a whole specialized vocabulary that applied to pastry.

Jay didn't have a particularly sweet tooth herself and it had crossed her mind that those who had a serious pudding habit to give up had it easy, diet-wise. Pasta, wine, roast potatoes, succulent sauces, surely you could carry on having them all if you'd surrendered a daily five hundred calories' worth of cheesecake, trifle and apple pie? This ice-cream dessert was for Win's benefit, a woman who had been known to possess in her freezer, all at the same time, every single flavour of Häagen-Dazs ice cream. Audrey, discovering this when running next door for an emergency loan of frozen peas, had suggested she simply get the company to rent her a shop's display cabinet.

'Don't we all want to know the same thing, April? Though I don't know how we could put it so it didn't sound rude. We can hardly come out with "What in hell's name are you doing with Delphine?" Now can we?'

'Bugger,' April said as she rinsed the colander of strawberries under the tap and water splashed all over her front. 'I see what you mean, but aren't you jumping the gun? He might turn out to be really horrendous and we'll end up feeling sorry for poor Delphine.'

Laughter spluttered from Jay. 'Poor Delphine? Tell me, when has it ever been "poor Delphine"?'

April grinned at her and handed over the strawberries. 'True, it would be a first. The girl who was Princess Perfect. Do you think she's dyed her hair yet?'

'Oh no, she couldn't! She always swore she wouldn't. Think how it would disappoint all those who made her promise she never, ever would. You couldn't help imagining hordes of weeping people, mourning the day she applied the first L'Oréal highlight.'

'Her "crowning golden glory". Remember Auntie Win brushing it for a hundred strokes every night with that soft silver brush? Imagine our kids putting up with that?'

'"Waist-length, like spun gold,"' April and Jay duetted. What *was* spun gold? Jay had never worked that one out. All she could think of was cotton reels of shiny gold thread that her mother had sometimes used for stitching sequins to spandex catsuits. It was wiry stuff, not something you'd want for hair.

'Waist-length gold what?' Ellie said, coming into the kitchen and peering into the breadbin for chocolate croissants.

'Delphine's hair,' April told her, wiping away laughter tears with a tea towel. 'She had fairy-princess hair right up till she was fifteen. Win used to say her hair was the colour of gold.'

'And your gran used to look po-faced and say "So are chips".'

Ellie didn't laugh. 'You're really horrid about Auntie Delphine. I thought she was really nice.'

'You haven't seen her since you were six,' Jay reminded her.

'So? She let me play with all her make-up. I remember her showing me how to put lipstick on properly. *And* she smelled nice. You shouldn't be so rude about her.'

Jay and April exchanged glances, recognizing a teenager in holier-than-thou mode.

'And we *don't* smell nice?' April teased, pushing her luck.

Ellie didn't reply, but simply raised her eyes heavenwards and shoved her chocolate croissant into the microwave, tutting that the oven was already occupied with potatoes and a hunk of beef.

'Well that's telling us,' April whispered to Jay as Ellie crashed around the kitchen in her pyjamas, assembling a plate, cup of coffee and an extra chunk of butter for the croissant which, brutally miked, was destined to be a scalded-chocolate disappointment.

From upstairs came the announcement that Freddie and Rory were now awake, in the form of an ear-splitting blast of heavy metal. The bathroom door slammed, the hum of the shower pump started up and Jay could already picture the thrown-down heap of soggy towel, the puddles on the floor, the outline of damp foot on bathmat and toothpaste splodges in the basin. Still, at least upstairs had rooms in which you could close the door on the shambles. When they'd bought this house and Greg had insisted on knocking down so many of the downstairs walls, she should have had a bit of a think about the all-exposed nature of open plan.

'Oh God, what will Charles make of this place?' Jay groaned, stirring the egg yolks into the vanilla cream and surveying the already mounting cooking fallout. 'It's practically a war zone. His flat looks as if no-one has so much as toasted a slice of wholemeal in it. And,' she added, scooping eggshells into the bin, 'I can just imagine Delphine giving me that look and telling me I could have made this ice cream days ago instead of leaving it to the last minute. I can't deny she'd be right.'

She'd done her best, down here in what an estate

agent would call the big kitchen-stroke-family room, but sometimes she could see the point of the days when you parked the guests firmly into a separate dining room and kept your culinary chaos way out of sight. Then you could legitimately leave them to converse politely among themselves while you retired to sob into the sinkful of debris in private.

'OK, so Delphine was the original domestic goddess,' April said. 'You can afford to be when you've got no kids and no job. It's what she was good at. You're good at . . . at other things.'

'See, you can't think of any.' Jay pointed the wooden spoon at her.

'Yes I can. You've made a lovely family and you run a successful business and you're a brilliant sister. Now stop moping and feeling sorry for yourself, open a bottle and pour us both a livener. You can face anything after a teensy glass of fizz.'

There'd just be time, Rory was sure, just time to go and check out if it really was the same house before they had to be home for the compulsory lunch. He was glad he'd got Freddie with him – a lone bloke hanging about would look extremely iffy, even with the alibi of the football he'd brought along to kick around. Two could just happen to be there. They could look more credibly on their way to somewhere else, even if they stopped walking and had a bit of a kick-around with the ball. If it *was* a hookers' hang-out, a lone man (OK, a lone *boy*) would look as if he was hoping to be invited in for a bit of business but was too scared (too right) to make an approach. And if it *wasn't*, well he'd probably have some old Neighbourhood Watch geezer coming after him and trying to give him the kind of good old-fashioned beating-up that never did *him* any harm back in the plod-on-the-beat days.

143

'There's the tree, the one with all the yellow flowery fluff stuff on it.' Rory slowed down as they turned the corner. The two of them stopped and consulted the picture in *Out for the Lads*. You couldn't see much of the building, just part of the tree, a bit of hedge and some of the gatepost which might be blue but had a lot of paint flaking off.

'Looks very ordinary.' Freddie was not impressed. 'I bet they've got it wrong. Either that or we have. From what you can see in the picture it could be more or less anywhere.'

'Well they could hardly paint it bright pink and hang a sign up, could they? Come on, let's get nearer and see what we can see.'

Freddie shrugged and sauntered along behind Rory, throwing the ball up and catching it. Rory sensed his cousin's lack of interest and felt a bit embarrassed. Freddie was currently on his second long-term girl-friend, which implied (though Freddie hadn't said) a genuine, grown-up, regular sex life, the sort that's so well established you take it for granted and don't get over excited about – except during *the* moments, presumably. The furtive curiosity of a virgin adolescent must seem light years behind him.

'OK, slow down.' Freddie surprised him by suddenly paying attention. 'We'll give it a good slow look, check it out for clues. It's probably just a family house with bikes and stuff and an off-roader full of baby seats parked in the drive.'

'But you never know.' Rory was still hopeful.

'No, you never do. Lucky we chanced to bring this football along.' Freddie grinned at him, running into the quiet tree-lined road and kicking the ball around, proving himself quite hopeless at keepy-uppy.

'God, you're crap at that,' Rory shouted, tackling him for the ball.

'Let's see you do better!'

'No worries, man.' Rory grabbed the ball and bounced it from his knee to his left foot and onto his right, keeping it going for several seconds.

'Hey not bad! You in the school team?'

'Shit, no. It's full of heavyweight jocks who are all wannabe sports coaches. Gym rats, always comparing six-packs.' He kicked the ball in a high arc, landing it just beside the flaky blue gatepost of Halcyon.

Freddie ran to get it, passing it back to Rory and narrowly missing the silver Porsche parked at the kerbside.

'Shot, wanker,' Rory shouted with sarcasm. 'If you'd hit that we'd have had to leg it.'

Aiming carefully, Rory kicked the ball back towards Freddie and managed to land it in Halcyon's garden, close to the left of the two downstairs windows.

'You or me? Or both?' he asked Freddie.

'Both. In case you need back-up. In case you're lured to the clutches of a big-breasted motherly type with a heart of gold and a leather whip.'

'Sounds like our history teacher,' Rory said as he took a deep, calming breath and pushed the gate open. 'Here goes nothing.'

Rory walked up the path followed by Freddie. He tried to walk in a nonchalant, don't-care sort of way, but when he heard Freddie tittering behind him he realized he was overdoing the swagger.

'Gosh, look, Rory, there it is, in that bush!' Freddie called loudly, making an overdramatic show of pointing towards a hydrangea bush beneath which sat the black and yellow football.

'Right! I can see it! You fetch it Freddie and I'll knock on the door and tell the owners what we're doing. We wouldn't want anyone to think we had no manners!'

He couldn't look at Freddie for fear of his face

cracking into helpless laughter. He tried to compose himself as he walked up the two front steps and rang the bell. He could hear it sounding somewhere far inside the house. Possibly, he imagined, in a little office somewhere where a uniformed maid sat waiting to greet customers, or where a spike-heeled madam did the accounts, stashing away wodges of cash out of sight and the snooping of the tax authorities.

Nobody answered. Freddie now stood on the path, looking slightly foolish and clutching the ball. They were both, it suddenly occurred to Rory, too old to be there, waiting like little lads to make sure it was all right to retrieve their ball. He waited a bit longer, trying to look into the front sitting room, past the heavy cream curtains. All he could make out was a big round gilt-framed mirror over the fireplace, a mantelpiece with what looked like birthday cards on it and walls painted the earthy orange-red colour of flower pots. There were pictures, but they were wishy-washy landscape efforts, nothing promisingly erotic. Disappointingly normal, really. Rory longed to open the letterbox and have a gawp into the hallway. He felt around inside his pocket and pulled out one of his mum's Dishing the Dirt leaflets that he'd written Samantha Newton's mobile number on. He didn't need it now – the number was committed to his own mobile and to his memory. Gently, he lifted the letterbox and leaned down for a quick shufti. A grey striped cat sat on the long blue rug in the hallway. It had its back leg up and was washing its bum. It gave him a look that was a complete sneer. Flustered, he pushed the bit of paper through and retreated down the steps.

'They're probably all asleep,' Freddie commented as together they walked back down the lavender-edged path. 'I mean, they must work mostly at nights, especially Saturdays.'

'Yeah. Either that or we've got it so completely wrong that they're actually a normal family who are out because they've all gone to the park or the pub or . . . oh I suppose to church.'

Bored now, the two boys half-heartedly kicked the football to each other as they ambled back towards home. Rory turned as he heard a gate click behind them.

'Hey, look there's someone coming out. I'm sure it was that house.' The man was medium height, greying, wearing a three-quarter-length dark brown coat and carrying a bunch of flowers. He pointed a remote-key at the silver Porsche and the lights flashed once, then he climbed in and drove away.

'Did you see that?' Rory said, immediately wishing he hadn't, as even to him he'd sounded like an over-excited small boy. Of course Freddie had seen – wasn't he standing right beside him?

'I did. I wonder why he didn't open the door when we rang. Probably in the bog.'

'Or on the job.'

'Nah, it was only a couple of minutes back. Unless he was just zipping up. He doesn't actually look . . . well like he's up to anything he shouldn't be.'

'True, though possibly a front. Perhaps he didn't want to be seen. Anyway, if he was a punter it wouldn't be up to him to answer the door, now would it?'

'Good thinking Rory, but, you know, I don't want to be a downer but I really don't think it's a knocking shop.'

Shame, Rory thought. To have been able to confirm it would have livened up the day no end. He smiled to himself as he walked, imagining astounding the family at lunch by telling them about it.

Reactions would vary, obviously, starting with Dad. He'd come out with something funny and rude, like:

'Ooh good – must pop round, ask if they fancy a nice extension.'

Mum: No comment but that 'not in front of (insert name of choice)' look.

Gran: A down-to-earth sort. 'Oh well, it's a job like any other. Someone's got to do it,' but old Auntie Win, she'd probably drop dead with shock.

Oh God, he was early. Terrific, no time for the last-minute lipstick. Jay heard voices in the hallway as she was transferring the ice cream from its churner to the freezer box. Ellie was, at last, dressed and showered and sweet-smelling and making a good job of laying the table prettily. She'd discovered some long pink narrow glasses that no-one ever used and placed them in a line down the centre of the glass table, each one containing a tulip from the bunch April had brought with her. They complemented the pink linen napkins very effectively, and for a fleeting moment Jay found herself considering whether or not to have a bash at napkin origami. Naff as it was, it would be so suitable a reminder of the absent Delphine, who could fold fabric squares into fans, swans and quite possibly a selection of the kings and queens of England.

''Scuse me, Mum, budge over, I need serving spoons.' Ellie shoved herself against Jay to get at the cutlery drawer.

'Careful, Ellie! You'll . . .' Too late. Caught off balance, Jay swerved with the ladleful of ice cream and it tipped, dropping a big pink dollop into the drawer, all over the sundries at the front: whisks, bottle openers, garlic press, lemon zesters and such.

'Shit,' she muttered, trying to scoop out a usefully salvageable amount of ice-cream. She plonked as much as she could into the bowl and slammed the drawer shut on the smeary mess, trusting that as most of the cutlery she possessed was already on the table, no-one would need to go looking for more.

'Granny moment again, Mum?' Ellie whirled away, laughing.

'. . . meet the others and have a drink . . .' Instead of installing the guest in the sitting room, out of harm's way, Greg was bringing Charles through to the kitchen. Briskly Jay grabbed a cloth, whisked it over the pink-smeared worktop and turned to her guest with her best, most welcoming smile fully installed.

'Charles! Hello, lovely to meet you.' Jay found herself shaking hands with a mid-height, mid-weight man with plenty of badger-grey hair and the kind of crinkled tan she'd always associated with leathery expats who scorn avoidance of the tropical midday sun. It wouldn't be the death of him, she thought, not now he'd got Delphine making sure he never left home in the sunshine without a hat. Disappointingly, he didn't in the slightest resemble either Roger Moore (as Saint or James Bond) or the Duke of Edinburgh, but, in a slightly formal though lightweight tweedy suit beneath a dark wool coat, he reminded her of the kind of MP who doesn't do 'casual' very convincingly.

'This feels like a blind date,' he said, smiling (nice teeth, well kept and presumably his own) and handing Jay a heavy bouquet of strongly scented lilies.

'More like a firing squad I'd have thought!' April ventured. 'All of us here lined up to inspect you when you're all alone and no Delphine for protection.'

'Absolutely. You're very brave. We admire that. Can I get you a drink?' Jay reached into the fridge for the champagne that she and April had made an early start on. Would Delphine, cross-examining later, be told that this bottle was already well sampled? That her cousins were a pair of lushes who couldn't even wait that extra half-hour till the chief guest arrived before downing a swift one? Charles, however, accepted his glass with neither a quizzically raised eyebrow nor comment beyond a thank-you, and April led him off to introduce him to Ellie and Rory while Jay hurriedly sluiced a cloth over the worst of any spillage and hurled utensils into the dishwasher. It felt odd, meeting this man whose bedroom she'd been inspecting only the other day. She'd looked in his cupboards, checked out his suits – probably even the one he was now wearing. For the first time she felt as if her job involved prying. She wouldn't go to the flat again, not till Delphine had taken up residence. It was all down to Anya, Katinka and Barbara from now on.

Jay could hear Imogen and Tristan clattering up the outside stairs and at the same time, Rory chatting to Cathy as he let Win and Audrey in through the front door. At least as far as Charles's future mother-in-law was concerned, the lilies would mean one of the approval boxes was instantly ticked. Win did so admire a man bearing gifts.

It was going well, so far, though it had probably been a mistake for Rory to sit Audrey down opposite Charles. Jay had planned to put Win on one side of him, April on the other and herself across the table, so that she and April could referee any overzealous cross-examination. Audrey, however, had muscled in, making Rory pull out her selected chair and settle her into it, so now they'd all been moved up, though not out of range.

As everyone sorted themselves out, April leaned across the table, past Tristan, and murmured to Jay, 'Well you've failed there; Delphine would have had individual place names printed up in gold.'

'Oh surely, hand-embroidered.' Jay whispered back as she handed round the starter plates piled with crab and grapefruit salad.

'Oh this is nice,' Win commented. 'Did you use tinned segments, dear?'

Jay tried to smile. 'The grapefruit? Win, please! This is a Raymond Blanc recipe! I think he'd faint at the very idea.'

Well that was true, she thought, not daring to meet April's eye, Monsieur Blanc quite possibly would. Of *course* she'd used canned segments, carefully rinsing off any hint of tinny juice. She'd made this salad before and it required the meticulous peeling of every tiny morsel of fine translucent skin from every slender slice. How many hours would that take on such a busy Sunday morning?

'So.' Audrey launched the bidding for information as soon as the starter plates were cleared and Jay, Greg and April were safely out of their chairs, busying themselves with the roast beef and vegetables. 'So, Charles, how long have you been a pilot?'

April grinned at Jay over the gravy she was pouring into its jug. 'She means "Do you qualify for a top pension?"' she whispered.

'Years and years,' Charles replied. 'Not for much longer though, I'll be pensioned off soon, just another year or so.'

'And your family, are they local?' Audrey chipped in.

'I think that's "Tick appropriate box for: wife/ children/inconveniently expensive dependants".'

'April, *shh*! Give me a hand with this lot and shut up!' Jay told her, taking the dish of potatoes to the table.

'I've a brother in Scotland but no-one else, alas,' Charles said, looking mock-sad. Strange that, Jay thought, what was amusing about being alone? Or was he being defensive in the face of interrogation? She didn't blame him.

'Oh that would explain you living in that funny penthouse,' Audrey said. 'I mean it's a single man's type of place, hardly Delphine's kind of thing is it? Have you thought of moving to a nice detached with proper neighbours once you're married?'

'Gran!' Imogen blurted out. 'That's like *soo* rude?' Jay looked along the table at Greg, who was doggedly cutting up his meat and refusing to meet anyone's eye. She suspected he was covering up an attack of hilarity.

'Was it?' Win opened her eyes wide. 'But Audrey was only saying . . .'

'My dear ladies, it's fine.' Charles smoothed away the possible (though unlikely, in Jay's opinion) beginnings of an apology. My dear ladies? Jay wondered if it was part of a pilot's training, to soothe ruffled old women.

He went on, 'Actually, we haven't quite decided yet exactly where to settle so we'll start off in my apartment and see how it goes.'

'Sounds like a good plan,' Imogen said. 'How did you meet Delphine?'

'Oh, didn't she tell you?' Charles said. 'At a dinner dance. We have that in common, you see, the dancing.' Jay blinked, trying to get out of her head a picture of Charles and Delphine whizzing across a polished floor, wearing Day-Glo spandex and sequins, competition numbers strapped to their backs and contorting themselves in a stylish lambada.

'Of course she's a *lovely* dancer, my Delphine,' Win purred. 'Always has been.'

'I intend to get a lot more involved in it when I finish flying. I'm a small investor in a little club in fact . . .'

'Oh for the dancing? Ballroom? How lovely,' Audrey said. 'There's not a lot of it about these days.'

Charles looked at her in a mildly speculative way before smiling (rather to himself, Jay thought) and agreeing, 'Indeed.'

'Lovely beef dear,' Win commented to Jay. 'Though a bit *pink*, if you don't mind me saying so.'

'Do you think so?' Greg said. 'I can't tempt you to a slice more, then?'

'Oh go on, twist my arm,' she said quickly, watching beadily as Greg piled another couple of very large juicy pieces on her plate.

You'd think no-one had eaten all week, Jay thought, as she and Ellie at last cleared away the empty plates. She surveyed the few remaining flecks of the phenomenally expensive joint of best organic fillet that could also have been tomorrow's cottage pie if Audrey and Win hadn't been stoking up their constitutions against their usual 'it's hardly worth cooking for one' theme. All the vegetables had gone as well, even the broccoli and the aubergine and cinnamon thingy that usually only Ellie liked. There wasn't a single roast potato left. Shame about that; tomorrow was to be the start of Weight Watching and it would have been delicious to exit the day's greed zone later that evening with a toasted fried-potato sandwich, topped with pepper, too much salt and a dribbly slick of tomato ketchup, munched on the sofa in front of *Midsomer Murders*.

'I'll just get the corkscrew,' Greg was saying as Jay took the meringue and strawberry concoction from the fridge.

'No! Let me, I'm much nearer,' Win trilled, leaping out of her chair and scurrying rather girlishly across the kitchen.

'No! Don't, I'll get . . .' April dashed after her, too late.

'Uuugh! What's this disgusting mess in here?' Win stepped back, appalled, peering into the drawer at the now congealed coating of abandoned ice cream that had blobbed over the contents. She sniffed at it, doing her substance-identifying from a safe distance.

'You were always hopelessly messy, Jay, but really, just look at this!' Win said, delving an experimental hand in, pulling out the corkscrew and delicately holding it in thumb and forefinger under the tap.

'I'm sure Jay has talents in *many* directions,' Charles said as, tight-lipped and fuming, Jay started to slice the meringue. She looked at him, a smile freezing suddenly as the man actually, to her amazement, *winked* at her. Smooth sod, she thought, and any more of that and he'll be promoted to 'slimeball'.

Thank goodness for Nigella's strawberry miracle, Jay thought as she concentrated on this unseasonal treat for her taste buds. Conversation was flowing fine without her for the moment. Win and Audrey were giving Charles a few minutes' respite while they listened to Cathy telling Imogen about safe yoga for pregnancy.

'I don't think she should do too much bending and stretching in her condition,' Win told Cathy firmly. 'Something might *give*.'

Later, Jay blamed herself for leaving the big glass kitchen door open to let in a much-needed blast of cooling air. She was just beginning to feel that the meal had gone smoothly enough (though without any doubt the ice-cream incident would get straight back to Delphine), just beginning to ask who wanted coffee and did anyone fancy another glass of wine when Daffodil clattered in from the garden, dragging something huge and black and flapping.

'Shit!' Imogen yelled. 'What's she *got*?'

Every chair scraped back as the cat hurled itself and its outsize prey round the room, finally letting go and allowing a fully grown black rook to flap onto the worktop.

'Oh God, what now?' Jay said to April who was uselessly giggling with Cathy, the two women almost falling off their chairs with laughter.

'Catch it, someone!' Audrey ordered, from the safety of the far side of the garden door. Greg and Charles made a lunge for the poor creature, Charles getting there just ahead, grabbing the bird by the claws. It bit him, hard, but he clung on, grinning at Jay over its head and giving her the dreadful impression that he was about to wring its blue-black neck and present it to her as a trophy, like a felled dragon.

'I hope your tetanus is up to date,' Cathy said, as soon as the bird, apparently unharmed, was safely sent flying free in the garden again. While Jay was hunting for plasters, Cathy held the injured hand under the tap, rinsing blood onto the remains of the potato peelings that hadn't quite made it into the waste disposal.

'Oh we pilots keep everything well up to date,' Charles told Cathy with a lopsided grin.

Of course she couldn't have expected it all to go right, Jay reflected later after everyone had gone. She, Cathy and April sat at the glass kitchen table, working their way through a final bottle of wine and polishing off bits of left-over meringue. On the worktop by the sink, in a cage too small for it, a half-grown white rat gnawed noisily at a carrot. Audrey had tripped over it on the doorstep as she was leaving. It had been abandoned there, with a mysterious note, like an unwanted Victorian baby. Win had said to let the thing go, but Jay hadn't the heart, not after everything else.

'It's not your fault.' April tried to console Jay. 'If Win hadn't been so keen to impress Charles with how sprightly she was, she'd never have leapt up to get the corkscrew from the drawer and seen all that ice cream in there.'

Cathy laughed, 'I thought it was funny, myself. Her face! Like she'd found a dead frog or something – definitely more appalled than when they found the rat.'

'Win and Delphine would never tolerate domestic spillage,' April explained. 'They're the people who buy every possible anti-splash gadget from the Lakeland catalogue and they fry eggs in little flower-shaped moulds for a perfect presentation.'

'And the bloody cat. . .' Jay groaned.

'Well it's what cats do. And you couldn't have known about the rat. Maybe we should give it a rub with a wand, see if it turns into something handsome. Old Charles wasn't a bad looker either, didn't you think?'

'Very charming,' Cathy said, pursing her mouth and looking cryptic.

'Hmm. Good choice of word.' Jay nodded slowly. 'Charming, bordering on the . . . *suave*, I'd say. One or two things he said, I wasn't sure quite which way to take them, especially, you know, just before he left and he gave me a sideways look and a sort of smirk and said it was all right, he'd chucked out the empty beer can from his kitchen.'

'He's got you down for a secret drinker, round his gaff,' April said.

'We didn't touch his drinks. I didn't even open his fridge.'

Bit of a near miss about the beer can, Rory considered as he settled into his bed with his remote control in his hand and the TV channels of the world to choose from by way of a bedtime story. Bloody Freddie, it was his mistake. He was the one who'd helped himself from the fridge. Of course it worked both ways though. If Charles had pushed it further, if he'd even *thought* of looking in his direction with a hint of accusation, he could have dropped a little hint of his own that he knew something as well. After all, if you want to sneak around in and out of hookers' houses on the way to visiting your future family members, you don't drive something as obvious as a silver Porsche Boxter. Not round here you don't, matey. No way.

ELEVEN

Weight Watchers

Jay woke abruptly, sat upright in bed and opened her eyes. It was still dark and for a second or so she had the sensation that she had gone suddenly blind. It used to happen a lot when she was a child – Audrey was a great believer in total darkness for sleeping and had lined all the house's curtains with blackout fabric. You took your life in your hands, negotiating strewn-about hazards like shoes and books, heading for the loo in the night.

What had woken her? Her heart was racing and she knew something had given her a bad fright. She rubbed her eyes and waited a while for them to get used to the dark, focusing on the window beyond which a foggy sodium glow overlaid west London's night sky with a grubby shade of brownish orange.

'Whassup?' Greg whispered. He put his hand on her back. The warmth and gentle pressure made her feel safer.

'Not sure; nothing probably. I think I was dreaming.'

She had been, she realized now. She'd been dreaming about a doll, a big one, so fat as to be almost globular and the height of an average four-year-old child. She wore an outfit like Alice in Wonderland: sky blue dress and white frilled pinafore, white tights and black patent shoes with rhinestones across the front. Her hair was waist-length, luminously golden blonde and . . . Jay lay down again and stared at the ceiling. That's what had woken her, it was the hair and the flash and the bang and the terrible thing she'd done to the face. She'd been curling up the doll's hair with Delphine's Carmen rollers which seemed mysteriously to be connected to the mains, so her head looked as if it was attached to an execution gadget of the type that rednecks in America's southern states might invent. After the flash she'd slowly turned the small figure to face her. The doll's chubby pink cheeks had gone black, the blue eyes that had had a vacant, slightly startled gaze had vanished, blown away, leaving bloodied caverns leaking trails of gore and sinew down the rigid porcelain face.

'Bad dream or a good dream?' Greg was waking up properly now. In the morning he'd be impossible to shift, sleeping late and feeling groggy and out of sync. Not good on a Monday, she recognized, it could throw his whole week out. He'd drink too much coffee then wonder why he got stomach cramps.

'Bad dream. I killed Delphine with her own Carmens.'

'Eh?'

'Heated hair curlers. I managed to electrocute her or something. Not that you can, only in dreamworld. She was a fat dolly in Delphine's dance shoes.'

Greg sighed and put his hands over his eyes. 'You've lost me now.'

'Well you did ask. You should never ask people to tell you their dreams, you know that. They're always either incredibly boring or completely barking mad.' Was it mad? Or bad? Only a jury could decide. Herself, Jay would plump for mad – she wouldn't really wish this fate on a dolly, let alone a real human.

She was feeling cross. It wasn't Greg's fault, he'd only been trying to sympathize, but she wasn't up to more explaining. She even felt annoyed with herself for being so contrary. But the thing with bad dreams was that you needed a bit of silent, thinking-through time to get rid of the demons they left behind. You needed time to reassure yourself that you hadn't done the dreadful thing you'd dreamed, not really. It was only pretend, nobody's fault.

Jay climbed out of bed and wrapped her comforting old cotton waffle dressing gown round her body, then slipped out of the room and down the stairs. Daffodil (still in disgrace after the rook) pattered along in front of her, swishing her brown tail out of the way of Jay's feet. On the middle landing she could hear Rory muttering in his sleep and hoped his dreams were less disturbing than hers.

It was years and years since she'd had a Killing Delphine dream. Certainly before Delphine went to Australia, so at least ten years. At their peak they'd turned up every fortnight or so, and for a time her cousin must have been the most serially slaughtered dream object on the planet. There'd been the Riding Accident (cruel to poor Cobweb, having him hurl himself into a canyon, but something had to be the weapon), the one with the crumbling cliff edge, the drowning (such a short but impossibly paralysed hand-stretch from the riverbank). The previous worst had been the one with the silver cake-slice that Win kept in a display cabinet alongside Delphine's under-fourteens Home Counties (South) Latin American Formation cup. When she'd settled from the sweating horrors of that nightmare, Jay had calmed herself by deciding it would have been impossible anyway, you really couldn't put a cake-sized cross-section of a person onto a small plate. You'd need a whopping great serving platter, and even then the flesh wouldn't stay in its neat wedge shape. It would flop.

Jay pulled a chair up to the dishwasher which was still warm from its late evening cycle. She felt shivery and slightly sick and peculiarly foolish. Dreaming about killing your cousin out of sheer spite was just so juvenile. Daffodil miaowed softly and jumped onto her lap, settling quickly and purring, pushing her head against Jay's hand, demanding fuss and forgiveness. This had been a real throwback dream. They'd been quite a feature of her teen years, starting, she was pretty sure, on the night of Delphine's eleven-plus results. Jay had passed hers easily the year before and was settling happily enough into the local girls' grammar school, hating some aspects (her too-big uniform, algebra, the sadistic Bingham twins) and loving others (English Lit, Thursday's semolina, hanging upside down from the gym wallbars). On the day Delphine failed her eleven-plus she cycled round to visit Jay on a brand new five-geared bicycle, all lights and bells and sparkly pink reflectors.

'Oh you passed then!' Audrey hadn't been able to keep the surprise out of her voice. Delphine was, school-wise, what even her fond mother could only describe as a 'doer, not a thinker'. Win frequently scolded Jay, April and Matt for always having their noses in a book, unable to understand why they wouldn't prefer to perfect the quickstep, as Delphine had, or turn themselves into a dab hand with floral arrangements.

'*I'm* going to St Miriam's!' Delphine had announced grandly, naming a small, private establishment where girls were not troubled with excess academic exertion.

'So why d'you get a bike then? It's ages till your birthday,' Jay had asked, understanding that Delphine had *not* passed the eleven-plus. Nobody in the area went to a private school unless they'd failed to get into the grammar and had parents who went pale and faint at the thought of their darlings attending Broom Lane Secondary. Even years on, when both schools became comprehensive, it was still the ex-grammar that was oversubscribed.

'I *got* it for being *me*,' Delphine had smirked, stroking a speck of dust off her gleaming dynamo light.

'It's silly to be jealous, you know,' Audrey had said later when Jay had spent the afternoon sulking on her bed with a book and refusing to fetch her own bike (second-hand, a bit undersized, slightly rusty) and go to the park with Delphine. 'And it's rather nasty as well. Delphine isn't as clever as you and she can't help that. I'm sure Win only wanted to make sure she felt as good as the girls who *can* pass exams, and show her that you didn't just get presents for being bright.'

But that was the thing, Jay had been given a congratulatory hug when she passed her exams. There was no big fuss, no celebration, just as it had been for her sister and brother before her. 'I'm not doing big presents, it's not as if you needed to be bribed to pass,' Audrey had said.

But looking at Delphine's triumphant consolation prize, even though Jay knew she was being shallow and greedy, right then she'd rather have sold her soul to have failed and got a bike. That night she'd woken up trembling with guilt from a dream about a tangle of flesh and metal. Even now she could still picture the black of the tarmac, the yellow of Delphine's cascading, spun-gold princess hair and the sparkle of sunlight on new chrome.

Ellie and Rory walked slowly and silently through the school gates together and trudged up the long driveway, heads down against the wind. Usually they arrived separately but today, Rory's first day back after his operation, it was as if each could do with the support of the other. Both felt nervy and each had the same reason. Tasha.

'She's mad you know, lost it big time,' Rory said for about the hundredth time since the previous afternoon when she'd crept up to the house and left the cage containing the white rat on the doorstep, then simply sneaked away again. 'I mean, what is she *on*?'

'I dunno. In the note she said it was a present.'

'But who to? You or me?' Then together they both said 'You' and laughed.

'Got to be you, she's your friend,' Rory said.

'No, it's you she wants. She's only being nice to me to get to you.'

They'd had versions of this conversation at least twice, starting the day before when Charles was leaving after lunch and Audrey had discovered the box with the cross rat squeaking away in it and gnawing holes. She hadn't completely freaked (all credit to her. They'd have expected an Old Person to jump onto the nearest chair and scream) but she hadn't looked delighted to see it. Nobody had except Charles, who had picked up the cage and quite recklessly put his face close to the bars to coo at the occupant.

'Oh a fancy rat!' He had been pretty much amazed (well who wasn't?) but not spooked or anything, opening the cage door carefully to stroke the creature. Even though he made sure his fingers didn't get in the way of its teeth, Ellie had thought he was mad, especially after Daffodil's rook had already pecked him. Suppose it was true that things like that ran in threes? Didn't pilots need their fingers to be in tip-top condition, Ellie had wondered at the time, would he get banned from flying if he had stitches and a fat bandage on the finger he used to operate some essential in-flight computer?

The note had said, 'He's for you. Be nice to him, Love from T.' Wildly, Ellie had thought, oh that could mean it's for anyone, but getting real, well it was hardly going to be a present for her parents.

April and Freddie had thought it was hysterical. Gran and Auntie Win had gone all pursed lips and suggested they set it free in next door's hedge, Greg had had the not-brilliant idea of letting Daffodil have a go at it, which made Mum give him a look.

It wasn't that funny though. How did Tasha know where they lived, for one thing? This worried Ellie a lot. It would be all over their year now that they lived in a big house with a Mercedes (her dad's), a Golf (her mum's and Moggie's) and a silver Porsche (the visiting Charles) all parked outside like some kind of executive fleet. Where was the Dishing the Dirt van when you needed it? Round at Anya's, ready for Monday morning and Mrs Ryan's Regular, that's where.

'We could pretend we don't know anything about it,' She suggested to Rory. 'Then she might think she'd got the wrong place.'

'That won't work. She'll have made sure she got it right. Our address was on the hospital notes at the end of the bed when I was in there. She must have got it then.'

'Or followed one of us.'

'Or asked your Amanda friend or almost anyone in your class. Anyway that's not the bit that matters. What are we going to do with the rat? Give it back to her?'

'She'll take offence. You don't know what Tash is like when she's upset. She goes all wild. She does things.'

'Tell her you love it then, tell her it's just what you've always wanted.' She'd have to. Ellie didn't want to get on the wrong side of Tasha. She might come round with a different sort of present, something much

163

spookier. She might bung a lighted firework through the letterbox, or dog poo.

They were on the school steps now. Ellie felt small whooshes as groups of people bigger than her hurtled past, eager to get inside to the fuggy warmth of the cloakrooms. She felt very tiny, even more than usual, as if she didn't take up enough space to count as a human, because she could hardly be seen. Perhaps she couldn't be. How brilliant would it be to be invisible? Or if you were only invisible to other people, but not to yourself, how would you know you were?

'If we say we like it, she might go and give us another one. Have you thought of that? I'll think of something, tell her it's really nice and thanks and all that but we can't keep it, make something up, whatever.'

'Tell her Mum won't let you. She can't argue with that.' Ellie gave him a look. What kind of a saddo would she be if she said something like that? Tasha-type girls didn't have mums who laid down rules about what and when. They had mums who shared their fags and shouted the place down for wearing each other's clothes and not washing them. If she said 'Mum won't let me' she'd never hear the last of it.

Ellie went into the girls' cloakroom and left her coat on her usual peg. She hoped it would still be there at going-home time. Sometimes coats and jackets weren't. She'd been lucky so far – hers was a bit small to fit most of the hulky great girls who did the thieving, but then they might have younger sisters who'd be happy to have her stuff.

'Good weekend?' Amanda was sitting on the radiator, picking at a small hole in her tights. She looked eager, pent up, something she was dying to say.

'Not bad,' Ellie told her, adding, 'nothing much happened.' You never knew, she might be in on the rat-present thing with Tasha. Maybe she'd got one as well. Unlikely, but best to make sure it came across as no big deal.

'Nothing?' Amanda's voice emerged as an excited squeak. 'What do you mean nothing? Who *was* he?'

Ellie took a quick look at herself in the mirror. Her hair was looking a bit lank. The phrase *rats' tails* came into her head. Her mum used to say that about hers when it needed washing. She didn't want to think about the rat. What were they going to do with it? Sell it on e-bay? Take it to the petshop and hope they'd make an exception to their new 'no live animals' policy?

'Who was who?' she asked Amanda at last.

'That boy you were with on Friday! The one you *kissed*? Duh?'

'*Him*? He was no-one, just my cousin Freddie.'

'God, Ellie, he was gorgeous! I thought he was like, *with* you? Disappointing or what.' The registration bell rang and the two girls picked up their bags and joined the noisy throng in the corridor. 'I was a bit pissed off, to tell the truth. I was going to text you and tell you but I've run out of free time. I thought you could have told me if you were going out with someone.'

'Oh I would, I would,' Ellie reassured her. She felt as if there was something going on here that she couldn't keep up with. All around her there seemed to be people who were fancying each other. Tasha was chasing Rory; Amanda thought Freddie was gorgeous. There was a girl in their year who'd had an abortion the term before. At lunchtimes there were couples under the trees by the railway, standing a bit apart from their groups of friends, sharing cigarettes, kissing sometimes, touching – not much, just enough to be claiming each other as their own. She didn't feel like doing any of those things. Maybe it was something to do with being a late starter, hormone-wise. Whatever it was, the idea of getting into a bed with a smelly boy rather than a good book did not at all appeal. She sometimes wondered if it ever would.

You couldn't miss the sign: a big 'Welcome to Weight Watchers' notice was propped up outside the pub like an oversized party invitation. A posse of teenagers lurked by the wall outside and Jay crossed her fingers that they wouldn't shout rude remarks at her as she went in. She could do without being greeted by, 'Oy, lard-arse!'

Temptation beckoned on the far side of the Red Lion's frosted glass door. You could turn right for the pints of lager and prawn-cocktail crisps option, or you could choose the path of virtue and go up the stairs to the function room. Here you would learn that the lager and crisps still *were* an option – albeit a risky one if you were keen to stay on that vital weight-loss curve – but only if you counted them into your daily total (possibly under 'treats': one pint of lager = 2 points, crisps = 6 points) and didn't even think of having that bag of chips (9 points, but no penalties for vinegar and salt) on the way home.

At the top of the stairs there was a queue – all female and every age from teens to seventy-plus. Jay joined it, looking at the bodies of the ten or so women ahead of her and recognizing Pat from across the road, close to where the Planet Man lived. Being here was surely brave of her: Pat was head teacher at a nearby primary school. If I was her, Jay thought, the last thing I'd want would be to risk running into off-premises school mummies when you're owning up to fat issues. This was the danger, Greg had pointed out, in picking the meeting place closest to home that the Weight Watchers website offered.

'Half the street might be there,' he'd warned. 'They'll hear you confess to your worst biscuit habits.'

Jay couldn't help wondering why, quite frankly, some of these women were here at all. Most of them looked perfectly normal-sized (if 'big-boned' as her mother used to call it) to her. One very pretty young girl with jagged blonde hair was wearing a short skirt that was barely pelmet-length and looking terrific in it, with legs that were far more sapling than tree trunk and a cute, perky bum. Perhaps she was a plant, bribed to come along and show everyone what could be achieved just by sticking to the diet. Either that or she'd once been as big as a heifer, and needed the constant back-up of WW, being even now only a Cadbury's Creme Egg away from spiralling into weight-gain hell.

'Hello? You at the back, are you new?' A curly-haired young woman in a tight seaside-rock-pink velour tracksuit called to her, leaning round from where she sat at a table at the queue's head, taking the subs.

'Er . . . yes, I am.' Every eye in the line-up was now on her, each woman blatantly sizing her up, comparing, calculating, possibly to the nearest ounce. In their various eyes she could see herself reflected: plumper, smaller, podgier, thinner-thighed, chunkier-armed. Pat, barefoot on the scales, waved to her and grinned, doing a rueful kind of 'welcome to Fatsos Anonymous' expression.

'Take one of these forms and fill it in please, my love,' called the pink velour. 'And then you need to get back in the line for paying and weighing.'

Jay took the form to a small table in the corner where a mountainous pale girl with mournfully droopy brown hair and wearing sack-shaped black seemed to be agonizing over her own answers. The questions didn't look that difficult. It was mostly a name and address kind of thing. The girl sucked on the end of her pen.

'I don't know what to put for my Goal Weight,' she confided to Jay in a nervous whisper. 'I mean, in an ideal world I'd be eight stone, I mean, who wouldn't? But, well I'm quite tall and, I mean, life's a long way from ideal, I find, don't you? Shall I put ten stone and hope for the best? What do you think? Or ten and a half? Or do we have to put it in metric? I'm not good at metric . . .'

Jay hadn't a clue. She smiled and said she thought ten stone would be fine. She could hardly be honest and tell the poor girl that, frankly, even twelve stone looked wildly ambitious.

The girl went on, 'I mean, I can always change it later can't I? Maybe I should ask Paula. I'm Holly by the way.'

'I'm Jay. Look, I shouldn't worry too much.' Jay tried to be encouraging, for surely if this bit was so anxiety-inducing, what on earth would the girl do when faced with a breakfast decision between Bran Flakes and Shredded Wheat?

'Why don't you just put down whatever you think is a realistic aim for now? Even if it's a lot less than you'd really like to lose. Then if you do better than that you can be really pleased with yourself.'

I'd be good at this, Jay thought as she signed her name and confirmed that she wasn't pregnant, breast-feeding or on medication, I'd be excellent at telling everyone else how to turn themselves into sylph-like beings, totally in control of their eating habits. It was when it came to her own intake that things went, quite literally, pear-shaped.

'You only want to lose a stone?' Paula-in-the-pink gave Jay a slightly disappointed smile as if she was sure she could (and frankly should) do better than that: it was only a matter of *will power*.

'A stone will be fine,' Jay insisted, 'I reckon that at

168

my age you *can* be too thin, whatever the Duchess of Windsor thought.'

Paula nodded but her bemused expression suggested that she'd filed Jay under 'mad' and she busied herself sorting out a membership card.

A stone surely *would* be enough. Jay was now wavering. She was certain she'd been perfectly comfortable a stone ago, whenever that was. And it wouldn't require an entire new wardrobe, just a lovely feeling that she wasn't squeezing into her clothes.

Paula briefly explained the Weight Watchers system: each item of food consisted of a certain number of points: a slice of bread was one point, a serving of sugar-free cereal was one and a half. Jay was allowed eighteen points per day and could more or less choose whatever she wanted as long as she stuck within the eighteen-point limit. 'Like counting calories you mean?' she asked.

Paula pursed her lips and frowned slightly. 'We don't talk about calories here. You'll find the points system a lot easier to follow than counting calories.' By which, Jay gathered, there'd be no tricky long multiplication. Paula then invited her to step on the scales for the awful moment of truth. 'If you take your shoes off today, remember to take them off every time,' she instructed her solemnly. Jay assured her, equally solemnly, that she would and went off, after the mercifully discreet weigh-in, to join several other members on the semicircle of chairs in front of a table displaying a basket of what she recognized as butternut squash. Holly was already there, fervently studying the Week One booklet they'd been given.

'Not at all a bad week, although one or two of you . . .' Paula began her presentation and looked at the back row, where two jolly ladies were giggling happily. 'What happened to you, Daphne? Time of the month, dear? Because that can always add a pound or two, don't forget. We mustn't be too hard on ourselves at those times. A couple of squares of Fruit and Nut can be such a comfort and only one and a half points gone.'

Daphne at the back was still cackling. 'I went to a wedding, didn't I!'

'Oh did you? How lovely. So did you relax and overdo it a bit?'

'Go on, Daph, tell her,' her companion nudged her hard. 'Tell her how many vodka and limes you had, go on!'

'Oh I shouldn't!' There was a general clamour for Daphne to tell.

'All right then, I had twelve, didn't I!' More hilarity from the back. All the women turned to look at Daphne, to see what a giggling, shameless, twelve-vodkas stalwart looked like. It looked like the picture of total, uninhibited enjoyment. Pretty appealing actually, Jay considered, watching Daphne and her friend consumed with unbridled mirth.

'Twelve!' Paula's smile was there, but was tight and forced as she sensed a revolution to be quelled. 'Ladies, that's more than a whole day's points!'

'Ooh I know!' Daphne was unrepentant. 'I had a lovely time though!'

There was still a mutinous buzz going round in which several of the women discussed whether Daphne would have done better, points-wise, getting thoroughly drunk on wedding champagne (fewer glasses for the same vodka effect) or could have improved things marginally by substituting diet tonic for the lime juice.

'Now.' Paula all but clapped her hands together for the class's attention. '*Ladies*. Butternut *squash*.' Her pearly-nailed finger pointed to the vegetable basket on her display table as she firmly quelled the atmosphere of mild anarchy and returned to her schedule. 'Terrifically versatile. If you're having people round for drinks you can make a few bowls of these lovely, delicious No-Point crisps to hand round and you won't have the temptation of the bought ones.'

No point? Jay wondered if she'd heard right. If there was no point, then what, exactly, was the point?

'. . . simply peel, slice thinly, give them a spray with Frylite and pop them in the oven! So easy and something different, I think your guests will agree, don't you ladies?'

'Butternut-squash crisps be buggered,' Pat snorted as she and Jay walked down the stairs together. 'She's dead right, they're different. But what a sodding palaver.'

'Well they sounded simple enough,' Jay admitted. 'But . . .'

'But what's wrong with opening a nice jar of olives? Or putting out the nuts for them but *not eating them*?' Pat suggested, eyeing the saloon-bar door with a certain amount of longing as they went out to the street. Daphne was already in there. Jay could hear her joyous cackle carrying over the usual pub din. Holly had gone in after her and Jay wondered if she'd manage to be all first-day devout and go for points-free mineral water with a slice of lime, or think what the hell, there's a whole week till the next weigh-in, and go mad with a pint of bitter and a bag of salted cashews.

'Exactly. I'm going to give this lot a go though, it seems to make sense, at least in theory.'

'Oh it does. I've done Slimming World but I never got the hang of it. Entirely my own fault rather than theirs. There was a loose wasp in the room when they were explaining the basics and I just didn't concentrate. After that I kept mixing up my Original days and my Green days and gobbled down so many sins I thought I'd have to go to Confession.'

Put into context, this didn't sound in the least bit unlikely, Jay thought as she walked up her own garden path. Possibly almost as many people, women at least, attended weight-loss meetings each week as went to church. Either way, you were gathered together to take in instructive words of wisdom from an inspiring congregation leader. With food indulgence described at some of these clubs as 'wicked' or 'naughty', eating a jam-filled doughnut represented little less than a cataclysmic falling from grace. It felt mildly uncomfortable, thinking like this, that one way or another Jay had now paid up to join the global congregation for collective worship at the altar of the modern, affluent-Western goddess called Thin.

TWELVE

Jogging

If she jogged to the recreation ground at the end of the road, and then ran all the way round it twice, Jay reckoned she'd have earned herself a dollop of butter with the marmalade on her breakfast toast instead of either nothing at all or a depressing and taste-free scraping of fatless spread. Diets that worked, she decided as she retied the laces on her trainers and smoothed down her unflattering navy Boden pull-ons, were all in the detail. Weight Watchers allowed you to accrue extra points by means of exercise and she was going to spend them on things that made life worth living (olive oil, good wine), rather than frittering them away on their suggested treats (a low-fat chocolate mousse or a small can of peach slices).

It wasn't far to the park. Surely no more than a couple of hundred yards, and there'd be few people about at seven in the morning who were likely to notice her and snigger at her efforts. She couldn't remember the last time she'd actually *run*. Possibly it had been when playing tennis in the sixth form at school or racing for a bus during university days. She'd certainly hurtled about after the children when they were small, playing French cricket on beaches, rushing to stop a

173

carelessly pushed swing from dashing their tiny brains out as they wandered too close. And every dutiful year she'd reluctantly joined in the ritual humiliation in the Mothers' Race at primary-school sports days.

She recalled now, that the mothers had been firmly divided into two camps. She was one of those who, when the call came for the dreaded race, merely put down her glass of wine, kicked off her shoes and padded to the starting line hoping she wouldn't trip over her skirt. The other lot, the *Über*-mothers, would already be there jogging up and down on the spot, streamlined in serious Lycra and sporting Prada running shoes, possibly with spikes. They'd been warming up, trackside, since the egg and spoon got started and would have collected their offspring, loaded them into the 4 x 4 and be halfway to Kodali violin by the time Jay and co. giggled into the home straight.

She pulled the door shut behind her as quietly as she could. Daffodil slipped out to join her on the path, miaowing an interest in this unusually early exit from the house and expressing concern that her keeper had overlooked something with regard to the provision of feline breakfast.

'I'll be back in a little while, Daffy.' Jay bent to stroke the cat's cool treacle-coloured ears. She wanted her to go back in the house. How embarrassing would it be, the first time she ventured out for a public display of activity, to have Daffodil trotting effortlessly alongside, barely having to break into a canter, racing up and down trees on the way while she gasped and plodded inelegantly, all hopeless human clumsiness. Talk about competition – fitness-wise cats won every time, paws down. This was clearly unfair, seeing as most of their lives they did nothing but laze around in patches of sunshine and sleep.

Jay shivered in her ancient Eric Clapton T-shirt. She had briefly considered wearing one of the yellow Dishing the Dirt polo shirts that she'd had made for the girls the year before, so that she'd be doing a useful bit of advertising as she ran. The idea had quickly been rejected; any potential customers were less likely to be attracted than terminally put off by the sight of her puffing along, sweating and unshowered.

Pausing only to look both ways along the road and crossing her fingers that she wouldn't meet anyone she knew, Jay set off at a comfortable jogging pace. The early air was crisp and bright and only lightly tinged with the kerosene scent of Heathrow-bound aircraft. Daffodil ran beside her for the first fifty yards then fell back, yowling a protest that her owner was escaping beyond territorial bounds. Jay whizzed along, enjoying the breeze on her face and trying not to notice how much her flesh blobbed up and down in rhythm with her pounding feet. No wonder it was called jogging.

It couldn't be good for you, it occurred to her, having all your essential organs bouncing around like this. If God had meant humans to run he'd have put livers and kidneys and other internal offal on springs. Unless that was what bits like the diaphragm and pelvic floor were for. That must be right. She pictured biology textbook drawings of muscles looking like swathes of bandages, cocooning and comforting. Was she hallucinating, she wondered as she huffed and puffed, trying to bring her mind back to what she was doing and where she was going. Was dehydration madness already setting in or did all runners go into weird trains of thought, like a crazed person's version of meditation?

Just before the park gates she heard a familiar mechanical whirring sound behind her, followed by 'Oi, darling, fancy a pint?' as the milkman whizzed past on his float, waving a carton of milk in her direction.

'Morning Bill!' She managed to summon up just enough spare breath to greet him.

'Keep it up, love! Next stop the London Marathon!' he laughed as he sped past, and Jay staggered into the park feeling the back of her throat burning dry with the effort of unaccustomed exercise.

'God, I'm unfit,' she groaned to herself. Where had those careless, youthful days gone when it had been no effort to race up and down a hockey pitch hundreds of times in half an hour? And thinking about the Marathon, could they really be true, those stories she'd read of people starting out for their first training session as utterly useless and feeble as she was, and ending up a mere few months later running twenty-six miles dressed as a penguin? How could that happen?

The park seemed crammed with early morning exercisers. A skinny young man all in white stood beneath the trees going through a slow-motion t'ai chi routine. A pair of shiny-sleek tanned girls in tiny shorts whirled past together on Rollerblades, reminding her of a TV tampon ad. There were runners everywhere – good, competent ones. No-one else seemed to have wobbly tummies and trembling legs. Joining the circuit on the path round the large play area was like being the one doing a badly co-ordinated breast stroke in the slow lane at the swimming pool while others sped past in a stylish crawl. Jay was constantly overtaken by fit, svelte twenty-something women with their hair scraped back into bouncy ponytails, wearing either serious cut-off-top-and-Lycra training kit or tight, dolly-mixture shades of Juicy Couture velour. The men were less of a pretty sight. Mostly they were pale, furry-legged middle-years ones trundling by clad in wife-beater vests and too-brief shiny shorts, looking unattractively larval in their limb exposure, huffing along with their air-punching fists clenched tight.

Dog-walkers were a different shape again, roundly swaddled in snug coats. They wove about at a leisurely pace, getting in the way, then stopping in mid-path to bend with their rotund bottoms in the air and pick up their poochs' messes, using hands encased in Tesco's carrier bags.

It occurred to Jay that you could usefully power-walk with a dog. A dog would haul you along at a good calorie-burning speed, then give you frequent welcome breathers as it slowed to sniff out rivals and pee on the trees. She didn't fancy the bit with the Tesco's bags though, shuddering at the thought of dealing with still-warm animal excrement. More crazy train of de-hydrated thought, she realized. Now she knew why everyone else ran along sucking liquid from bottles.

Agonized with exhaustion, Jay trailed towards the gate after her final lap and faced the much busier road. As if the good-natured derision of Bill the milkman hadn't been bad enough, now half the neighbourhood seemed to be on the lookout for someone to tease. Pat, her Weight Watchers companion, was across the road in her driveway, stowing her briefcase into her car boot. 'Glad to see you're taking it seriously!' she yelled. 'You'll be down to Goal Weight in a fortnight!' Jay, exhausted and breathless, simply waved a limp hand at her.

Cathy was also out by her gate, putting her box of newspapers on the pavement ready for the recycling truck. 'Don't forget to cool down properly,' she advised. 'Eyes closed in Child Pose would be good – it stretches your back and releases tension . . .' she was saying as Jay staggered into her own front garden, where the postman was hovering on the doorstep.

'Morning Mrs C.,' he said, handing over a pile of mail, 'Mostly junk today plus a couple of bills and your Toast catalogue. Oh and a nice pink airmail one from

Australia. Don't see many of those these days, what with e-mail and cheap rate phones . . .'

Jay leaned on the door frame and panted, stretching first one leg down and then the other, trying to catch her breath. She had a vague feeling she might have overdone it.

'You all right Mrs C.?' the postman asked, slightly nervous. 'If I was you I'd have a nice cup of tea and a sit-down. That'll sort you out.'

Cup of tea be buggered, Jay thought as, legs trembling, she let herself into the house and was greeted by the smell of bacon grilling. Greg was buttering wholemeal bread. He looked at her enquiringly, eyebrows up, and she nodded with what felt like the last of her strength. Two slices of bread (medium cut) had to be three points. Two slices of grilled bacon, six points. So it was half a day's worth of food points but she'd earned them, she thought as she sank into the kitchen sofa and kicked off her trainers, boy had she ever earned them.

'Thing is, Tasha,' Ellie began, wondering how to continue without risking Tasha's wrath. It wasn't the best moment, being in the middle of the biology class, but it might be the only one she got that day, or even that week. Tasha was like a sort of elf, flitting about fast between her chosen people and putting spells on them. You might get her attention for half an hour, you might think you're the Best Friend of the Day but then you wouldn't see her again on close-up terms for ages. She'd chosen to sit next to Ellie for biology (staring out Amanda till she backed away to the far corner of the room) and somehow Ellie had to get her to accept the rat back again. Now. Nobody at home really wanted it, though her dad had got it out to play with a couple of times and said something about designing it a good cage. He'd doodled some sketches on a bit of paper and muttered something about (surprise, surprise) perspex. Right now the poor rat was living in an old fishtank left over from when Imogen had kept a couple of terrapins years ago. It kept standing up on its back legs, sniffing the air above it, leaning its long slim paws against the glass and showing its pinkish tummy. It looked a bit sad in the makeshift house, as if it knew it should only be temporary but was worried that everyone had forgotten about fixing it up with a real home.

She began again while someone was asking Mr Murray a question. 'Thing is, Tasha, we've, like, got a cat, you see and . . .' She couldn't get any further. Mr Murray had stopped listing the different types of bone joints on the board and was expecting some kind of response to a question he'd asked. She hadn't a clue what it was and looked down at her notes to avoid catching his eye.

'Ellie. What about you? Any ideas?' She'd known he'd ask her, just known. Typical. She looked up at his list. Bones. Think, Ellie, what could he want to be told about them?

'Hinge?' she guessed, then looked properly at the board. Hinge was already up there. They all were, as far as she could see. What was it he'd asked, then?

'We were talking ball and socket joints, Ellie.' He sighed, in his teacher-specialist am-I-completely-wasting-my-time way. 'I simply asked you for an example, which you'd *know* if you'd been *listening*.' He smiled, the chilly sort he often did with the cold stary eyes that meant he was getting angry, and that she shouldn't even think he'd be happy if she smiled back. But she did anyway, it seemed only good manners. Mr Murray glared.

'Hip joint,' she said quickly. It had to be that – it always was. That or shoulder. There were only the two, weren't there? Why was he asking them stupid

179

questions like that? Mr Murray was smiling again, but not at her and not so coldly. Beside her, Tasha was gazing wide-eyed at him and running her pointy scarlet tongue over her top lip. She pulled gently at a tendril of hair and twirled it round her finger. Ellie kicked at her beneath the desk. What was she doing? Pretending she was out on the pull? Was there any man on the planet whom she wouldn't consider fair game?

'Yes, hip joint. Or you could have said shoulder.' Mr Murray came back to earth at last and returned to the board just as the bell rang for the end of the class.

'There y'go, I got you out of a detention for sure,' Tasha said, aiming her huge wolfy grin at Ellie. 'You owe me one. How's the rat? Brilliant isn't he? My brother breeds them. They win prizes at shows.'

Ellie sighed, beaten. 'He's fine. He's lovely. Thanks, Tasha.'

Well what else could she say?

Upstairs in her little office, Jay forced herself to confront her Weight Watchers daily food diary and write down the shaming breakfast truth:

Bread (very thick-cut, chunky wholemeal): At a guess, four points.

Bacon (two large rashers): Six points.

Brown sauce (a good-sized dollop): Probably one point.

Butter (thick and melted into the hot bacon): At least another point.

Twelve points gone left only six for the rest of the day, although she had earned back a good two by running (well she called it running, an unkind observer, one who lacked any genes of generosity might snigger and call it 'staggering'). If she was to keep within the Weight Watching guidelines she would have to stick to No Point soup, a tuna salad and sliver of skinless chicken. It could be done, just.

A thank-you card from Charles had arrived in the same post as Delphine's letter. The front of it featured a photo of a Siamese cat watching a caged budgie, which she took to be evidence of a sense of humour rather than a comment on Daffodil's delinquency. He was effusive about the food ('exquisite') and about the company ('delectable' – a strange word to use if it encompassed the watchful, silent Rory, gushing Win and Ellie noisily slurping Coke) and hoped they'd meet up again soon, although he was 'Horribly busy, off to Singapore in the next few days and with fingers in so many pies.'

He must mean this club he's involved with, she thought, wishing he'd been a bit more forthcoming about it. Possibly he would have been if the cat-plus-rook hadn't interrupted the conversational flow. By now she could have been up to speed about whether he was involved in the kind of thing where gentlemen of a certain age sat on gnarled leather grunting behind the *Daily Telegraph*, or something more to Delphine's taste: a hall with parquet and a glitterball where ladies (also of a certain age) took their partners for the military two-step.

Delphine's carnation-scented letter told Jay that in two weeks she would be back in England. Not only would she be back, but she'd be here in the house occupying the spare room next to Jay's office. Why? Surely at this stage in life she wasn't preserving her maidenly virtue? What was wrong with moving in with Charles right from the off? Superstition, probably, she decided. Delphine and Win had always been keen on touching wood and coaxing black cats across their paths.

'You don't mind, do you? I don't want to stay with

Mum – she'll only fuss.' Delphine had written. 'I'm a bit beyond all that.'

Jay could only sympathize there, really. It would be hard not to agree with Delphine on this in spite of initial horror at having her on the premises for a front-row view of her family's disordered existence. With Delphine comfortably installed in her mother's bungalow's second bedroom (musk-rose-chintz over-load, accented with gilt, frilled broderie anglaise cushions lined up to attention, corners up, on the bed), Win would be sure to go into princess-pampering overdrive. She'd be straight back into shoving cedar shoe trees into all Delphine's footwear and getting up Before God to concoct the muesli that Delphine hadn't tasted since the morning she'd left the house under an acre of white tulle and satin to marry Peter Bicton. She'd been barely nineteen then, she and Win both triumphant that all their efforts had succeeded. This was life's great prize they'd been aiming for since Delphine had come top in domestic science at thirteen and started amassing cookery books, small domestic gadgets and Tupperware.

The two of them made an annual pilgrimage to the Ideal Home Exhibition with the same reverence that other folks went to Lourdes. April and Jay used to mock. In their bedroom, during occasional futile attempts to put away their hopelessly untidy possessions, they'd parody Win, singing 'She'll make someone a lovely little wife' while they tried to stuff clothes into overfilled drawers. Delphine's years of ballroom dancing had, when she'd become a teenager, been topped up with evening classes in cake decor-ation, floral art and home furnishings. If you had to concoct a list of things Delphine would never, ever do, Jay reckoned at number one would be: slinging up a pair of IKEA tab-top ready-made curtains, hemmed with iron-on Wundaweb. She'd feel cheated at the waste of a chance for lining, interlining and triple goblet pleats.

'Brains are all very well, Jay,' Win had gloated when Jay had come back from university for the wedding weekend. 'My Delphine's got herself nicely married without faffing about with too much education.'

For Win, this wedding knocked into eternal oblivion any starred double first in Classics or Law. There would be no glittering career on the planet that she'd rate higher than housewifery. She'd leaned in close to Jay and, in a spirit of genuine generosity, whispered her sure-fire tip. 'It doesn't do to look too *clever*, dear. Always remember men like to think they know more than we do.' Jay had managed to keep a straight face and solemnly thanked her aunt for the advice. It was *Win's* day, after all. Hers and Delphine's.

Peter Bicton might have thought so too, seeing himself as rather a bit-part player in the event. A few years later he'd admitted to a lifelong passion for his second cousin and decamped from the rag-rolled, stencilled, pot-pourri-stocked cottage in East Sheen to live with her on a scruffy smallholding near Norwich. He told Delphine he could no longer bear having a kitchen where real live wandering hens weren't welcome, retrieved his pheasant-blood-stained Barbour from where Delphine had banished it to the loft and drove off to the substantial bosom of his first love.

Jay, on her way up the stairs to sort out the third-time bride-to-be's accommodation, checked her watch and calculated that Delphine was quite possibly now sitting on her sunny terrace near Dunsborough, Western Australia, sipping Earl Grey tea and nibbling on a piece of toast with the crusts cut off. The marmalade would have been decanted into a small white bowl with a silver spoon and there'd be one of those beaded nets over it to keep the flies off. Delphine, even if she was alone, would have a starched linen napkin on her lap and her tea – leaves not bags – would be (and Tristan would approve here) poured from a small chubby teapot into a bone china cup. How on earth, Jay wondered, would she fit into the food-on-the-run chaos of their household? Would she shudder at the lined-up schoolbags and discarded shoes in the hall? Avert her appalled gaze from Ellie dipping her buttery knife into the honey? Would she understand that Jay's mental Ideal Home also featured a family who didn't festoon every radiator with trousers that Must Not Be Tumble-Dried, even though these were battles that were not only lost long ago but were also not really worth fighting?

Delphine's room (as Jay now thought of it, even before she'd told the family to expect the guest) used to be Imogen's before she'd moved into the basement with Tristan. It had a small en suite shower and loo – all chic white mosaic tiles with lots of sparkly chrome and mirror. This was currently home to a pile of supermarket boxes containing many of the childhood leftovers that Imogen had sorted when she'd moved into the flat, but had neither wanted with her nor had the heart to throw away. When she came to stay, April never minded stepping over them (she'd said it was just like home) but Delphine wouldn't be happy without a clear route to the facilities and a certainty that *all* the floor could be got at for hygienic mopping.

Where to put the boxes? Jay considered. The loft space was tiny now that the glass bedroom and bathroom took up so much of the roof. All cupboards were already overoccupied. Ideally she'd have that woman from *The Life Laundry* round. She wouldn't be one of those who wept and whined to keep every trinket, oh no. She'd go to a health spa for a few days, then come back when it was all over to luxuriate in the empty spaces. So long as she still had the family photos, the diamond earrings Greg had given her (she'd wear them to the spa, just to be sure) and a few of her choicer items of clothing (OK, Trinny and Susannah could join in for that bit), she'd be perfectly happy.

Jay opened the shower-room door and peered into the first box. It contained soft toys, dozens of them. Pandas and teddies, a fat furry owl, grubby pink and blue bunnies and a rakish-looking Rupert Bear. Moggie would just have to be persuaded that she didn't need them any more, that some other small children could give them some love and attention. Otherwise they'd be there for years, forgotten till way after Mog's own child had got well past the cuddly-toy stage. Jay had Dishing the Dirt clients like this, people who stored their life souvenirs on shelves, in boxes, in plastic bags, all heaped into cupboards. At some point it would occur to them that they wanted Jay's girls to give everything a thorough blitz of a spring-clean but instead of chucking stuff out, it was the cupboards and shelves they wanted polishing and then all the stuff was to be put back again till next time. Why, she and Barbara frequently wondered, did people want a dark understairs space expensively scrubbed out simply to stuff into it a pile of grubby Sainsbury bags full of outgrown toddlers' clothes or old gas bills?

Jay ran down the stairs and out through the kitchen doors and down the spiral metal staircase to the basement.

'Moggie? Are you in there?' she shouted into the open doorway, hesitating on the mat. Strange how rude it would seem, crashing into her own daughter's premises without knocking first, even though only a couple of years ago she'd been the one who'd had to stride into her room and haul the girl out of bed so that

185

she wasn't late for her A-level exams. It was doubtless due to her sharing her life with Tristan – that tricky privacy balance that coupledom required.

'Mum? Oh brill, you're here.' Imogen rushed at her, coat on and bag over her shoulder ready to go out. 'I was just coming up to get you. I'm late, we have to go *now*. Got your keys?' Imogen pulled Jay, tugging her out through the door and slamming it shut after them both.

'Where are we – *you* – going? What's the rush? I needed you to come up and sort out . . .'

'No, Mum, no time. Tris was supposed to come with me but now he can't, he phoned. He's got a 'mergency leak in Sutton. You come instead, *please*? I need some-one.'

Imogen had somehow hustled Jay back up the stairs and into the kitchen and was shoving her jacket at her. '*Please* Mum, I don't want to go by myself.'

She was looking close to tears. 'Moggie, what is it?' Jay asked, frantically pulling her jacket on and grabbing her keys. 'Is it the baby?'

Oh please don't let her lose it, Jay prayed silently, conscious of how few years ago it was that she'd pleaded, every time Imogen left the house with a gruesome, sexed-up, mouth-breathing boyfriend: please don't let her get pregnant.

'It's my scan. At the hospital this afternoon. Tris was supposed to come and now he can't. I wish he could.'

Full-scale tears threatened as they hurtled out of the front door. Why, it crossed Jay's mind, did Imogen always do everything at last-minute racing speed? How would she ever slow down to a toddler's pace?

'It's all right Moggie, of course I'll come with you. I'll be thrilled to, actually.'

Imogen had been born at this same hospital nearly twenty-one years before. Jay remembered all too clearly the rush-hour traffic jam that had made her sure at the time that her first child would have to be born at a bus-stop pull-in.

'You'd think there'd be privileges,' she remarked. 'Surely you count as an Old Girl, like school.'

'What, like Frequent Flyer points?' Imogen laughed. 'I wouldn't mind being upgraded to private patient class.'

'Oh I'm sure you'll be all right. In a ward you get to meet all the other mothers and compare birth experiences.'

'Yuck. I don't think I'll want to go on and on about it.'

Jay looked at her. 'You'll be surprised. It's all so mind-boggling, you sometimes wonder if you'll ever talk about anything else ever again.'

'Not me, matey,' Imogen said, lying back deeply in her seat and putting her feet up in their habitual place on the dashboard. 'Me and Tris will just want to get back to normal life. Besides . . .' She looked pensive.

'Besides what?'

'I don't think there's anyone my age. The midwife said they're usually either fifteen or forty. Boring.'

'You'll be OK, there's bound to be someone. Anyway we're here.' She turned the Golf into the hospital's gateway and slowed to go over the speed bumps to the car park.

'Careful Mum, don't bounce the car. I had to drink a litre of water for this scan and I don't think there's room for it.'

Jay wasn't the only patient's mum in the waiting room. Imogen had been right – two of the girls didn't look much older than Ellie. The only other customer was a smartly suited woman with a briefcase that bulged with files, one of which was taken out and studied fervently, as if even here where life was slowed to a baby's growing pace she couldn't afford for work to come second. Jay, in her pregnancies, had more or less relaxed for her hospital check-ups, thrilled to use each waiting time to catch up on magazines full of celebrity gossip and problem-page delights.

'Do you want a photo?' she said, nudging Imogen and pointing to a sign on the wall.

'What? Oh of the baby? Ooh yes, but you have to put money in the machine for a voucher. Have you got any on you?'

Jay handed over the cash and Imogen paid for her voucher, then sat clutching it tightly as if it was a winning lottery ticket. It was better than that, Jay thought, feeling a rush of tender mumsy thoughts towards her daughter. It was a ticket to a picture of an exciting, brand new, tiny life.

'Ms Callendar?' The radiographer opened her door and called to Imogen. 'Come through here dear and bring your friend with you if you like.'

'Come on Mum, come and have a look at your grandchild.'

Jay sat beside Imogen and watched as the gel was rubbed over her tummy. The bump was definitely showing now. It reminded her of a tiny version of one of those smooth, swelling Wiltshire hillsides. She crossed her fingers and wished for Imogen an absence of stretch marks, puckered flesh and aching legs.

'Look, Moggie, that's its head!' Jay exclaimed as the image came up on the screen.

'Where? Which bit? It all looks mad to me.'

The radiographer pointed to the screen. 'Look, there's a hand, and these are its legs. Everything seems to be in the right place. If you want to know what sex it is, that'll take a little while.'

'No, no don't tell me! I want it to be a surprise,' Moggie said, her eyes shining with excitement.

'OK, Imogen, I've done a couple of pictures, one for you and one for Granny.'

Jay, on being handed the photo, almost looked round for another person. Who was 'Granny'? It was her. It didn't sound anything like as bad as when Greg had said it. In fact it sounded a bit wonderful. She was actually related to this little black-and-white paper scrap. Amazing. Truly amazing.

THIRTEEN

Chips

'Ellie?' Jay called up the stairs, trying to catch her before she raced out of the bathroom, down the stairs and straight out of the house to school. 'Do you remember if I ever asked you to put Dishing the Dirt flyers through the doors in Masefield Avenue?'

'Not a clue!' came back the immediate reply. No thinking had gone into the response, that was obvious. Ellie didn't do multitasking yet. If she had gone to clean her teeth then that was exactly what and only what she'd be doing. There was no spare compartment in her adolescent brain for anything else. It would be as much as her morning mind could take to remember what came next, as in brush hair, get coat, grab bag, go to school. The more time Jay spent with teenagers the more she understood that thinking about and doing more than one thing at a time was a skill acquired only in adulthood and perfected only by women.

'I don't remember asking her to do it,' she commented to Rory back in the kitchen. 'In fact I'm sure I didn't. We haven't sent any out for ages.'

Strange. The woman who had called had definitely said she'd had one through the door. These days new clients were usually word-of-mouth contacts, from ads in the local paper or from Yellow Pages. Sending out door-to-door flyers had been something she and Barbara had done way back at the beginning when they'd first been setting up the business. By the simple means of cash incentive, Rory and Ellie had been persuaded to deliver most of them and had shamelessly conspired to exaggerate how long it took in a brazen attempt to boost their earnings.

Rory gathered up his toast crusts and put them in the bin. 'Masefield Avenue?' he asked. 'Er . . . where's that exactly?'

'Oh you know, up past the park, a couple of roads before the station.'

Rory opened the dishwasher (warily, as if it was a dangerous, unfamiliar beast) and painstakingly stashed his plate and mug inside. He was gazing inside the machine, lost in thought, as if he was noticing it properly for the first time and possibly wondering what it did. Jay, watching, realized she could be witnessing a significant stage of development being achieved here. She held her breath while he carefully closed the door again. Was it possible that he would, please God, at last turn into a Tidy Person? First stop the dishwasher, next the unexplored jungle terrain beneath his bed? If only.

'Ah. Right. Yeah I think I know the road.' Rory did a lot of overemphatic nodding, then picked up speed and dashed past her yelling, 'Gotta go . . . late, bye! Oh, and the post's here!' There was a scraping sound in the hallway as his bag was dragged across the polished floor (he would surely have worn a groove in it by the time he'd got through his A levels) then the door slammed shut with the usual wall-shaking brutality, leaving only the sound of the lonely white rat scuffling in the sawdust at the bottom of its tank, and the occasional glug from the coffee machine. It was very nearly possible to hear the house sighing with relief.

Jay picked up the mail from the doormat, poured a heap of Special K into a bowl and added a handful of raspberries. These were straight from the fridge and too cold. She'd intended to leave them on the worktop all night so they'd be up to room temperature, but someone had tried to be helpful and put them away. Too chilled and they had little flavour, not to mention setting her teeth on edge. Win had had a point, all those years ago, mixing up Delphine's breakfast at body temperature. This breakfast was two Weight Watchers points, she worked out, crunching through the cereal. It didn't seem a lot to sustain a body through a hectic morning, but ten pounds had now gone, so something among all these diets and the agonizing scurrying round the park must be working.

There was yet another pink envelope in the post. Delphine again, revving up in pre-wedding, pre-moving mode. Why couldn't she just phone, Jay wondered, or did she find calculating the appropriate time, given the different hours, completely impossible? It was a card this time, a picture of an appealing, wide-eyed pony almost identical to her long-ago pet.

'Remember Cobweb?' Delphine had written inside. 'Didn't we have some good times on him?'

Hmm, Jay thought, remembering the stressed afternoons at Mrs Allen's and Delphine's manipulative bargaining that guaranteed she'd never have to clean her own tack or haul her own heavy saddle on and off her pony.

'I wanted to ask you if you'll be the Matron of Honour or whatever it is you have at Register Office weddings. If it's yes, get something peachy to wear. See you next week, Delphine.'

And if it was no? Jay felt old rebellions stirring inside, a mild huffiness at being bossed around by a cousin she hadn't seen since Delphine had gone off to

Australia ten years ago with Bill Durant (husband number two, succumbed to liver failure three years back), and had communicated with, till these last few weeks, only at Christmas and birthdays. But then, it couldn't be no, could it? If it was, she'd have to phone Delphine and tell her and be callously aware she was being pointlessly hurtful, and what kind of a person would do that? After all, who else was Delphine going to ask? How many non-family old friendships would she still have over here that she could so casually revive when she needed them? So it would be yes, of course it would. But . . . peachy? That was a puzzle. What did that mean, exactly?

Jay put the card on the table and zapped around clearing up the kitchen, ready for Monique to come in later in the morning and give it a proper clean. In fact, she decided, she would treat the house to an all-out blitz before Delphine got there, or better yet, she'd treat herself and Delphine to one. It would be a perfect pre-wedding trip out for the two of them, an all-dayer at a spa and then home again to a spankingly scrubbed-out house.

'What do you think she meant by peachy?' Jay asked Barbara as they drove the van over to Masefield Avenue to talk terms with their potential new client. 'Do you think she means the colour? Or is peachy a sort of Australian term for cute, do you think? I'm way too old for cute, but oh please God, don't let it be the colour.'

Barbara frowned and looked at Jay. 'Heavens I hope it *isn't* the colour. You can't wear peach, not with your browny-blonde hair. You'll look like a trifle.'

'Thanks, Barbara, don't wrap it up for me will you? You're right though, peach only looks good on six-year-old bridesmaids with cream tights, yards of tulle underskirts and freesias in their hair.'

'But weren't you thrilled to be asked?' Barbara said, giggling. 'It must mean that her man's been in touch and told her you've passed the entrance exam. What did you think of him? Was he the Perfect Man for Ms Perfect Cousin?'

Jay thought for a moment. 'Well he was . . . really nice. The sort of man you say "Oh he's a really nice man" about. I think he did that trick of making sure everyone liked him without actually giving much away about himself.'

'Clever knack that, not one that most women have, that's for sure. Maybe it's just a man thing. You must have found out *something*.'

'Well I'm racking my brains, but he managed to sidestep any probing about ex-wives, children etc. Very metaphorically nippy on his feet – must be all that dancing.'

'Do you think he'd fancy you in peach?'

Jay made a face. '*No-one* would fancy me in peach! Mind you, I've been Delphine's bridesmaid before. Peach or no peach, believe me, getting to choose my own outfit is definitely a plus.'

'Why? What did you wear last time then?'

Jay shuddered, remembering, 'Elastoplast pink. Duchesse satin, something called "ballerina length" – not good on a short person – skintight bodice with dropped waist and pearl beads sewn on the shawl-neck bit. I looked like a chrysalis that's been out in the rain. I was away at university and stupidly sent the measurements instead of getting back home to try it on. And by the time I did, well, let's just say Delphine ordered me to starve for five days so all the fifty-six buttons would fasten. I was a little bit pregnant with Imogen.'

'Did you tell her that?'

'I did. She got into a panic that I'd throw up halfway down the aisle, or faint in front of the altar or something, and Auntie Win had a right old go and said I was very selfish, getting myself pregnant for Delphine's big day. As if I'd done it on purpose, specially for that. Mum was great – she said it served them right for not getting *her* to make the frocks, after all the years she'd spent running up glitzy little Latin American numbers for Delphine's competitions. She very sniffily told Win that a first-class dressmaker who really knew her stuff would have allowed a bit extra for "give".'

'Or for lying. Think how many people must swear they're a size ten when what they really mean is they hope to diet down to it.'

Jay laughed. 'I can relate to that, Barbara, don't knock it. It's not called Goal Weight for nothing!'

Barbara steered the van round the corner and pulled up at the house. Jay looked up at the mimosa tree that waved its graceful slender branches out over the pavement. 'This reminds me of somewhere . . . Heavens, surely it can't be the place I saw in Rory's magazine?'

'What, the one you said was a brothel?' Barbara peered out of the van window, checking out what looked like an ordinary family home. 'Looks perfectly normal to me. Nice and big but nothing special.'

'It does doesn't it? The real one's probably nowhere round here. Pity, but all the same let's get inside quick, have a shufti!'

'I keep rooms,' the proprietor of number thirty-six announced as soon as she'd opened the door to Jay and Barbara. The term had a grand Edwardian ring about it, as if the house was a warren of gloomy bedsitters each containing a gas ring and a genteel governess of good family, who had fallen on harder times than her upbringing had led her to expect.

Mrs Howard was a small, bony woman in her mid-sixties. Her head darted forward and back, nose leading as she spoke, reminding Jay of a skinny budgie on a perch. Disappointingly, she was nothing like the brash bawdy-house madam Jay had been hoping to meet. It would have been great fun to have been greeted on the doorstep by an aged siren with fluffy high-heeled mules, a long cigarette holder, scarlet slit skirt belted with wide black patent and a deeply cut translucent black frilly blouse. A classic caricature definitely, but nothing wrong with that, it was very Beryl Cook, and if it was good enough for her . . . The vision should have been topped off with piled-up ginger curls and a filthy laugh. This lady was all tidy Marks and Spencers box pleats and high-necked crisp white blouse and looked very much as if she would order Jay and Barbara from the premises if they so much as accidentally flashed a leopard-print bra strap. Men who visited the house wouldn't be punters, they'd surely be referred to as 'gentlemen callers'.

'. . . girls who work in the theatre, they're mostly from abroad,' she was continuing as she showed them into her sitting room. This sounded more promising. What on earth would girls 'from abroad' be doing on the stages of London theatres? Unless you counted all those bouncy Irish ones who'd been recruited for *Riverdance* a few years back.

'These days,' she seemed keen to explain, 'the younger girls are on such short contracts they need somewhere to stay where they won't be molested or get lonely, and they tend to move on so it's not worth their while setting up home in flats. Being so close to the station, we're handy for the West End, you see, and cheaper than central areas.'

Jay looked around the room, taking in the fact that it was meticulously tidy and that there were relatively few knick-knacks on the surfaces. There was something mildly impersonal about it, as if paintings (Lake

196

District landscapes, a 1920s Thames pleasure-boat scene) had been chosen to match the decor. There was a decided preference for Laura Ashley. The walls were papered with a sort of pale terracotta, patterned to look like rag-rolling. Her aunt Win would be pleased by the many floral cushions, the creamy damask curtains and the peach-striped sofas. Jay tried for a second, and failed, to imagine herself wearing this colour to Delphine's wedding. She was more of a grey-blue person really, absolutely not this. She'd have to wait and see what Delphine was intending to wear and tone herself in with something.

'It's really only the communal areas that need your services, and then the girls' rooms as and when they're vacated. Some stay a while, some are off after a few days,' Mrs Howard went on, leading the way up the stairs. 'The girls like their privacy so while they're here I have to trust them to keep their own rooms up to scratch.' She turned and gave them a wry smile. 'Some of them though, frankly you wonder where they were dragged up. And if you say anything you come up against the language barrier. What does it take to run a duster over a shelf?'

Jay bit her tongue to stop herself from blurting out, 'About ten quid an hour.'

The three bathrooms – two on the first floor and another one between the two attic rooms – were all strangely void of real signs of habitation. There were no toothbrushes on the shelves, no Tampax boxes, shampoo bottles, towels, shower gels, flannels or loofahs strewn about. Jay imagined the inhabitants behind the closed bedroom doors, shyly peering out to see if the coast was clear before scuttling into the bathroom, clutching sponge bags and towels and trussed up in big velour dressing gowns. It was probably miles from the truth – when the occupants were around, the place would surely be vibrant with polyglottal girly chat, the air full of clashing scents and shower steam. Just now, though, with everything quiet and empty there was a strange air of deadness and sterility – like, she imagined, an old boarding-school dormitory a day before term began. The kitchen was a jollier place – the dresser hung with a lively selection of brightly coloured mugs, the walls a pretty sky blue and a big noticeboard covered with photos, messages, lists, postcards and fast-food flyers.

'It would have to be afternoons, for the cleaning,' Mrs Howard told Jay and Barbara. 'The girls sleep late,' she said with a smile. 'They need their rest, you see, working so hard at night.'

Oh if only, Jay thought, catching Barbara's eye, if only it were true, that behind those ordinary cream-gloss doors upstairs there were chambers all kitted out with exotic, erotic delights. It would make such a change from the tame suburban tastes of most of their clients. She imagined running Henry's nozzle under a bed and clanging it against abandoned handcuffs or tangling it in the laces of a leather basque. Instead of the usual bedroom shelves holding books, photographs, make-up, she pictured a row of vibrators, arranged neatly in size order. The big snag would be finding staff who didn't have scruples about polishing them . . .

Rory waited till the morning break. It had been hard to concentrate in French (bloody Jacques again, up to nothing much with his *cousine* Dominique, taking their *chien* to the *village* to buy some *crêpes* and eat them by the *rivière*).

'Freddie?' Rory whispered into his mobile, even though he was under the trees on the far side of the football pitch and miles from anyone. 'Freddie can you hear me?'

'Whassup? It's early, man.' He'd woken him. Didn't you have to go to school during your last year? Was hours of free kip-time the way they got you to stay on after sixteen? Well punted, that.

'Freddie it's nearly eleven.'

'So? Got nothing till two. Whaddya need, cousin?'

'That house, that one we went to with the tarts, except they weren't and I shoved that bit of paper through the door, they've only rung Mum and she's gone round there.'

'So? It was just a house. What's she gone there for?'

'Someone phoned about cleaning. I just said.' He felt slightly silly now. He'd overreacted. It *was* just a house. An ordinary big family-type place. The cleaning was just a job. Life was boring, predictable, unthrilling. He so wished it wasn't. He so wished that house had been crawling with stonkingly gorgeous pouty Albanian hookers offering porno services he'd only (so far) dreamed about. It was very handily local – he'd be tempted to save up and make a visit. But better than that, much better, he so wished – and his heart actually squeezed itself extra hard, he could feel it – he so wished Samantha Newton thought of him as more than the dim tosser at the back of the class who'd had trouble that morning translating '*Mon chien est noir et blanc*'. He'd looked at her as he wrestled with the language. She had her hand over her face as if she was trying not to laugh. He couldn't blame her, if he wasn't the one being so lame, he'd be laughing too.

'Maybe you'll be able to find out what that Charles bloke's connection is,' Freddie said, sounding a bit more awake. 'You been back to his swanky pad yet?' Rory heard him lighting a cigarette, then inhaling deeply on the first blissful one of the day.

'I'd forgotten about him. He probably just knows the

owner. Dull as. And no, I haven't been back. Seen it, done it.'

Even to himself, his voice sounded gloom-filled. Someone should be taking care of him, treating him gently, feeding him Prozac before he turned into one of those teen suicide statistics. He sighed, reminding himself of one of the olds you saw on the bus every morning who sighed their annoyance at having accidentally got on before the pensioners' free travel kicked in and then sighed that schoolkids were in their space (sighed even more if someone let them sit down, as if they'd hoped for a bit of lively confrontation about Manners These Days). Then they sighed at having to get up off their comfy seat when they'd got to their stop and sighed when they made it safely to the pavement. God, if he was like this now, what would he be like at seventy? He'd be all sigh, no breathing.

'You all right Rory? You sound a bit down, man.' Rory could hear Freddie peeing, then the flush of the loo. He pictured him striding about in his boxers, wandering between the bathroom and his bedroom, idly scratching his balls and flopping back on top of his bed, flicking the remote at the telly. Freddie, at ten, had had a Ryan Giggs duvet cover. He'd taken it with him on a school trip, unable to be apart from it and bravely oblivious to teasing. Rory tried to imagine the grown-up Freddie lying on Ryan. It was a bit of a gay picture he was conjuring up there, not at all like Freddie. He'd probably got a Kylie one now, which could pretty gay as well, he supposed. Could you get J-Lo ones? Or Beyoncé?

'I'm OK,' Rory muttered eventually. 'Just . . . life, you know.'

'No luck with the chick?'

'No, none at all. Not a hope. Given up.'

'No don't do that. You see it, you want it, you gotta make it happen. Gospel according to Freddie.'

If only it was that easy. Getting a snog off Samantha Newton would be the equivalent of being a sub for some part-time club in a minor league being called up to play for Man. United. She was going to be the sort who only went out with men born under the Amex Platinum sign. When she was an independent grown-up she'd never get on a plane and turn right. She was destined to be forever pursued by drooling rich suckers who'd fork out to shower her with life's most expensive things. He'd have to impress her something massive even to get a look-in.

Rory trudged back across the soccer pitch trying to get himself in the mood for Geography. Not easy. When he thought of mountain ranges all that came to mind were the superb rising mounds on the front of Samantha Newton's body. Scaling those peaks, now that would be something. But first, she'd got to notice him. Got to be impressed. A small idea was taking shape. A very small idea that was uncurling and gently feeling the air like a butterfly's damp new wings. And it all fitted perfectly with the gospel according to Freddie.

Jay changed out of her work jeans and into a light-weight unlined linen skirt, ready for the Weight Watchers weigh-in. OK, she conceded that Paula had warned them that they were only fooling themselves with the clothes thing, but surely you wanted to come away from the meeting feeling that your subs weren't entirely a waste of money? Putting on something that weighed next to nothing was only human nature, and would make it the nearest thing to getting weighed stark naked in your own bathroom. She drew the line at abandoning her underwear in the pursuit of

201

offloading a couple more ounces, but she could sympathize with those who did.

Pat had told her about a woman who'd been weighed at her first class wearing a big fake-fur coat and gradually over the weeks had shed bits of clothing till she was down to a strappy sundress and nothing else. She even got her long hair cut short. Only then did she confess she'd actually lost nothing at all over the entire time. '*And*,' Pat had said in real outrage, 'she'd been awarded her seven-pound pin! Bloody nerve, bloody mad or what?' Jay could only agree; if you could get applauded as slimmer of the week simply for putting your coat on a table, what was it all about?

She looked in the mirror, pulled her stomach in and turned sideways to see if she was noticeably skinnier. Hard to tell. Surely by now everyone she knew should be shrieking with amazement at her svelte shape? What was the point if even she herself could barely tell any difference between her body-plus-eleven-pounds and her body now?

Jay didn't hang about after the weigh-in. She was meeting Greg for something to eat at All Bar One and besides, didn't feel much like staying to be taught ways to Make Friends with Tuna. She'd already had enough tuna to last a lifetime. If every dieter on the planet was scoffing the stuff at the rate she'd been eating it then soon there'd be an environmental crisis for the poor fish, and they'd be as protected and mollycoddled as dolphins. Holly (still mountainous but sticking to the diet and very optimistic) asked her where she was going and had looked doubtful. 'All Bar One isn't listed in the Eating Out Guide,' she warned. 'Do you think you should be going there? You won't know what to have. You'd be better going to a Harvester.'

'Ye gods,' Jay said to Greg as she took her first sip

of the champagne he'd ordered. (Why? Were they celebrating or was he feeling guilty about something?) 'I'm never going to one of those classes again, somehow I'm just not a team player. I can see it makes sense but . . . hell's teeth, I've had it with adding up points for every mouthful and bargaining with myself: "If I run up the stairs instead of the escalator at Oxford Circus, please may I have a Twix bar?" Aaagh!' She gulped the tingling wine, savouring the creamy biscuity flavour and half longing to glug down the whole bottle in minutes, like a chilled beer on a hot summer day. She'd only hiccup, she told herself, she'd feel sick and past hunger. And she didn't want to be past hunger.

'You never go to Oxford Circus,' Greg pointed out. 'Well you haven't for ages anyway.'

'Oh I know, I know. It's just a what-if.'

'And you never eat Twix bars.'

Was he being deliberately obtuse? 'You never order champagne without a good reason either, come to that,' she told him.

He smiled and took her hand. 'I just fancied some. I thought you might. But I think I'd have clouted you over the head with it if you'd said "Ooh I can't, the diet, the diet . . ."'

'No chance,' she said, squeezing his fingers. 'No bloody chance. So what is this about?'

'Oh nothing, just felt like celebrating being a lucky bastard. Getting another baby in the house without it being you having to go through being pregnant, being glad the kids seem to be coming along OK.'

'You sound like those people in *Bridget Jones's Diary* that she describes as Smug Marrieds.'

'Yeah, well so what?' Greg laughed. 'I am. And by the way I left Mog and Ellie sorting out those soft toys you wanted cleared from the shower room.'

'Well that's a minor miracle and worth celebrating on

its own. Did they have binbags? Had they put anything in them?'

'Now that I couldn't say. They were giggling about when they used to play *Animal Hospital* with them and line them all up with bandages and Elastoplast and invent gruesome operations for them.'

'I remember that. Not long ago for Ellie, really, and even Mog doesn't seem that many years past that stage. Odd to think she'll have her own soon.'

'She said she's looking forward to playing with the baby,' Greg told her. 'At least she's young enough to still remember how. She'll be fine.'

'She'll need a lot of back-up,' Jay said, wondering how it would all work out.

'I know, but that's what we're for. But for tonight let's not feel all grown-up and responsible. What do you want to eat? And as we're not driving anywhere, shall we have another bottle?'

Excellent idea, Jay thought, having a look at the menu and a bit of a think. She wasn't giving up though, not quite yet. Just about everybody swore by the Atkins diet. No carbohydrates, low carboyhdrates, modified versions and the nicest of all where you could still drink wine. The steak would be suitable, lots of lovely protein there, she thought, and delicious with the tomatoes and caramellized shallots. Not chips though, absolutely not. Her tummy rumbled its own opinion on this and she sympathized with it. Well maybe chips tonight, she thought, giving her middle a reassuring pat. She could start it all off properly tomorrow, and leave Weight Watchers with a glorious bang at approximately thirty-six points for the day.

The house was almost in darkness. Apart from the unevenly flickering bluish glow coming through the windows from at least two televisions, there was no sign of anyone being home. It wasn't particularly late, just typical that teens who were sprawled on beds and sofas almost comatose with TV viewing could never be bothered to reach out a hand far enough to switch on a light.

'When the house needs light they never switch them on, but once on they never think to switch them off again,' Jay commented as she slid the key into the lock.

'That's teenagers for you,' Greg agreed, laughing. 'But don't be hard on them, it's their job to be awkward sods. Bloody hell, what's all this?'

Each side of the glass staircase was lined with soft toys, leaving only a narrow pathway up the middle. Pandas and elephants and the outsize tiger Imogen had won at the fair were there, Pooh and Piglet and Eeyore were cuddled up together and a family of Pound Puppy beagles spilled over onto a Bagpuss.

'Would you look at this?' Jay said, picking up a pale grey seal, long-ago souvenir of the Cornish Seal Sanctuary. Each one of the animals had been 'treated' in *Animal Hospital* style, all carefully bandaged and plastered and splinted. It must have taken the girls all evening.

There was a note halfway up the stairs: 'Promise no. 1: They'll all be well again in the morning. Promise no. 2: Then they can go to the Charity Shop. (Boo-hoo, sniff-sniff) Love, Ell & Mog xxx'

FOURTEEN

Dr Atkins

It didn't feel right. Surely this couldn't possibly work. Surely you couldn't have a whopping great cheese and herb omelette with crispy bacon and a big tomato on the side and still get thinner? It defied all the laws of food physics, if there were such things. Guiltily, but feeling blissfully sated, Jay stashed plates in the dishwasher and washed the grill pan, stowing it and the omelette pan away in its drawer. She did all this at top speed, out of a vague fear that the calorie police would catch her destroying the evidence of overconsumption and condemn her to fat-prison as punishment for actions contrary to the due slimming process.

'God, that was good,' Greg said, leaning back in his chair and patting his middle. 'Can we do this every morning? And what's for lunch? A roast swan and a couple of cows?'

'Only if you don't have rice, bread, potatoes or pasta with them,' she told him. 'Otherwise you could literally eat a horse.'

'Did that once,' he said, pulling a face. 'Well not a whole horse, obviously. In Belgium on a work trip. It was chewy and a bit gamey. Not pleasant. I kept thinking of Shergar and wondering if he ended up as a *plat du jour.*'

There was actually nothing new about this kind of diet, it occurred to Jay, in spite of all the media fuss and furore about it and all the medicos going into health-warning overdrive. Many years ago when her mother and Win had embarked on one of their regular spats of weight loss, they'd simply decreed 'No Starch'. It was just that one basic rule. That was the way diets were done – no faffing about with calorie-counting, fat units, zone calculation, blood-group-appeasing and what have you. No-one mentioned. carbohydrates unless they were working in a food lab. Nobody had heard of cholesterol, antioxidants, lipoproteins or omega-3 fatty acids. Free radicals would have been a slogan on a demo banner. And in practice what Audrey and Win were cutting out was only bread and potatoes and pastry. As Jay remembered from plain-cooked home meals and school food, pasta came in the form of canned spaghetti, rice was for puddings or an occasional kedgeree, and bread was white sliced.

Audrey hadn't had a great deal of interest in food. It was functional stuff, fuel for getting through the day. Providing it for her family was a chore like any other domestic ritual, very much on a par with cleaning the bath. She'd have suggested to anyone who confessed to enjoying cooking that they get themselves a proper hobby. The only point she could see to standing at the cooker stirring a tricky sauce was that it gave her time to read her library books while she did it.

Win had had an extreme mistrust of 'Continental' food (linking it with overheated Continental climate and unreliable Continental manners) and considered much of it to be deeply suspect and likely to cause stomach troubles. When Delphine went on her school's ski trip to Austria she'd been given a note for her teachers instructing them not to let her eat anything unfamiliar for fear of it being a potentially fatal challenge to the grumbling appendix. Delphine, in a rare spirit of adventure, had torn up the note the second her mother was out of sight and later become an accomplished and adventurous cook. The day she'd persuaded Win to sample the Hungarian goulash she'd made in domestic science had been a turning point in their household. Win took full advantage after that, graciously ceding kitchen space and fattening herself up comfortably during her daughter's teenage years, as Delphine cooked her way through the recipe books of nearly every European country.

'As long as she can boil an egg and has a light touch with pastry, you don't need much more than that,' Audrey had remarked one Sunday lunchtime, after sitting down to sixteen-year-old Delphine's excellent crown roast, stuffed with apricots, saffron rice and aubergine. She was reacting to Win queening it (as ever) with 'Of course Delphine is practically *Cordon Blue*' and warned, rather gracelessly considering she was tucking in greedily at the time, 'She'll find the day-to-day stuff less rewarding than all this fancy business.'

She didn't actually say 'You Mark My Words' but they were there, hovering, just waiting in the wings.

Win smirked and wagged a finger at her. 'The way to a man's heart is through his stomach. When my Delphine's married, her husband won't have to be embarrassed when he invites the boss round for dinner. They'll get no less than *Oat Cuisine*.'

Jay and April had raised their eyes heavenwards and giggled, partly thinking of Delphine's daily muesli but also certain that the route to a man's heart involved a knack with zips, fancy underwear and alcohol rather than a talent for cutting flower shapes out of carrots.

'What day's Delphine getting here?' Greg asked, pouring a final cup of coffee before retiring to his office to start a day's work.

'I was just thinking about her,' Jay said. 'Next Monday. I've got to pick her up at Heathrow.'

'Why you? I thought Win would be rushing down there in a limo, all red carpet and welcome balloons for the prodigal daughter.'

'Win's got her chiropody appointment. Apparently it's an event carved in stone and completely unmissable. She says she can only get her corns filed every six weeks and if you miss an appointment they won't give you another for months and months.'

'She could go to a private place, surely, and choose her own times? Delphine could fork out.'

'I suggested that, but she says she likes to go to this particular Wendy person who's got a gentle way with the clippers and she always sees the same patients in the waiting room for a chat and a grumble. Anyway, I don't mind, I think of it as part of the matron of honour's duties. I'd probably have had to drive Win anyway – she'll only get flustered and lost. Last time she went to Australia I had to hand her over to the ground staff after she'd checked in to make sure she made it to the right plane. If I hadn't she'd probably have ended up in Rio.'

After Greg had gone down the garden to his office, Jay went back up the stairs to give the spare-room shower a final scrub-up. It was all looking pretty good up there now that the boxes of toys had gone. Anya had shampooed the carpet and the sky-blue linen curtains had come back from the dry-cleaners. There was a new silky throw on the bed, not unlike the one at Delphine's fiancé's flat, and Jay had replaced the tatty old bedside lamp with a simple chrome Anglepoise. The drawers were lined with geranium-scented paper and the wardrobe was equipped with every kind of hanger, from padded satin (memories of Delphine's childhood bedroom) to trouser rails. The shower room was stocked with a Clarins selection of cosmetic goodies and fat white towels. Jay reckoned she'd done everything short of folding the loo-roll end into a V.

Surely, she thought, standing at the doorway to inspect her handiwork, even domestic supremo Delphine couldn't find fault with all this? And if she did, well it wasn't for long. Jay would bite her tongue, smile and let any stinging remarks wash straight over her. It would all go towards making her a Better Person. A few weeks on and Delphine would be mistress of that sleek top floor of the Swannery, all married off (again) and with a whole new domain to make her mark on.

Barbara was due round at any minute to go over the bookings and work out a new rota that would include a regular slot for Mrs Howard and her 'kept rooms'. Jay went downstairs, kicking Rory's football boots to the inside of his room as she went and hoping he could manage not to overspill too much into the rest of the house and risk tripping Delphine headlong down the glass staircase. She was going to hate that as it was, and would be sure, Jay could almost bet on it, to give them all a lecture on proper staircase safety and the benefits of good old-fashioned stair-runners fastened by brass rods.

Barbara gave the doorbell her usual three long rings and Jay went to let her in. She was holding a cat-carrier from which an insistent Burmese miaow could be heard and Daffodil ran up to have a curious sniff at it, following the two women into the kitchen.

'We've got trouble with Mrs Caldwell again!' Barbara said, sounding remarkably cheerful about it.

'Oh God, what's happened now?' Jay said. 'Is Monique still folding the knickers the wrong way?'

'No. Worse than that.' Barbara stifled a giggle. 'You know Mrs C. likes shirts all folded to look just like when she'd first bought them? Well . . . you won't believe this . . . Monique's gone and folded them all perfectly and then stuck pins in them!'

'*Pins*? But why? Or do you mean like some kind of voodoo doll-type-thing?'

'No, no, pins like you get in men's shirts when you've just bought them, you know, holding the sleeve to the body, part of the packaging, all that?'

'Yeah I know, and there's always at least three still there after you think you've got them all out. So whatever did Monique do it for?' Pointless question, really. Monique had simply run out of patience. It happened, and in most cases she could hardly blame the perpetrator. It shouldn't be part of any cleaner's remit to tidy away used condoms (however carefully knotted) from beneath a bed, or to hose down a patio on which a Labrador with a stomach upset has spent many productive hours.

Mrs Caldwell's problem was that she was a 'follower' – a woman who couldn't simply trust her cleaner to get on with it, couldn't just take the opportunity to disappear to the shops or go to work or trot off out to the local beauty salon to have her nails buffed or her fanny waxed. Oh no. She had to stay on the premises and trail round after the cleaner, refolding towels, moving a vase an inch to the left, tweaking a rug. They'd lost one of these clients only a year before, when she'd picked up a folded J-cloth from the cold tap by the sink and rehung it over the hot one. Sandrine, a fiery girl from southern Spain, had grabbed the cloth, soaked it in scalding water and shoved it down the front of the woman's cashmere sweater, then slammed out leaving her screaming and with Dishing the Dirt's Henry the vacuum cleaner still grinning stupidly at her from the middle of the kitchen floor.

'Monique did it out of pure logic, really,' Barbara continued, 'I went to pick her up after Mrs Caldwell phoned in a fury. Monique was completely un-apologetic and said that if Mrs C. had wanted her husband's shirts to be just as if they had come from the shop, then she was only doing what she'd asked.'

'Well, you can see her point. That's what Mrs Caldwell said to us, too.'

They'd lose this one, for sure, Jay thought, even as she gave in to a growing urge to laugh. At this very moment Mrs Caldwell was probably running her finger down the options in Yellow Pages and then dialling On All Floors for an emergency quote. Quite possibly, Jay fancied, she'd end up with Spanish Sandrine – in which case, heaven help her. She also imagined Mr Caldwell fresh from the shower (unwelcome thoughts of droopy pale naked flesh here), dressing in the morning, pulling a shirt from the shelf in the wardrobe and scattering his bony bare feet with pins. The pins would vanish into the three-inch eau de Nil shagpile. For weeks after, the Caldwells would be spearing their tender soles with the lethal spikes.

'Well you can't please everyone, I suppose,' Jay said. 'What about giving Monique a go at Charles Morgan's flash pad next Monday? You'll be there to keep an eye on her, and she is very good.'

'I thought that too. At least on a first visit he won't have done anything to upset her . . .'

The kitten Barbara had brought with her was the last of the current litter, on its way to the vet for the second of two vaccinations. 'Couldn't do it before – she was sneezing a bit but she's fine now and raring to go,' Barbara said, opening the kitten's basket and pulling out the wide-eyed grey-blue creature. She handed it over to Jay. It sat on her lap gazing round the kitchen and blinking its big amber eyes.

Jay stroked its wedge-shaped head and it rubbed its face eagerly against her hand.

'Please tell me you've got a home waiting for it, Barbara.' She sensed there was a sneaky reason why Barbara hadn't just left it in the car, and was overcome by appalling temptation. Daffodil was getting very dependent. She leapt into the cars every time anyone left the house; she followed them up the road and yowled for them to come back to her and at night she tried to get into bed between Jay and Greg, purring and dribbling and kneading her claws into the duvet cover. The cat was overseeing the visit of the newcomer, sitting on the floor, staring up at it with something that could well be longing.

'Look, Daffy, what do you think?' Jay carefully put the kitten on the floor – it had been struggling to get off her lap and get at the bigger cat. The two animals stalked around each other under the table, checking out relative size and threat level, then Daffodil patted gently at the kitten with her paw and rolled it over, batting the animal's soft little body, then washing its plump tummy.

'It *did* have a home but I was let down,' Barbara admitted. 'The deposit was paid and everything, but the woman was moving to Ireland, and at the last minute decided she didn't need the hassle and expense of transporting a cat. So if you're interested . . .' She gave Jay a sly look. 'Bargain price? Just the vet fees so far? You'd be doing me a huge favour.'

'Barbara, I couldn't!' Jay protested, trying to voice a bit of common sense. 'We've got the rat, the cat, a baby coming, Delphine arriving any minute . . .'

'Delphine!' Barbara snorted. 'What's she got to do with it? She's only visiting for a teeny while! You don't have to put a saucer of cream down for her! Go on, you know you want to, and look – there's no hostility at all between the two cats. They've already taken to each other.'

This was true – well so far anyway. Daffodil was calmly standing by while the kitten investigated her food supply and took a greedy nibble from the bowl, turning her little grey head sideways as she crunched loudly on the biscuits.

'But Daffodil's past the litter-tray stage – we'd have to start all that again . . .' Kittens were a lot of work – they needed training up and large doses of utterly spoiling affection so they'd trust their humans and be a joy to live with, rather than bad-tempered and spitty.

There was a thumping on the outside staircase, then Imogen and Tristan ambled into the kitchen. 'Close the door, quick, Moggie,' Jay said. 'We've got a kitten in here.'

'Oooh! What a sweet blue furry baby!' Imogen scooped up the kitten and cuddled it to her. 'Is it a friend for Daffodil? She could do with one. She's very bored. She ripped up my *Cosmopolitan* yesterday, all over the floor.'

'She's called Cicely,' Barbara told them, firmly shutting the cat basket. It seemed to be a done deal. That basket wasn't going home with an occupant.

'She could be *our* cat Tris, couldn't she?'

Tristan looked concerned. 'I don't know – what about toxoplas-whatsit and pregnant women? You can't go messing about with cat litter, not right now. And cats get jealous of babies.'

Imogen's eyes filled with easy tears. 'Oh but . . .'

'Tris is right, Moggie. And make sure you wash your hands when you put it down.' Jay told her. 'But . . . well we could keep it up here, train it and settle it and then when the baby's a bit bigger you can take it downstairs to live with you.'

It seemed simple enough. What was one more pet? It wasn't as if it was a fierce great Rottweiler. No, that would be next week, when the scariest creature in the house arrived by Qantas.

It had been Freddie who'd been saying about how girls love to be impressed, so it was him who'd put the idea into his head. Rory decided this was so in order that he'd have someone to blame, even though he knew he was the one who'd really cop it if anything went wrong. There was no reason why it should; he'd make sure they cleared up everything. He'd go back the next day and double-make-sure that everything was all sorted, right down to polishing the forks. He'd see that the floors were clean and the rubbish taken away, every single bit. He'd run the waste disposal till whatever was in there had disappeared so far down the pipes that not even forensic bloody murder-expert geniuses could trace anything back to him other than plain cold tap water. He wasn't planning to involve the bed, not this time (though to get real, of course if she was completely insistent he couldn't actually see himself saying, 'Oh no, absolutely not, Samantha, a shag was the last thing on my mind.'). He'd save that for another time and another place. And there would *be* another if he could get her to turn up for the first one – what girl wouldn't be impressed?

All he had to do (all? He felt sick at the thought) was ask Samantha Newton, get her to say yes. He'd have to invite a couple of others as well, but they couldn't be his usual crew. Alex and Mart would be hopeless – they'd get overexcited and bounce on the bed and start mooning off the balcony and chucking down paper aeroplanes or something. And they'd whine for a pizza and beer rather than what he'd got in mind. It had to be someone with a bit more sophistication than that.

Tragically he was going to have to invite that spoon Hal Clegg, which was tricky because it meant he'd have to find a girl for him. Hal was so not likely to be able to find one for himself, being as how he was the type who spent his Saturday nights revising his French verbs. He'd have to ask Samantha about that, maybe her friend Shelley would come, which would provide something else good to look at but have the not so perfect downside of producing a bit of a girl-on-girl double act. They'd sit together and giggle and whisper like they did in class and sort of . . . pair off, not like *that* but so you couldn't get one away from the other. Big risk, just like using the premises, but it had to be now or no chance ever again.

Food was the easy bit. He'd just decant some Marks and Spencers stuff into the Charles bloke's dishes and bung them in his microwave. Considerate, that, because he wouldn't mess up the oven. And Samantha and Shelley wouldn't have any idea he hadn't cooked it all – he'd tell them he'd made everything at home and brought it along. They'd need wine. There was loads in the little room at the back of his dad's office, he'd just have to raid that and pray he hadn't nicked something that would taste like cat's pee if you drank it before the year 3000. It was all going to cost a bit, but as the ad went, Samantha was sooooo worth it.

Katinka sniffed in the van all the way from the station. Jay, parking outside Mrs Howard's, handed her the box of tissues from the glove compartment but Katinka refused. They'd all get streaming colds at this rate, Jay thought, pulling out a wad of the tissues and stuffing them into Katinka's hand. This was like taking small children around. Any minute now she'd have to resort to cramming a tissue over the girl's nose and shouting 'Blow!' at her. Mrs Howard wasn't going to be impressed by a constant sniffer and they could really do with this gig, now that Mrs Caldwell and her folding fetish had buggered off to another company.

Mrs Howard at least looked delighted to see them. She was, Jay could tell, the wonderful sort of woman who tidied up the place before cleaners arrived. You'd never have to sort through a week's strewn-about news-papers and a sea of socks in this house. They should be through in a couple of hours, no problem.

'A nice cup of tea before you start, ladies?' Mrs Howard asked. Katinka immediately plonked the Henry down on the hall floor and brightened up. Jay wanted to get them well under way before they slowed down for a break, but Katinka was always happier and speedier after coffee and a biscuit. Two of Mrs Howard's lodgers were making their way down the stairs. They were tall girls, very leggy and pretty. They said hello and then carried on talking to each other in a mid-European language. Jay followed Mrs Howard through to the kitchen but Katinka and Anya lingered, chatting cheerily to the two girls as they collected coats from the hooks on the hall wall.

'That's nice, isn't it?' Mrs Howard said as she switched the kettle on and offered Jay one of the high kitchen chairs by the counter. 'Someone new for them to chat to. My girls don't get to meet others who speak their language around here. They don't get out in the evenings either, well they do for work but not socially. They're always so busy, poor things, but in the day-time, when they're up and about, they're good company and they like to have somewhere safe to be.'

'Safe?' Jay was curious. Were these suburban avenues, perhaps especially this square mile where each road was named after an English poet, full of leering predators? Were there hundreds of men who, like her, had mistaken this place for a house of ill repute?

Perhaps, at night, the gatepost was thronging with raincoated potential punters lurking in the shadows and kicking themselves for getting it so wrong.

'Well, you know, they're pretty young girls, a long way from home and working in the entertainment business. Someone's got to take care of them.'

Jay began unloading her box of cleaning products while Mrs Howard bustled about putting flapjacks on a plate and measuring spoonfuls of tea into her flowery teapot. The girls would feel spoiled, she thought, wondering why all their clients didn't treat them as royally as this. It would make a nice change for them to feel cherished, if this kind of treatment continued, so long as they didn't take too much advantage and start hanging around the kitchen like hopeful, hungry puppies. They'd soon suss that Mrs Howard was the caring sort and could well end up being cooked a three-course lunch every time they came to clean.

'You bring all your own equipment, do you?' Mrs Howard asked, looking over the selection of products and dusters that Jay had unpacked on the worktop. 'Because you don't need to, there's plenty in that cupboard over there.'

'Ah but you see, the girls are used to what we've got,' Jay explained. 'If they come up against unfamiliar brands everywhere we go then you'll never know if they're putting neat bleach on your floor or washing-up liquid down the loo.'

Katinka and Anya were in very giggly spirits. Jay found it hard to get them to concentrate as they chatted away to each other. When they were up in the top bathroom she could hear them shrieking with laughter.

'Happy souls, aren't they?' Mrs Howard commented, coming into the big terracotta sitting room where Jay was giving a hand, polishing photo frames.

'They're not always so noisy.' Jay felt she should

perhaps apologize. Another time, there might be sleeping people to consider. She'd have to have a word.

Anya and Katinka were still in high spirits at the end of their couple of hours. They were off to the Dachshund Man in the afternoon so she hoped they'd still be feeling energetic enough to get round his book-filled, musty house with appropriate gusto.

'You two sound very happy,' she said as they loaded the van. 'What was so funny?'

'Is the girls,' Anya told her in little more than a whisper and glancing back at the house, smirking. 'They dance.'

'I know, Mrs Howard told me. Some kind of theatre work.'

Anya looked puzzled. 'Theatre? No, *club*.'

Jay was backing out of the driveway and turned round to see where she was going, in time to see Katinka miming the removal of her bra.

'Club like no clothes,' Anya went on, patting her knees. 'Sitting-dancing, for the men!'

'*Lap* dancing? Those girls who live there?' Jay slammed the brakes on, unable to drive and think this through at the same time. Wow – the things that went on in the leafy suburbs, after all. Here was a perfectly-respectable looking house, owned by a woman of perfectly run-of-the-mill niceness, sheltering a selection of exotic dancers. It wasn't exactly the bawdy premises as reported by Rory's *Out for the Lads* magazine, but it was astonishingly close.

'A *dinner* party? Uh?' Samantha didn't have to look quite so astounded. You'd think she'd never heard the term before. Perhaps she hadn't. Perhaps he'd really miscalculated her grown-upness and she'd rather munch a Macca on a bench down the town square than sit at a table with all the right poncy cutlery, nibbling bits of squid and rocket and talking about something remotely intelligent. Rory tried to control his breathing. This was his big chance and he wasn't going to blow it now by stammering and backing off and blushing and looking like a total dick.

'Yes. In this penthouse I use.' How nonchalant did that sound, or was it just ridiculous at his age?

'You know. It's just usual stuff,' he shrugged. 'Food, wine, music, conversation, all that.'

He tried to keep his voice perfectly normal, as if she was the one who was being completely off the wall for not getting it, not him. It wasn't easy. In the empty classroom she kept looking over his shoulder towards the door as if he'd got her trapped in there. More likely it was because Shelley Caine was right outside, ear-wigging at the gap in the door and geeing up to have a complete giggle-fest.

'So, like, you can cook then?' She sounded doubtful but not completely a lost hope. Put it this way, Rory told himself, she hadn't actually said no straight off.

'Yeah, course I can cook.' He tried to make it come out in a 'Can't everyone?' sort of way, but at the same time hoping he'd pitched it so she wouldn't expect Marco Pierre bloody White.

'OK then.' Samantha suddenly beamed her full thousand-megawatt best smile at him. 'I'd love to come,' she said simply, and so, oh so very, very unexpectedly. Almost enough to turn him into a believer, just name your god, your religion, he'd take it.

'I've got a dress that needs a try-out,' she went on, slinking off towards the door, yellow hair wafting out. He leapt past her, pulling open the door to let her out ahead of him. Might as well start on the gentleman stuff now. They liked that sort of thing, dinner-party-type women.

She looked back over her shoulder at him. 'Let me

know nearer the day, what time and where you want me and everything,' she said, dazzling him again with the teeth. Oh he would, he promised, he would.

Result! Fucking result! Rory punched the air, accidentally clipping the edge of the door frame as he did but not, in the exhilaration of the moment, feeling even the slightest pang of pain. He reached into his pocket for his mobile and punched in a text to Freddie.

'Sorted. What next?'

FIFTEEN

Rosemary Conley

Rory was looking at himself reflected in the glass-fronted cupboard opposite the table. He was stock-still and zombie-ish, his mouth gaping unattractively and his fork suspended in the air as he lost all animation, stuck frozen with the piece of juicy pink steak halfway to his mouth. She couldn't be saying what he thought she was saying. And if she was, why did she and Dad think it was so funny?

'A houseful of lap dancers!' She was all amusement and curiosity. 'Only a few innocent tree-lined avenues away!'

'I might have to escort you to work,' Rory heard his dad saying. 'Help you carry your mop.'

Oh huge joke. So what about the Charles bloke, then? They didn't know about him, did they? What had he been doing there?

The steak finally made its way into Rory's mouth. He had to pretend nothing was out of the ordinary (apart from that his mum was now Official Cleaner to a cathouse) or she or Ellie would start asking him what was wrong. In his head he was jumping, no, *leaping*, to a good dozen sleazy conclusions. He hadn't much taken to Charles, partly out of suspicion (and oh how right, well how *nearly* right) about what he was doing coming out of a brothel. For one thing he'd almost completely ignored Ellie and Freddie and himself, as if when he was working out how best to do his impressing of Delphine's family he'd put 'talk to teenagers' right down the bottom of the list. And although Rory had been listening really hard, hoping to catch a clue or even a mention about what his connection with Masefield Avenue was, he'd hardly given away anything at all about himself. All they knew after he'd been and gone was more or less what they knew before he'd arrived. He flew planes and was going to marry (why, for buggery's sake when there was all that aircrew totty?) Auntie Delphine. Oh and they knew he bought flowers in great big impressive bunches and that he was 'interested' in dancing. Well you could bloody say that again.

'Dancing', my knob, Rory thought. What was it Cathy had said after he'd gone? Oh yeah, that he wasn't a 'high divulger'. Well you wouldn't want to divulge that actually you were a club-owning pimp, would you? Not to a bunch of total strangers, some of whom were about to become a set of in-laws. No wonder he'd been a bit shifty about his 'club' venture.

Should I say something? Rory wondered. What would Freddie do? Keep schtum or blurt it out for a laugh? He'd go for the laugh, every time, that was Freddie. So would he . . .

'Um . . . so that place, sorry I wasn't really listening,' he began, shrugging a nonchalant lack of interest. They were all attention. That was the trouble with having really polite parents, they did actually stop what they were gossiping about and listen to you. Sometimes, when you were wittering on, you just wished you had parents who said, 'Oh give it a rest, Rory' instead of saying, 'Oh I see' and, 'How do you feel about that?' and stuff.

'That house in Masefield Avenue.' He munched on some salad. Perhaps they'd tell him not to talk with his mouth full, then he'd be able to cop out. Silence: they were all ears, all three of them. 'Is it that one with the blue fence, called something beginning with an "H"?'

He didn't want to look at his mum. He reached across for a piece of garlic bread that he honestly didn't feel much like eating.

'Halcyon. That's the one. Why?'

He looked at her. She was trying not to laugh. Why? Oh yeah – she'd been poking about in his room. She'd said she'd seen what he read. She'd been in *Out for the Lads.*

'No reason.' He shrugged. 'It's just I saw Delphine's beloved fiancé coming out of there before he came to us for lunch, that's all.'

'*Charles*?' They both shrieked it together, his dad cracking up into laughter again. 'But you can't have!'

'I *did*!' he insisted, 'It was his car outside and everything. Me and Freddie saw him coming out of the gate. He had the flowers. And then he came here, straight after.'

'Why didn't you say something? Why didn't you say "Hello, I just saw you in Masefield Avenue"?' Trust Ellie to ask the tricky question.

'Well . . . er I wasn't sure. I didn't see the car when he arrived, not till he was going and only then cos we went to the front door because of the rat.' He could feel himself getting hot. Ellie was looking at him with her face all screwed up with hard thinking.

'So what were you doing down Masefield Avenue anyway?'

He was just about ready for this one, thank goodness.

'We'd been down the park to kick the ball about. We were on the way back.'

It would have to do. It wasn't what you'd call a short cut and they all knew it, but if they asked anything else about *him*, well, he'd just have to remind them who was the one who was turning out to be a bit iffy in this conversation. It wasn't someone whose name began with 'R', that was for sure.

'Delphine can't possibly know, can she?' Jay asked Greg while she was lying in the bath that night up to her neck in enough hot bubbles to obliterate all trace of any lingering Eau de Flash (pine). 'She surely can't have any idea that the man she's going to marry has some kind of involvement with a houseful of lap dancers? She'd go ballistic. It's so *not* her. She was always a bit prissy about sex. Same way that Win is.'

Win's advice regarding men had been firmly old-fashioned and ruthlessly trade-led.

'A man won't expect to pay for goods if he's already used them for free,' she'd warned the two girls on the day that Delphine (then sixteen) was getting ready to go on a date with a twenty-two-year-old man from her Latin American formation troupe. Audrey was amazed at Win for allowing Delphine to go, certain that this was someone far too old for her. She was, though, so deeply curious to know if the girl was going to glam herself up to look as if she could lie about her age, that she'd sent Jay round with a swatch of Lycra fabrics for Delphine to look at for a dress for her next dance contest.

Jay had sat on Delphine's bed, crumpling the satin rose-swagged quilt and watching while she did her make-up and put her hair up in an arrangement of artistically dangling Carmen'd curls. She *did* look older, Jay would be able to report back, a good ten years older. She not only looked older but as if she was a relic from another generation. Whereas Jay and all her friends were a raggy mixed bunch of Goth, punk, New Romantic and charity-shop treasures, Delphine always looked as if she'd been worshipping at the Jackie Kennedy shrine and tended to get herself up in co-ordinated separates, pointy court shoes, pale, sheer tights and rigid on-the-knee A-line skirts. She was also keen on trims – pocket flaps and bows and collars and superfluous bits of frill always seemed to figure somewhere. Win approved deeply (not something a normal teenager would aspire to, surely?) and was forever pointing out to Jay and April that it always paid to be 'well groomed'. The term made Jay think of poor old Cobweb, who would have appreciated Delphine's attention with a curry-comb a lot more often than she'd been prepared to give it.

'I think your mum means you shouldn't shag on a first date,' Jay giggled to Delphine as soon as Win was out of hearing range.

Delphine had looked horrified, 'I wouldn't . . . do . . . *that* even on a twentieth. Not without . . .'

'A condom?' Jay ventured cheekily.

'Without at least being very nearly engaged,' Delphine had hissed, still outraged. 'I'm not that cheap.'

'Sex isn't about price,' Jay had told her, with all the high-minded hopefulness of seventeen. ''Cos that's what you and your mum make it sound like. Swopping sex for an engagement ring is just the same as prostitution.' It sounded a good enough argument.

'Well no-one *has* to have sex,' Delphine had pointed out. 'For payment, for rings or for irresponsible fun. I just don't intend to till I'm ready. Men respect that. And right now,' she said, twirling in front of the mirror and admiring her rather formal slate-blue shift dress with matching long jacket, 'what I'm ready for is what

226

I'm having tonight. I don't know about the sort of boys *you* go out with but *I* prefer a man who thinks I'm worth being taken out for dinner and being given flowers and chocolates and being treated like a *lady*.'

With that, she'd smirked at Jay and flounced out of her immaculate floral bedroom, leaving a trail of expensive grown-up scent. Jay, whose various impoverished sixth-form boyfriends never came up with anything more in the way of sustenance than a half of cider and a packet of dry-roast nuts from the rack beside the optics, could only shrug and marvel at this sophisticated parallel dating universe that *ladies* like Delphine inhabited.

'If Delphine doesn't know, I don't think you should be the one to tell her,' Greg now advised. 'Maybe she'll be perfectly happy with Charles and never need to know anything about it. Maybe there's nothing *to* know and he was just delivering a . . . a, I don't know, a misdirected letter or a Neighbourhood Watch poster. On the other hand,' and he chuckled, a deep-down dirty laugh.

'On the other hand what?' Jay asked.

'On the other hand it could be he's using his convenient working travel arrangements to link up with the dodgiest of the Russian Mafia and recruit a whole string of hookers for the London meat trade. He could be running a whopping great vice empire going on out there, starting with Masefield Avenue and ending up who knows where, maybe, ooh, all the way to Surbiton?'

'Oh sure. OK it was a fun notion at first, but,' Jay laughed, 'I think not, somehow. I mean, look at the men around here – solid, respectable, a bit dull. A whole lot of Sunday car-polishers, *Archers*-listeners and armchair football pundits.'

'Gee, thanks,' Greg said.

'Not you! But you know what I mean. I know you can only speculate on other people's debauchery but if it was all going off in Masefield Avenue, Mrs Howard would have to have one of those special rails for tying up dog leads outside, like they've got outside Waitrose. Dog-walking is about the only chance for men from round here to get out on their own, unless they've tunnelled out to Homebase for DIY bits. They're always being hustled into cars to do quality time with the kids on the school run, or they're dragged down the tennis club with the keen wife. Two of the pubs along the main road have had to close for lack of traditional early evening bloke custom. All the men are rushing home to get the chicken breasts into a tangy marinade and knock up a *salsa verde*.'

Reluctantly, Jay hauled herself out of the hot, bubbly water and wrapped herself snugly in a towel, patting gently at her tender tummy skin before giving her thighs a brisk, hard rub. It was important, it said on the instructions that were in the pack of anti-cellulite cream she'd bought on the way home from Mrs Howard's, to keep the circulation stimulated. A hot bath was just the thing, she imagined, though she suspected if she'd read to the bottom of the page she'd find she should have finished off by standing under a freezing shower scraping exfoliating grit into her skin. That particular approach seemed too brutal and Scandinavian for her. Ideally she imagined there should be a snow-fringed ice-strewn lake for her to plunge into, just to add that extra effective tingle. Horrible. Thank goodness for living in a moderate climate.

'Of course, being embroiled in the vice trade might explain . . .' she went on, pulling on a strappy silk nightie for Planet Man and his telescope to admire before wandering into the bedroom, where Greg had now started playing with the TV channels. He didn't look up (so much for the skimpy silk), so she guessed he was in eager search of football or a film with guns and spies. She sat on the bed, blocking his view. '. . . it might explain how Charles can afford all those fab paintings, and that glitzy place he's got to live in. Doesn't explain what he's doing marrying Delphine.'

'How about that good old-fashioned word, "love"?' Greg said softly, leaning over to kiss her. 'Remember that?'

Jay then felt bad. Of course it would be love. Why shouldn't it be? And *what* else would it be? Just because Delphine had been a difficult, spoiled, over-bearing girl who'd somehow been a blight on a good bit of Jay's younger life, it didn't follow that she was completely unendearing to the rest of the world. Or that she hadn't changed over the past ten absent years. She'd have softened in that time. She must have: how could she not, losing her second husband after only five years? Win hadn't been oversympathetic, exactly, when Bill Durant's liver had gone into final booze overload and abruptly stopped working. She'd said it was a perfect moment for Delphine to come back home, but Delphine, understandably uppity about the word 'perfect', said she'd got used to the sunshine and had all the emotional support she needed, thank you very much, from the Yallingup Tango Troupe. Jay remembered Win being quite miffed that her con-solation skills were not to be called on, saying, 'I never liked that man; he was always scratching himself somewhere.'

As she switched off the bedside light, Jay promised herself she would do her best for her cousin, make sure that her stay with the family was as much fun as it could be, and help send her off to her new life with as much generosity of spirit as she could muster. It couldn't be that difficult. And it would be the proper grown-up thing to do. Whatever Charles was up to, either it would all become clear or it wouldn't.

The kitten was miaowing on the landing. Barbara had suggested shutting it in the kitchen so it wouldn't have any choice but to sleep in its own basket, but she hadn't taken into account that their kitchen didn't actually have a door. Ellie climbed out of bed and picked up the little yowling creature and took it back under the duvet with her. It settled immediately, snuggling down beside her and purring and closing its eyes. It was four in the morning.

'Poor baby Cicely, are you missing your mummy?' Ellie whispered to it as she stroked its paws. 'Why didn't you curl up on the sofa with Daffodil?'

But Daffodil was likely to have slunk out through the cat flap for her usual pre-dawn wander. Cats, Ellie thought as she tried to get back to sleep, had a whole secret life that their owners could only guess at. Rory was being very cat-like at the moment, smiling to himself at something secret that was happening in his own head. Usually if there was something going on he'd drop a few clues – he wouldn't be able to resist – but this time, well . . . nothing except this sly half-smile. It was there all the time which was so completely *not* how he'd been for the last few weeks, when he'd had no light in his eyes and had barely smiled at anything. She wished she knew what it was, if only to help him keep whatever secret it was safe from Tasha. If Tasha saw him looking like that, all cat-with-the-cream, she'd worm it out of him. If he'd told *me*, Ellie thought, I could help him to distract her from burrowing into the truth somehow. Unless it *was* all about Tasha? Were he and Tash . . . were they seeing each other? Had Tash finally got round him and persuaded him that she was exactly what he wanted? This thought landed in her brain with all the force of a dropped bomb, this certainty that this was what was happening. She felt quite sick. Completely left out, as if she was just some little child who wasn't being let in on grown-up secrets. Bloody sodding Tasha, she whispered to the sleeping kitten, I just hate her.

It was a last-ditch attempt before Delphine day. Not an ounce was budging with the low-carbohydrate diet. In fact two sneaky pounds had crept back on board and she could feel others clamouring on her personal quayside, all packed and ready to join them. This was purely, Jay felt, because although it was pretty easy to avoid bread, potatoes and such during the day, by the evening you were in dire need of a bit of ballast. According to one of the books she'd been reading, a tiny miscalculation in carbohydrate grams at this point meant that all the otherwise harmless full-cream milk, the cheese, the avocado, the steak and the eggs were suddenly diverted from their job as basic fuel to larding themselves permanently onto your hips. With a family that was used to meals which regularly featured rice or pasta, and didn't include much red meat during the week, it would hardly be either easy or fair to inflict daily chunks of flesh, slabs of fish and endless, endless chicken on them all. How to have spaghetti Bolognese without the spaghetti? A risotto without the rice? Not possible. And besides, as quick lunches go, Jay was heartily sick of avocado and prawns or yet more tuna.

'Rosemary Conley. Now that's the one for us,' Pat across the road told her when she found Jay dispiritedly bagging up more organic broccoli in Waitrose. 'I'm doing OK at Weight Watchers but the Conley class has an exercise section as well, so that should gee things up even more, I feel.'

'That means you can't just slope off after the weigh-in,' Jay pointed out. 'Which also means you've got to listen to the talk bit.'

'Well yes,' Pat conceded. 'But you never know, it might be useful. Someone might have come up with a no-calorie cheesecake.'

So here they were, signing up for a five-week special offer in the hall of what used to be a school but was now an adult education centre. The dark-panelled walls held lists of the names of girls who'd excelled in exams over the previous half-century, all meticulously signwritten in gold.

'I'm up there.' Pat nudged Jay and pointed to the top of the 1976 list of A-level stars on the wall opposite. 'But they spelled me wrong. Look at that: "Patrickia" Andrews, I ask you. I feel like bringing in a pot of gold paint and crossing out the "k".'

'I think you should,' Jay said as they handed over their cash and received yet another diet-guide booklet full of you-can-do-it cheer and promise. 'I think we should sneak in very early one morning and just do it. We could do it really neatly with car paint and a stencil.' She meant it. Why put up with something so annoying, albeit close to frivolously trivial, that could be so easily changed?

The Rosemary Conley diet didn't pussyfoot around with points and sins.

'We're talking calorie control, and we're talking getting those fat percentages down,' Vanessa, the leader, told the class newcomers with back-to-basics, no-nonsense briskness. 'Keep the calories below fourteen hundred and whatever you eat, look at the packaging and make sure the fat content's always under four per cent. That's four grams per hundred,' she added, just to make sure the maths had sunk in. 'And if you're in doubt, refer to the books you'll be given that show you all the calculations. OK?' Vanessa beamed and turned her attention to the whole class. 'And now ladies . . .' she rallied them, 'let's talk turkey rashers!'

A brief talk about dry-fried low-cal turkey-rasher breakfasts was followed by a comparison of supermarket pizzas, showing which ones were possibles for inclusion in the diet and which ones were not, all illustrated with packaging which was passed round the class.

'I'd have thought that on any low calorie diet the simple word "no" would apply to pizza, wouldn't you?' Jay whispered to Pat as they prepared to get going with the exercise section of the class. They'd been advised by Vanessa to stand at the back for this first session and just 'try to keep up as and when and don't worry if you find it tricksy; my ladies have been learning this routine for a few weeks now,' leading Jay to dread being expected to achieve *Chorus Line* skill after the first couple of classes. Instead, the steps were not too hard to follow, though the energy required was deceptive: it was only when they took a breather to get water that she realized she was a lot more puffed than she'd expected to be. Low-impact aerobics was replaced for the last ten minutes by stretchy floor exercises and ended with a peaceful, relaxing cooldown on the mats. Jay would, she decided as she lay and looked at the peeling ceiling, come again. But never, even under threat of severe torture, would she breakfast on turkey rashers.

It was all set. So long as he could find out for sure that this Charles bloke (sleazy pimp, as he now thought of him) would still be away (and Rory was as sure as he could be, because his mum had said Charles was off to Hong Kong this week), then it was all on for the night

233

of Friday week. A Saturday would have given him more time to get food and stuff (and himself) ready, but then it wouldn't give him any time to sort out any bits of clearing up afterwards. This way, he'd even be able to leave the washing up till the next morning, when he'd come back in and completely obliterate all trace of people. Not that there'd be much. It was only going to be him and Samantha and Shelley and that divvy twat Hal Clegg who apparently all the girls 'really liked', according to Samantha, because he was just '*sooo* hilarious'. Rory couldn't see it himself. What was funny about a bloke who was so far into the clouds that in Art he'd actually asked whether Blu Cantrell was a light blue shade or a dark one? If Rory'd said it everyone would have thrown wet paint at him and called him a tosser for not being able to tell the difference between a pigment and a pop star. But oh no, Hal comes out with it and they're all laughing along, highly amused. Still, whatever floats their boats. So long as the guy was useful. He'd even volunteered to nick some of his dad's champagne for them so that was a good start. There was just one more essential thing Rory had to do for now and that was sort out the keys. Charles had had them copied for Barbara and left the other set with his mum so that she could take Delphine over there when she got here. It was a risk that he'd nicked them but at least she wasn't needing them for a few more days yet.

Ellie seemed to be suspicious, which was a bit worrying. At home, she kept looking at him sideways and half-starting to say something. Whatever it was he wished she'd just come out with it, so he could get his lying over with and convince her there was absolutely nothing going on, nothing at all. Tasha was also hanging around a lot, which was a problem. It was like she could sniff out that there was something going down and she was working on getting it out of him. Not a chance, he thought, wondering if he ought to wear garlic round his neck to fend her off like you do with vampires.

It was lunchtime. Rory sauntered out of the last class of the morning (Chemistry) at his usual don't-care pace. It wouldn't do to rush, even though he risked finding himself short of time. He didn't want anyone following him. As he ambled casually towards the school gate he realized he was enjoying himself hugely, feeling quite excited and playing the part of a spy-type person inside his head, a man with a secret mission and everything to lose.

At the gate he had a quick look round to see if there was anyone around that he knew. Nobody. Now he could run. He sprinted fast up the road, round the corner and across the main road into the High Street. Still no-one, not unless you counted a few of the sixth-form girls pointing at skirts in Topshop's window. They wouldn't notice him, or anything else; they were on a completely different kind of mission.

Carefully (and needlessly, even he would acknowledge it now) he looked around again before he dodged into the doorway of Bowden's Hardware and slid in through the door. There was a resinous tang of paints and wood shavings and he breathed it in, savouring the atmosphere for a moment.

It didn't take long. Luckily there were no customers ahead of him at the key-cutting counter. You could be there all day if you were stuck behind someone getting five door keys and a spare for the car.

As the cutting machine ground away, Rory got absorbed in a wall full of paint charts. Idly he picked out a few shades of purple, ranging from a deep lavender through to sumptuous aubergine, and imagined having these colours on his own room walls. Would they make a good background for the arty black-and-white photo stuff he was planning? Possibly not. A request from the key cutter for £6.50 brought him back to earth.

'Oh, er, right. Thanks,' he mumbled, sorting money from his pocket.

'I'll take those, for you, shall I?' A harsh and familiar girly voice cut across his thoughts and long pale fingers, decorated with fright-pink nail varnish, reached forward and took the keys out of the hands of the technician before Rory could get them. 'Tasha! What are you doing in here?' He didn't really need to ask – the sly sod had obviously followed him.

'Why shouldn't I be? Free country innit?' she said pertly, grinning a challenge at him. 'And what are you looking so guilty about, Rory Callendar?' Teasing, she dangled the keys at him then snatched them back as he lunged to grab them.

'What we got here then? Two sets of keys. Hmm. One with a tiny little label. "The Swannery"! Oooh I know where that is. Big new block by the river with a posh bit on the top. You shouldn't leave keys around with labels on, you know, Rory, people could take them and break in, couldn't they?' She backed towards the shop door, still holding out the keys, just out of range. At this rate he was going to have to rugby-tackle her and pin her to the ground outside in the precinct. Not a good move.

It was undeniable that he'd been stupid about the label. He'd just quickly tagged the keys the night before in case somehow in the night they got mixed up with all the others his mum had in her key cupboard. He didn't know what he'd have done if she'd found it – just tried to convince her she was losing it in the granny-brain department, he assumed.

'So what are you doing with these?' Tasha said, linking her arm through his and almost dragging him out of the shop and back in the direction of school. He surrendered, hopelessly.

'I'm getting some spares cut for my mum,' he told her. 'She's too busy to do it herself so I said I would.' Not bad, he thought. Surely that would do?

'So why's *she* want them?'

'She's cleaning the penthouse.' Shit. He hadn't meant to say that. Just any old flat would have done. Now he'd given something away.

'*Cleaning*? Your mum doesn't do cleaning.' Tasha laughed. 'I'm not a complete muppet, Rory.'

'She does! You've seen her, driving a Dishing the Dirt van!'

'Yeah but . . . OK,' she said suddenly, letting go of him and handing over the keys. 'OK you can have them back. I believe you,' she said. Quickly, so fast he barely knew it had happened, she kissed him briefly on his mouth and skittered away into the school grounds, giving him the faint taste of minty gum and lipstick and a feeling that she wasn't going to leave things at that.

One of the Henrys had gone missing, along with a floor mop, a bag of dusters and J-cloths and the standard box of cleaning products that went on every job. Monique, it turned out, had been in overnight charge of a van and had been due to meet Barbara that morning to clean Charles Morgan's apartment.

'Bloody Monique,' Barbara said down the phone to Jay. 'She went out with her boyfriend in the van last night and decided it would be a good idea to drop off all the stuff ready for today. Probably wanted it all cleared out so they'd have space for some back-seat action, though she says they were moving a carpet. So what does she do? She can't get into the flat so she parks all the kit in a dustbin ready to pick up in the morning. And guess what – the bin men have been.

We're going to be late starting at the Swannery now and it'll run into Mrs Prentice's time for her Regular. Have you got any spare stuff at your place? Selina and Mandy are out with my other van.'

'I have. Now Mrs Caldwell's off the list one of the vans is here, all loaded up and ready to go. I'll bring it round to the flat now.'

Oh this was a great start, Jay thought, thanking her stars that Charles was out of the country. What a terrific example of non-efficiency this would have presented. She could just see Delphine cackling about it, telling her how typically disorganized she'd been, employing someone who managed to lose the entire tools of the trade. What was Monique thinking about? Was her brain completely ruled by her hormones? She'd have done better to leave the lot in the Swannery's doorway. Someone would probably have taken it all inside, if only to keep it out of the way of the rain. It was hardly a place where people were going to pounce on it gleefully and have it down the next car boot sale before you could say 'nicked'.

Charles actually being on the premises was quite a shock. Jay wasn't surprised to see the Porsche in the car park – she assumed he'd left it safely parked and gone off to work in a taxi. To arrive at the open door and find him standing there waving her in was not what she'd intended. Bugger, she thought, while at the same time beaming a jolly hello at him as he stood there, obviously on his way out with one of those pilot's bag-on-wheels.

'Jay! Lovely to see you again. Change of plan! Being sent to Singapore to bring a bus home. Regular chap was taken ill over there and I'm down as a spare,' he explained. 'Didn't mean to be in your way, just come on in and feel free. Your hard-working colleagues are already here.'

'Shame you won't be here tomorrow when Delphine gets here,' she said. 'You two are going to cross in the sky.'

'I know. Can't be helped but duty calls. I'll be back in a week though, just in time for the big day. Still,' he laughed, 'it'll give you two girls chance to catch up and for Delphine to haul you round the shops.' He looked at her in a mildly calculating way for a moment, then said in a lowered voice, 'Er . . . do you know a little shop called 'Agent Provocateur'?'

'Er . . . yes . . . underwear.' Good grief, need she know about this?

'Absolutely. Delphine might like to pick up a few little somethings there.'

'Um . . . Charles, I hope you don't mind me asking . . .' Too bad if he did, she was going to anyway – when would she get another chance?

'This club that you . . .'

He laughed, a bit of a surprised one, in her opinion. 'Oh that! Just a little investment to supplement the pension.' He made for the door, looking back at her with a rakish grin. 'Purely investment, nothing "hands-on" as it were. Ciao, see you at the do!' And he was off, his bag clattering along behind him like a toddler's dog on wheels.

'Girls' indeed, she thought, as appalled at being so described as she was amazed to be pointed in the direction of saucy knickers. 'Girls' was even worse than 'Ladies'.

After Charles had gone, Jay cornered Barbara in the main bathroom where she was clearing a smart selection of male cosmetics out of the mirror-fronted cupboard.

'Nice stuff here. Expect he gets it duty free,' she said.

'Why didn't you tell me he was actually *here*?' Jay asked, still feeling flustered.

'Why? What's the difference? I'd still have needed you to bring the stuff. And anyway, he was on his way out. Another five minutes and you'd have missed him.'

'I don't know.' Jay sat down on the edge of the bath. 'It's just this thing that I don't want to be seen as Delphine's cleaner.'

'Your problem, sweetie, it's between you and your inner therapist. There's nothing wrong with it, even if he does see you as that. If it makes you feel better, just walk away, right now, straight out of the door. You aren't down for this job.'

Out in the hallway, Monique was singing to herself as she unhooked an armful of coats out of the cupboard.

'OK, I'll see you later,' Jay said. She'd got the Dachshund Man to talk to about all the jars of marmalade he'd rescued from the bin last time they'd cleaned out his larder. Some of them were over three years out of date. There was also a tin of syrup he wanted to keep that had swollen to dangerous proportions.

'Whatever she got up to last night,' and Jay indicated Monique, 'it's put her in a lively mood!'

'Oh she's been singing and smiling away since the early hours. It's driving me mad,' Barbara said with a grin. 'Plus, she seems to have been offered another job. She told your Charles person that she's not really a full-time cleaner, she's a dancer, and he's given her a card and told her to go and see someone he knows at some club. I don't know what it's got to do with him, or what he's up to, but it looks like one way or another we could easily be down one member of staff again.'

Well he didn't waste any time or opportunity, this Charles. He'd got in quick with Monique. Jay imagined him in a club in the pre-opening hours, giving the assembled lap dancers a warm-up talk like a football manager before an important Premiership match. She shuddered, imagining him demanding for the paying punters something along the lines of 'More thrust', 'More writhing'. Unavoidably, and before she could stop herself, she had a vision of Delphine, doing a slinky tango in baby-pink satin underwear, a swirl of satin ribbons and rippling marabou, with Charles partnering her, dressed to fly in his pilot outfit, all gold brocade cuffs and a sharply angled cap.

SIXTEEN

Magic Pants

There was the usual disorientating chaos in Terminal Three at Heathrow. Jay had arrived too early. She spent twenty minutes browsing in the bookstalls, nervously opening and shutting books without making sense of any words. Unable to concentrate enough to focus properly, she tripped over passengers' bulky hand baggage that had been parked in the middle of the floor as their owners flicked through magazines. Any real concept of time quickly vanished in the flaky dry air conditioning and harsh strip light. People here felt compelled to shop to relieve the tension, she thought as she tried to decide if there was anything she might need from Accessorize. What with that, and endless grazing in the coffee shops and bars, no wonder so many found it next to impossible to make it to their departure gates on time. They were too busy distracting themselves from the atmosphere of anxious antici-pation and mild panic that air travel induced in even the calmest, most seasoned voyager.

She wouldn't have minded, she thought as she heard the swoosh of an espresso machine, a cup of something hot and strong and a big, gooey, comforting Danish pastry. And of course she couldn't be fancying anything more off limits – that was the downside of diets. Whichever one she picked for the day, low-carb, low calorie, whatever, she couldn't hope to get away with a concoction of sugar, processed fruit and far too much butter.

Up on the Arrivals floor stressed and crumpled passengers, newly hatched from the snug, stale shells of aircraft, emerged through the airside doors and were scooped up by those who'd been pacing impatiently, waiting and craning for the first view of friends, colleagues and relatives. Jay stood close to the chrome rail that divided travellers from greeters, between two drivers, each carrying a placard with the name of their quarry scrawled in felt tip. One of them smelled strongly of a recent cigarette, and he fiddled with something inside his trouser pocket that Jay politely assumed was a lighter.

Delphine, looking as spruce in her cream trouser suit as if she'd merely made the forty-minute hop from Manchester, strode into view pushing a trolley laden with a pair of matching blue leather suitcases bound with pink straps. Of course they were matching, Jay thought as she moved forward to greet her. Did she really imagine that this perfect cousin would arrive with the kind of assortment of mismatched baggage, duty-free carrier bags and lumpy packages that Jay herself always ended up travelling with?

'Delphine! Over here!' Delphine, perfectly made up and with short sun-streaky blonde hair, turned towards her and smiled.

'Hi, Delph! Great to see you!' Jay hugged her cousin. 'And ooh, you smell gorgeous!' she told her. 'You'd never think you'd spent twenty hours travelling.'

'Hello Jay. Been a long time, hasn't it?' Delphine stepped back slightly to inspect her, brazenly looking her up and down, taking in, Jay imagined, every inch gained over the years, every last ounce, every frizzing, grizzling hair. Was she, Jay wondered, about to tell her she was a lot less than all right?

'You look really well.' Delphine decided, smiling. 'But where's Mum?'

'Chiropodist! Didn't you know?'

'*Chiropodist*?' Delphine laughed. 'Her only daughter comes home after ten years on the other side of the world and she's gone to have her bunions trimmed?'

'Corns filed, actually, but yes, I'm afraid she has. It was unmissable, apparently,' Jay told her. 'Come on, let me push the trolley. The car's through here.'

'You look just the same, apart from the hair. Suits you short,' she remarked to Delphine as they loaded the baggage into the back of the Golf.

'You don't look the same,' Delphine said. 'You look . . .'

'Older? Fatter? Well I am. So are you. It's what happens.'

'I was going to say, softer,' Delphine told her, climbing into the passenger seat. 'But I see you're as bristly as ever.'

Oh don't start, Jay thought, switching on the car engine, or it's going to be a very long few weeks.

'So you met Charles, then,' Delphine went on as they got under way. 'What did you think?'

Ah, a tricky one. What could she say? Very nice for a pimp? Unfair, that. Jay negotiated the selection of roundabouts at Hatton Cross and concentrated on getting into the right lane at the lights.

'We had an excellent lunch for him,' she said eventually. 'He was very good company, very easy to get on with. How . . . how did the two of you actually meet?'

'Thought you'd have asked him that,' Delphine said. 'Obvious question, really.'

She was right, it was, and of course she, or possibly April, had asked him. She had a feeling that Delphine already knew this.

'We met at a dinner and dance in Perth. Charles was there with some friends.'

'I didn't know people still had dinner dances. It sounds like one of those Masonic ladies' nights that Win used to go to.'

A bit of a time warp, that, she thought, remembering Win getting togged up in sparkling finery a couple of times a year to go to what she called a 'do'. She always used to get Audrey to come round, ostensibly to stitch up a bit of hem or advise her about jewellery, but April had said it was just to show off. Then she'd sweep out of the front door with her escort, trailing a fur stole that she boasted was mink but Delphine, playing on her cousins' love of felines, told them was actually Abyssinian cat.

'It wasn't Masonic. It was the Perth Latin American Society Ball. I'd been giving a tango seminar in the city.'

'A . . . what?'

'I've been a dance teacher for the past five years. Didn't you know?'

Jay laughed, 'I'm surprised I didn't. Win still does that thing she does when she talks about you.'

'Oh heavens, does she? Not the old "my *Delphine*"? You'd think I was still twelve!'

'I suppose it's just a mother thing. Most of them do it. I expect I will, and then Imogen in her turn,' Jay said, contemplating the idea of laid-back Moggie turning into a version of her great-aunt Win.

'A mother thing? I wouldn't know,' Delphine said. Jay bit her lip.

Delphine had been only in her early thirties and not long married for the second time when she'd gone to live in Australia with Bill-the-boozer. There was so much about her that Jay no longer knew, such as had it been a sadness, or not, that she had no children? As the car pulled up at the house, she wondered if they would now become close enough for things like this to come out. One thing she suddenly remembered as she parked, switched off and opened the door, was that Delphine used to sneeze in the presence of cats. *Not* good timing then to have acquired a new, attention-needing kitten.

'I brought a cake. One I made this morning,' Win announced immediately as Jay let her and Audrey in through the front door later that afternoon. 'I didn't think *you'd* have made one,' she added, peering past Jay to see if there were unexpected telltale signs of baking – flour scattered across the floor possibly, viscous eggshells all over the worktop, a searing smell of burning perhaps. She looked satisfied to have been proved right.

'That's kind of you. Delphine's upstairs, having a shower and a bit of a lie-down. I'll give her a shout.'

'She'll be very jet-lagged,' Win told Ellie, who had arrived from school minutes ahead of her aunt and grandmother. 'It stayed with me for weeks after I got back last time I went over there,' she said, sitting down on the kitchen sofa and stretching out her legs, rotating her ankles as if she was remembering being on the plane and doing her anti-thrombosis exercises.

Delphine followed Jay down the stairs. She'd already unpacked, showered and was now dressed in sleek black trousers and a soft pink cashmere sweater. How had she managed, Jay wondered, to have not a single crease in an outfit that was straight from a suitcase? Had she packed each item with tissue paper or sneaked in a travel iron?

'You look amazingly unruffled,' she commented to her.

'I hung it all up in the bathroom while I was showering,' Delphine told her. 'Works every time. Got to smarten up to face Mum, you know what she's like . . .' Delphine said, taking a deep breath as they approached the kitchen.

'I don't know why you didn't come to stay with me. I've got a lovely spare room you know,' Win started in as soon as the greetings were over.

Delphine grinned past her mother towards Jay. 'I thought I should stay with my matron of honour,' she said. 'We've got outfits to co-ordinate.'

'I could have done that. I'm your mother. And I'm good at hats,' Win sniffed, helping herself to a second slice of her own lemon drizzle cake.

'I know but . . .'

'Well it's true we've got shopping to do.' Jay came up with an instant brainwave. 'And we're not just staying here, I'm taking Delphine to a spa for a bit of pre-wedding pampering,' she told them, 'The weekend before the big day.' She glanced at Delphine, who looked relieved at this solution.

'Suits me. And also I've got to go to the apartment and do some sorting out as well, and Jay's helping me with that. So you see . . .'

'Yes I see.' Win sighed, surrendering all hope of her spare room being occupied by anyone other than her own fat poodle. 'Still, at least you're here, and in one piece. You're looking very well, I must say. Not spreading into middle age yet, like Jay has,' Win commented, surveying her daughter with satisfaction.

Audrey looked at the ceiling and tutted. 'Win, you've no manners have you?' she told her sister. 'And when someone's travelled twelve thousand miles, do they really want to discuss what shape everyone is?'

'I'm only saying,' Win went on, 'that Jay was getting quite plump. You've lost a bit of weight lately, haven't you dear? You're almost looking quite trim these days, compared.'

'Yes, you do look quite well,' Delphine said, sounding unflatteringly surprised. 'Though I must share with you one sure-fire tip for your shape: *side-fastening* trousers.'

You were supposed to say thank you for comments like that, Jay conceded as she felt Win and Delphine and Audrey staring at her hips. Somewhere in the midst of that lot you were supposed to sift out a compliment. She tried very hard, but failed to interpret anything but the negative. All that calorie-counting, all that carbohydrate avoidance. Right now she wondered if it had all been worth it.

'It's only going to be a small affair. Just our family plus Charles's best man,' Delphine told Jay as they pulled into the lane beside Harrods and waited their turn in the car-park queue. 'But all the same, I want it to *look* right. I know just the colour I want you to wear.'

'But surely . . .' Jay began, for about the fortieth time. She didn't get any further. She never did. This time it was because it was their turn in the queue and she had to climb out of the car, hand her keys over to the attendant and drag out her handbag from under the seat. Delphine climbed out of the passenger door, clutching her own, much larger, handbag containing the essential pieces of fabric for which a co-ordinating outfit had to be tracked down for Jay.

It was going reasonably well, so far. Delphine had only upset Greg once, commenting that now he was older, surely it was time to move on to less dramatic tastes in household decor. 'You'd find adding a selection of soft furnishings very *soothing*,' she'd told him, as if all the glass, chrome and steel in the house represented an overlengthy attachment to juvenilia, as suspect as if he was still hanging onto posters of the Bay City Rollers.

'I don't want to be *soothed*,' he'd replied, patiently but aping her tone. 'If I want to be *soothed* I'll have a large Scotch and soda, thank you very much.'

Jay had stepped in here, fast, diverting Delphine by taking her upstairs for another look at the bridal outfit. Delphine had brought with her from Australia a loose, lacy coat in a sort of bricky pink, with a matching sleeveless dress underneath. The price of it almost took Jay's breath away and she wished she thought it as stunning as its cost deserved. Instead, she only just managed to stop herself saying that it rather reminded her of the late Queen Mother. So Delphine, she could see, was still dressing older than her years. As a child she'd preferred nice neat skirts and blouses to jeans and T-shirts, then there'd been the Jackie Kennedy teen phase. Jay had assumed she'd now have sort of caught up with herself and in middle age have landed in a clothes realm where she'd always been comfortable. And yet, even now, she seemed to want to be looking ahead to the next generation. Another few years and the going-away outfit she'd be shopping for would be the one she planned to wear in her coffin.

'So you see,' Delphine explained to Jay about the colour, 'that's why I want you in something peach. It'll *tone*.' Oh it would, that was undeniable. But not, in Jay's opinion, attractively.

'But shouldn't it be the bride in the lighter colour?' she'd suggested, brightly, thinking it would be quite useful to get something in a rich cocoa brown, perhaps with, if Delphine insisted, peachy accessories. But no. It had, for some deep reason, to be a particular pinky, orangey, pale peach.

'You'll look like . . .' Imogen had started.

'. . . a trifle,' Jay had finished for her. 'Yes I know, Barbara has already pointed this out and found it hilarious, thank you very much.'

'Well the two of you together will, definitely,' Imogen agreed. She'd even, brave girl, said the same to Delphine, who had simply looked at her in a chill way and said, 'Don't be silly.'

At least the cats weren't causing any problems. 'I'm not allergic to short-haired pedigree cats,' Delphine had declared. 'Only cross-breeds. Burmese have very fine fur and don't shed much of it.'

It was a difficult season to buy for. Late spring could be as freezing as February or as flaming as June. Delphine stalked ahead of Jay through the Harrods halls of designer wear, occasionally flicking a rail or two here and there and tutting at what she saw.

'Should have brought you something from home,' she said, dismissing with a sniff the top-flight couturiers of all Europe. Eventually, Jay persuaded her to go along to Harvey Nichols and guided her surreptitiously in the direction of the Ghost concession.

'They're doing the colour you're looking for this season,' she told Delphine. 'I happen to know. Let's just see if there's anything . . .'

And, oh joy, there was. Jay tried on a selection of peachy dresses and jackets till she found the perfect (to her) combination of bias-cut dress and an embroidered jacket that nipped in and out at the waist and had delicate fluted sleeves. For choice, she'd have gone for the dress in a less pound-enhancing colour but Delphine liked it though she tweaked and twitched at the fabric, hauled up the hem that trailed almost to the floor and deplored her cousin's shortness, plumpness and general lack of posture.

'It's being a cleaner,' Delphine said loudly. 'All

that stooping with a mop.' The assistant, who'd been counting on a sale, tittered and went to help another customer, leaving the two women squaring up to each other in the changing room.

'What's wrong with cleaning?' Jay demanded.

'Nothing! Don't get in an egg about it!' Delphine said. 'All I mean is . . . I know exactly what you need. Quick, get changed. You need to try this on with Magic Pants. We'll go get some.' Jay hauled the clothes off, handed them to Delphine who told the assistant to keep them for her, and allowed herself to be hustled down to the underwear department.

'We're supposed to go to Agent Provocateur,' she told Delphine, reminded of Charles's knicker request. Or did he want Delphine in a velvet basque? Or a pearly thong like a . . . lap dancer. Don't even go there, she thought, as Delphine pointed her in the direction of some decidedly *non*-exotic pants.

'I've got plenty of fancy underwear already, thanks,' Delphine said, rifling through a rack of big, functional knickers.

'There! That's what you need under that dress!' she declared, hauling out her choice. 'They'll take pounds off. It'll make all the difference. Buy at least two pairs.'

Well it was worth a shot, Jay thought, though she did wonder where the flesh actually *went*. Would it squelch over the top of the pants, or squidge un-appealingly out beneath the legs? Or did it go inwards, pressing against her internal organs so that she absolutely wouldn't be able to eat? If that was how they worked perhaps she should wear them all the time. Leaving no room for a fully functioning digestive system would certainly solve the problem of how much to eat. Putting even a tiny morsel of sustenance into her mouth would simply be out of the question.

*   *   *

251

'So how're you two getting on?' April, on the phone, sounded gleeful for gossip.

'OK, so far. The odd tetchy moment but we're surviving,' Jay told her sister. 'Are you coming down for the do?'

'Wouldn't miss it for anything. I want to see how the Club King is with Delphine. Do you think he's one of those people who has two completely separate lives?'

Jay laughed. 'Well if he does I hope he's good at *keeping* them separate.'

'Hey but,' April sounded halfway serious, 'don't you think you should say something to her?'

'Me? Are you mad? What could I say? "Oh, by the way Delphine, did you realize that bloke you're marrying, he's got an interest in the kind of dancing that would melt your collection of formation medals." And suppose we're wrong?'

'Wrong? He's inviting your cleaners to audition for him, how can we be wrong?'

'True, true, but . . . Delphine's happy. Maybe she always will be. How can we spoil it for her?'

'How? Come on Jay, she's spoiled things enough for you over the years . . .'

'Yes . . . but that was then. Honestly, unless she does something really, really terrible then I'm not going to be vindictive.'

'OK, your call. But I'd say . . .' and April giggled, 'I'd say that making you wear pale peach could arguably come under "really, really terrible" . . .'

It was going OK so far. No real arguments, no more than a few fizzing comments. You weren't sure till later if they were bitchy or not. Maybe that was what ten far-apart years had done to the two of them. Jay and Delphine had grown up enough to get on reasonably well together.

Jay was conscious of trying hard. She cooked meal

after meal, pulling out all the stops she'd got as if she had something to prove. She told herself she was just doing her best to be a good, welcoming hostess, but it was a strain. Even Greg had started wondering if it was ever going to be all right just to slob out with a takeaway Chinese again.

Jay took Delphine to the Swannery to have a look round.

'I can't believe you're moving into somewhere you've never seen!' Jay said as they drove over there. 'It seems odd that I've been inside and you haven't. I wouldn't have thought it was . . . well wait till you see it.'

'I know what you mean,' Delphine said as they wandered from room to stylish, minimal room. 'It needs warming up a bit. A lot more colour perhaps but . . . no clutter, no *bits*.'

'I just wanted to ask you though . . . these paintings . . .' Jay led her cousin up the metal spiral staircase to the office area. 'Are they actually . . .'

'Original? No,' Delphine told her as she admired the Picasso. 'Charles was married before, to an artist. She specialized in exact copies, for people who have to store the real things for insurance purposes. Sad really, I mean if you've got a genuine version but you have to hang up a fake, it sort of cancels out the pleasure of owning the real thing.'

She looked out of the top window, down to the outside terrace that ran all the way along the length of the sitting-room windows. 'The outside's a bit bare too. I'm going to fill it with plants. Tubs and tubs of traditional English roses and bulbs.'

'Not hanging baskets though.' Jay couldn't keep her voice from showing how appalled she felt at the thought. Win, whose garden was a hymn to concrete and gravel, was keen on hanging baskets (cats couldn't dig in them and they didn't need weeding). She bought four fully planted, ready-to-flower ones at the garden centre each spring, two for the front porch, two for the back door.

'Oh I don't know, I can just see it. Six mixed baskets of petunias and fuchsias. Multicoloured.' She looked at Jay's stricken face and laughed. 'Joke! You don't know me at all now, do you?'

Probably not, Jay conceded privately, but, looking round this gloriously minimal place, she'd be willing to put money on it being up for sale within six months, during which Delphine would be wheeling Charles round a selection of plushly carpeted show homes out in the various small towns of Surrey.

SEVENTEEN

Swimming

The girls were coping very well without her, Jay realized. Dishing the Dirt was at last functioning exactly as she and Barbara had always planned. Strange that it had taken the reappearance of Delphine for that to happen. Just shows, she thought, organization is the better part of method. Anya and Katinka really could run the show almost on their own; each one, for this couple of weeks, had been designated to be in charge of two other girls and simply get on with the job with no fuss, no problems. She was in charge, but from a distance. She was, at last, not having to be 'hands on' as Charles would so succinctly put it.

Delphine had gone to the Registrar's office, to make sure that all the relevant official details were intact. There was only so much you could do from Australia and by way of your future husband. She had to take her various documents along in person and had made Win feel useful by taking her along as well.

Jay lay on the sofa, relishing being completely alone in her own home for a couple of hours. Daffodil and Cicely were thumping about in the kitchen, miaowing a lot and bickering away over a catnip toy. Rory and Ellie were at school, Imogen was at a lecture and Greg was out at a site meeting. Just before lunch she and Delphine were due at the Body and Soul spa hotel a couple of miles away for a weekend of pampering and pre-wedding bodywork. She closed her eyes, relishing the absolute relaxation. Then the doorbell went. Pat from across the road was on the step, looking keyed up and eager-eyed.

'Pat! Hi, how are you? We're not on for an extra Conley class this morning are we?'

'No, not that . . . you know what you said about painting the "k" out of my name on the old school wall?'

'Yes . . . but . . .'

'Well I've got the paint! And a day off! And I've checked with the caretaker, there's no-one in the hall this morning. If you've got a spare half-hour . . .'

And so here they were. Two properly grown-up, otherwise responsible women sneaking into council premises with Waitrose carrier bags that concealed brushes, gold paint and sandpaper.

'If we were blokes no-one would bat an eyelid,' Pat said, peering into her bag and searching for the right brush. 'We should have overalls and a ladder, just to be on the safe side.'

'We're righting a wrong,' Jay reassured her. 'They can't argue with that.'

The two of them worked at the name. It wasn't as easy as they'd first thought. Changing 'Patrickia' to 'Patricia' meant a lot of moving of letters. Somehow, over more than an hour's careful concentration, they removed the 'k', then obliterated the 'c' and the 'i', replacing them carefully with the gold paint so they took up the right amount of space.

'Not a bad morning's work,' Pat said, standing back and admiring their efforts. 'We could almost set ourselves up as calligraphers.'

'If there was any call for it that was at ground level. I'm not going up beyond first floor. But you're right, it's not bad at all.' Jay agreed. 'We've done you proud. But a whole morning – oh God.' She looked at her watch. 'Look at the time!' Delphine would have been back at least half an hour. No-one was home. She'd be sitting on the doorstep fuming.

And she was. 'Where the hell have you been?' Delphine said as Pat screeched up in her car and dropped Jay off. 'I was only gone an hour and you didn't think to leave a key, did you?'

'Er . . . sorry about that. Been painting the local school hall.'

'Oh, you do that as well, do you? I'll keep you in mind for the flat. I'd love to see you up a twenty-foot ladder. That ceiling – I'd rather like it pink. Now – are we going to get ready for my wedding or not?'

This was going to be harder than he'd thought. The house was full of people all the time. Mum had gone into domestic-efficiency overdrive in the days since Delphine had got here. She was either doing unusually fancy things with food or she and Delphine were all over the house surrounded with magazines, talking about wedding outfits and the best place to get shoes. And even if he had the place to himself he could hardly stash all this food away in the kitchen fridge. Someone was going to notice four boxes of Marks and Spencers chicken in white wine sauce, a big bag of rocket and Parmesan salad, two packs of dauphinois potatoes and four individual sticky toffee puddings. Worse than that, someone was very likely to eat them and then he'd be stuffed – this lot had cleaned out his bank account.

In the end, after hiding the food under a rhododendron in the front garden where it would stay more safely chilled than if he hid it under his bed, he retrieved it quickly for fear of foxes and cats dragging it all out, and went down to the basement to see Imogen.

'What's it for?' she asked, eyeing the contents of his carrier bags with a look that was too much like sheer greed.

'I'm doing a sort of dinner. Not here, at someone else's house. I just wanted it all to be out of . . . well out of Mum's way, you know?' He trusted she'd get it, understand that whatever he was up to she was being asked to keep it to herself. She knew what it was like – it wasn't that long ago that she was starting to go out with Tristan and sneaking him into her bedroom at all hours of the night, and then out again before the house got under way in the mornings. He'd known about that and never told, and she knew it. She owed him.

'OK. For Friday is it? Tris and me'll try to keep our hands off it all, but you know, sticky toffee pud . . . well that's going to be tempting.'

'Oh Moggie, please just don't, right?'

She laughed. 'Don't panic. I'll keep it safe for you. Hope she's worth it.'

Rory grinned at her, feeling embarrassed. 'Oh she is. Well, I don't know. I think she might be.'

Oh God, Samantha looked fantastic. Rory didn't think she was wearing a bra – how could she be with a halter-neck dress, unless it tied up round her neck and got tangled up with the dress-strap bits? If she was, and he was required (well he could dream) at some point to delve about inside the clothing, he hoped he'd be up to sorting out the underwear thing. The great naked swathe of skin on her back was just so gleaming and strokable he was finding it almost impossible to stop himself running his fingers across it. Shelley had, as Hal had so inelegantly put it, scrubbed up nice as well. She didn't seem to mind his clumsy compliment and both girls had gone giggly and swung in towards each other as they laughed, the way they always did. Why did they do that, he wondered, as he slid the dish of chicken into the microwave? Why did they always lean against each other as if they might fall over? Or did they do it for effect? Their hair, both of them with plenty of the long blonde stuff, it sort of swung together for a moment, like something you just wanted to get hold of.

'Fabulous place.' Samantha wandered around, holding her glass of champagne and looking as if the flat was just made for her. She so fitted in. She'd so fit in if she was lying naked under the crisp white sheets on that huge bed. Then she said, 'Whose is it?'

Tricky one to answer, that. 'Um . . . someone in the family.' he shrugged. That would do. It wasn't even a lie, well not exactly.

'And don't they mind you using it?' Shelley chimed in. What was this, cross-examination time? Couldn't they just sprawl on the sofas and look model-ish?

'No, it's cool. I told you.'

Hal wasn't saying much. He wandered round and had a look but then completely relaxed and just started in on the beer, seeming pretty much at home. That was the great thing about blokes, they didn't have that stupid curiosity that girls had. Girls had to ask, had to probe, had to know every last bit about everything.

'Can we smoke in here?' Samantha asked, looking at the massive windows. 'Or should we go out there?'

Shit. One thing he hadn't got, the key to the terrace doors. He wished he had, he really didn't want to leave this place with the stench of fag in the air. That sort of thing stayed for ever. He'd have to look in the kitchen cupboards and find some air-freshener.

'It's fine,' he had to tell Sam. 'You can smoke in here, no problem.'

They must be mad, Ellie thought. Completely stupid, stonking crazy. At first she'd thought it wasn't true. It couldn't be, Rory wouldn't do anything as blatantly idiotic as that. But Tasha had that light in her eyes that always glowed when she was really believing the thing she was saying and there was no way Ellie could pretend to herself that they were wrong.

'Everyone's going,' Tasha told her. 'You have to come, it'll be rad.' And she did have to go. How else could she be sure they wouldn't just wreck the place? She felt responsible, even though she told herself she definitely wasn't. She tried to phone Rory but he'd turned his mobile off. She could, she thought, just stay at home, watch telly and go to bed. Homework was a possibility even, but no way would she be able to concentrate on it, not while she knew what was going on out there, this party up at the Swannery. Good thing Mum and Delphine had gone to the spa for the night, otherwise she'd have felt she ought to tell them. She wouldn't have wanted to but she'd have felt she should and she'd have spent all evening being twitchy, waiting for the disaster that would have to happen and then the disappointed fallout. Instead, there was only Dad to deal with.

'All right if I go round Amanda's?' she said casually over their pizza supper (which she could hardly eat).

'Sure. Want a lift?' Greg asked.

'Nah, 'sfine. I'll get the bus.' He wouldn't argue – there was football on Sky. He'd mentioned it that morning when he'd told Jay and Delphine that he wouldn't have time to miss them.

Ellie raced out of the house and round the corner before her dad got the chance to look out of the window and see that she was heading the wrong way if she really was going to Amanda's. She wondered if she should have dressed up a bit. But what was the point? She was on her way to stop the party, not to join it.

Side by side on loungers by the pool, Jay and Delphine lay wrapped in warm towelling robes and sipping champagne.

'This is bliss,' Jay murmured, closing her eyes. She almost wanted to swim but they couldn't for another half-hour, till the fabulously expensive gloop plastered all over their faces had taken effect, knocked the promised ten years off them and been absorbed for a lasting assurance of money well spent.

'Wonderful,' Delphine agreed. 'And so was the aromatherapy massage this afternoon and the pedicure. My toes are still tingling.'

'And tomorrow – what have you got first? I'm on for an anti-cellulite holly and lime wrap at nine thirty.'

'I haven't got cellulite – I'm going for the Pilates class.'

'What do you mean you haven't got cellulite? Everyone our age has cellulite.' Maybe she doesn't know what it is, Jay thought. Surely every woman over twelve has got it? Just a little bit? She should have hung onto those patches, shown her what they were for.

'Not me. It just seemed to . . . well it passed me by, that one.' Delphine was adamant.

We can't argue about cellulite, that would be juvenile, Jay thought, finishing the last of her champagne. It would be really juvenile. It isn't important. This sort of thing doesn't matter at all.

'It was all the dancing. It kept me in trim. You should try it, you can learn at any age, you know,' Delphine continued, parting her robe and holding up a taut-muscled leg for Jay to admire.

Something clicked in her head. Call it the champagne,

Jay told herself, at the same time as she also, realistically, told herself that the truth was that old demon, envy.

'Well it's easy to keep trim, if you've only yourself to think about,' she snapped. 'When the rest of us are racing about being the family gofer, working, running the house, bringing up the children and hoping they're going to get by, you don't have a lot of time to spare for personal preening.' Hardly fair, a small voice was telling her, seeing as she'd spent the last few weeks thinking about little else, all for the sake of impressing this got-it-easy cousin. How pointless was that? As Ellie would so accurately put it.

'Oh, sorry, was it something I said?' It was a classic teen Delphine moment, Jay recognized, yet another moment where she was left feeling that whatever she did, it didn't quite come up to standard.

'Yes, actually, it was. Do you know, Delphine,' Jay could feel fury rising, 'did you ever realize, *ever*, just how much you were up there as the great example of Perfect Womanliness when we were younger? And you know what? Even now you're here getting the bloody better of me with your perfect body and making me wear Big Pants and your mother going "Oh she's marrying a *pilot*" as if that was some goddam *qualification* on your part, better than a PhD . . .'

'Hey, hey hang on a minute, what do you mean "perfect womanliness"? What the fuck's all that about? You mean you ever, ever once, *envied* me? Hah!' Delphine laughed and poured the rest of the bottle into their two glasses.

'Cheers!' she said, raising her glass. 'Here's to family misunderstandings!'

'*What* misunderstandings? You spent your whole teen years – and even before, remember how you were with Cobweb? – being a complete cow, always so sodding superior, always getting the better. *Everything* you had, everything you did, there was either you or your mother crowing away. And me? Undersized, underweight, underachieving in the fields that you lot counted as important, pregnant as a student, no big, white, show-off meringue wedding . . .'

'Well the marriage hardly lasted,' Jay ignored this, up there on a roll she might never be on again.

'Even now, Win gives me that look every time I cook something, as if I should have phoned you for the recipe before I even peeled a potato. And you should hear what she says about my job!'

'You do cleaning. Someone's got to do it. I never thought it would be *you* though,' Delphine chuckled, taking a long deep mouthful of her drink. 'You weren't exactly born with a duster in your hand. That bedroom you and April . . .'

Oooh such a satisfying splash! Jay was certain she had the yoga, Weight Watchers, Rosemary Conley, Dr Atkins and a sack of grapefruit to thank for the strength and balance that sent Delphine hurtling, in one swift move, from her lounger straight into the pool. What she hadn't reckoned with was Delphine's own flexibility and reflex (all that dancing, again) that enabled her to make a last-minute grab for Jay's robe and send her, only a second later, flying into the water alongside her. Vaguely, Jay was aware of other swimmers, no longer gently breast-stroking up and down the pool in costly, exclusive serenity but scurrying away at a swift crawl, out at the other end of the pool and away to the safety of the steam room.

'You stupid cow! Didn't it ever occur to you that *I* envied *you*? So much for you being the clever one! Couldn't even work that one out, could you?' Delphine was shouting, flailing about in the water, tangled in her heavy towelling robe, the towel that had been wound round her head coming undone and starting to float on the water. Jay swam out of reach of Delphine's wind-milling hands, making for the steps. She could see big, astounded eyes watching them from the steam-room window. Hands had rubbed away the mist from the glass and the audience was lined up, enjoying the show.

'What was to envy? Everything we'd got you'd got a better version. You got a new bike for failing your eleven-plus, you got Cobweb, sailing lessons, dance classes, ice-skating with your own boots not hired ones, endless fancy clothes . . .'

'Endless mother input.' Delphine said slapping her hand down on the water's surface, setting up a tidal wave. 'Can't you imagine what it's like to be so much the centre of someone's life like that? Don't you think I was absolutely deadly jealous of you for having April and Matt and a mum who just let you get on with it? And then later when we were all grown-up you had a husband who stayed the course and all those kids, *and* you're getting a grandchild. Do you realize I couldn't fucking *fart* in our house without Mum being there flapping and fussing that I'd eaten one bean too many!' Delphine's mouth hitched sideways, remembering, and laughter started to bubble out. And it was too much for Jay as well. She could feel her face twitching un-controllably and the giggling rose up with no hope of stopping. Helplessly, she gave in to it, clutching the pool steps for support and watching the towelling robe float about her like a giant white lily pad. Delphine was completely convulsed and the two of them sat on the steps, weak with unstoppable laughter, trying uselessly to stand up and drag the seeming acres of soaking towelling out of the water with them.

'Mrs Callendar?' Delphine and Jay looked up and saw the spa's front-desk receptionist staring down at them.

She looked stern, increasingly appalled as she gazed about her and took in the scene of the soaking be-robed women, a towel floating far away across the pool, the empty champagne bottle on its side, an upturned lounger and the collected, smirking audience emerging (now there was someone safely in charge) from the steam room.

'There's been a phone call from home. And . . .' she looked around pointedly, 'I really think you'd better collect your things and leave.'

'Oh Lord. I hope there isn't too much damage,' Jay said for about the fortieth time in the taxi.

'We can't know till we get there,' Delphine reassured her. 'They can't . . .' and another giggle escaped her. 'They can't be much worse than us,' she said.

But that was the difference, Jay thought, Delphine didn't know that they *could* be much worse than them. They were teenagers; they could go far beyond grown-up limits because they *had* no limits. That's what they were all about, teenagers, about finding their own level. Unless you'd been Delphine, of course, who hadn't had a chance to make her own limits. Win had set them all out for her, laid down the rails and sent her gliding off smoothly along them. We should have taken her in hand, Jay thought now, April and I could have roughed up those edges for her a bit, helped her escape and loosen up.

The police were still there, leaning against their squad car, two of them smoking. There couldn't be much wrong, Jay thought, if they'd got nothing better to do than stand around smoking. There was movement in the shadows too, and she recognized the sneaky shuffle of guilty teens making a getaway.

The fire engine didn't seem to be in use either. There was only one man sitting in it and he was listlessly tapping the steering wheel in time to some unheard music.

'Mum?' Ellie came running out of the Swannery's main door. 'Mum? Tasha's a bit hurt and they've made a mess.' She looked at Delphine, tears in her eyes. 'Sorry Delphine, I did try to stop them.'

Up in the flat the smell of burnt food was overwhelming and the kitchen was full of wafting smoke. There was a chill breeze from somewhere high up and Rory was sitting on the desk at the top of the spiral staircase, looking at where three large uniformed firemen were dealing with something beside an open window.

'Mum? Sorry and everything. I was just . . .'

'He was doing a bit of entertaining.' A pretty girl in a silver halter-necked dress and spiky sandals interrupted him. 'It was really cool till *they* all turned up.'

'They shouldn't of,' the other girl said, grumpily.

'Shouldn't *have*,' Delphine and Jay said both together, then laughed, stopping themselves, trying to be suitably serious.

'What's the damage?' Delphine asked Rory.

'Well the worst is Tasha. When the chicken caught fire she tried to open the window to let the smoke out. But the alarm had gone off so the fire people came. And she was a bit drunk so she . . .'

'She sort of fell out,' Ellie finished for him.

Rory looked exhausted, Jay could see. Whatever scam he'd been up to, it was now far too much for him. That wasn't to say he should get away with it, not at all.

'OK! Pull her in!' The biggest of the firemen lurched backwards towards them, swinging the window and a young girl with him. He hauled her upwards and she slumped to the floor in front of them, looking pained. 'You've broken them!' Tasha wailed as a scattering of pearls fell out over the top of her trousers and trailed themselves across the floor like droplets of mercury.

'What's that? Your necklace?' Jay asked her.

Delphine spluttered beside her. 'It's not her necklace! It's her knickers! She's got one of those pearl thongs on!'

'She was . . . was hanging from them,' Ellie told them. 'She opened the window and sort of tried to climb out to get down to the balcony and got caught on the window catch. She was swinging there for ages. That's why they had to come and get her down.'

'Not enough elastic,' Delphine sniffed. 'You see?' she said to a terror-stricken Tasha. 'Now that'll be a lesson you won't forget. Sensible knickers. They can stop you getting into all sorts of trouble.'

'I'm sorry, Delphine. We'll clear it all up.'

'Yes you will. And you won't involve your mother's workforce. It'll be you and your mates. You've to do this by tomorrow afternoon and be there in time for my wedding. Understand?'

EIGHTEEN

Cake

'And you're *wearing* that?' April whispered.

'Well of course I am. I love it.' Jay twirled in front of the mirror and adjusted the feathered headband. It wasn't *that* bad. Not entirely her choice maybe, but when you're just the bridesmaid, that's the way it is. Anyway, how tricky could it be to slide a souped-up Alice band over your hair and do your best to live up to a bit of trimming? She really did like it (well, quite) – the feathers were the brick-pink of Delphine's outfit and included a strand of seed pearls that toned in with her own dress.

'OK – I give in. It looks great. That peachy shade though . . .'

'April, don't start. Delphine and I . . .'

'. . . are new best friends. Yes, I get it. All you needed over the years was to beat each other up and get it out of your systems. You should have done it at ten. And again at eleven, twelve, and so on.'

'Mum?' A voice hollered up the stairs. 'Rory's back. He's all filthy. How long have we got?'

'About an hour. Plenty of time for him to shower and change, don't worry about it Ellie.'

Ellie came into the room, pretty as a thirteen-year-old

could get in a short blue pleated skirt. It wasn't so far off the sort of skirt she objected to wearing for games at school, on the grounds that it got the girls leered at by men who hung around the perimeter fence on netball days. She was wearing it with knee-length brown suede boots and a tight little flowery jacket.

'This OK?' Ellie said, suddenly conscious that her mother and April were staring.

'Yes, fine. You look gorgeous, Ellie,' Jay said, hoping she wasn't going to do any crying. And this before the actual ceremony. 'I'd better go and offer Delphine a hand,' she told April. 'I think that's what I'm for, being matron of honour.'

'Oh you are. And I know what I'm for – I'll go down to the kitchen and pour us all a sharpener, just to get it all nicely under way.'

Jay went carefully down the loft stairs, watching her step in the new, spindly-heeled cream shoes. She was happier in footwear that was more substantial and doubted she'd ever wear these again, but she loved the dress and jacket, just . . . the colour.

Rory felt gruesome. All that cleaning. You didn't want to do that on a Saturday morning, not ever, not that early. He'd scrubbed and polished and vacuumed and scraped the food off the microwave shelves and off the kitchen walls. And all the time he'd thought of Samantha Newton and how he hadn't even got a snog. But . . . in the back of his mind he knew he'd got a score chalked up on the wall for later, however much later it was. It was there. She'd loved the place. She'd loved the risk he'd taken. She'd screeched a lot when it all went wrong; she'd left before he got to say anything to put it all right, but maybe that was cool enough. He knew, deep inside, that she'd got him down as someone who'd always try to show her the good – no, the

269

excellent – time she deserved. It was just a matter of saving it for later, for the right time.

'Ah. Sweet,' April said under her breath to Jay as Charles put his arms round Delphine and did as he was ordered by the Registrar: kissed his bride.

'Well it is, isn't it?' Greg said to her. 'Or are you a hundred per cent cynical about this?'

'No,' she said, smiling. 'Only ninety per cent. The man's a pimp, no question.'

Well they looked happy enough, so perhaps they would be. Jay tweaked her sliding headgear back over her ear and settled it into place. Charles looked exactly like a properly smitten bridegroom should. His new mother-in-law was beaming and triumphant in a pale blue dress and a navy straw picture hat circled with turquoise pansies.

'Don't they make a perfect couple?' she trilled at Audrey and Jay as, later, they all took their places for lunch in the San Pedro restaurant.

'Lovely, dear,' Audrey agreed. 'And third time lucky, let's hope.'

'Oh I don't think we need to hope, this one's got sterling qualities.'

'It takes more than money, dear,' said her sister, but Win was in full sail; nothing was going to sink her delight.

They hurt, the magic pants. They might be compressing her tummy flat but they sure as hell hurt. Jay sat beside Charles feeling that if she stood up she'd leave the lower half of her body behind her. She was definitely being cut in two. In absolute agony she dutifully munched her way through a couple of lettuce leaves from the side of the pâté starter, a teeny sliver of the sea bass and managed to down a bit of the peach dessert by sort of sucking at it, in the hope that it

270

would turn into mush that would take up no noticeable room in her insides.

'No appetite?' Charles muttered to her, watching a waiter take away a good forty pounds' worth of food that she'd normally find luscious.

'I'm fine. Just a bit . . .'

'Yes it is exciting, isn't it?' he said. 'I feel very lucky.' He squeezed her hand and she smiled at him. Whether he was being new-cousinly or habitually letchy, it didn't matter. She'd made the decision to say nothing to Delphine about her suspicions and she'd have to follow through by doing her best to think well of him.

'You're not eating much. You're surely not dieting at a wedding?' Delphine said as she and Charles prepared to leave for their honeymoon in Scotland. What was it about people? Why, today of all days, were they gawping at her food intake as if keeping a close eye on a budding anorexic?

'No – just these knickers you made me wear. They're killing me.'

'You should wear them all the time. You'd be down to a proper weight in no time.'

'Hey, what kind of a comment is that for your matron of honour?' April cut in.

'Only being cruel to be kind,' Delphine said. 'Though I'm not always right.'

'God, that's a first,' April said. 'Tell me what you're wrong about, quick so I can remember for later!'

Charles came up, claiming his bride and leading her to the car for the start of their honeymoon.

'See you all in a couple of weeks,' he said. 'And thanks so much for being here, everyone.'

'Bye, Jay. And thank you,' Delphine said as she kissed her. 'And you were absolutely right, you know.'

'I was?' About what? About her being a cow over Cobweb, about her having a charmed childhood, what?

'Oh completely,' Delphine said, hands on Jay's shoulders and a look of sincere affection. 'Peach does nothing at all for you. Makes your hips look like a side of pork.'

Delphine disappeared into the white Mercedes and hurled her flowers into the family. Imogen caught them and Greg, beside Jay, groaned and said, 'She'd better not be getting married, I can't afford it.'

'You would though, Greg, you would.'

'Bugger a wedding,' April said to Jay. 'I heard what Delph said to you. Go and take those tight pants off *right now*. There's only one way to deal with a comment like that.'

'I know, you're right,' Jay said, laughing and wondering where she'd left her glass. 'Cake and champagne. Diet another day.'

THE END